PUFFIN BOOKS

TIME BOMB

I've never told this story to anyone
because when I was twelve I swore an
oath in blood that I would never tell it.
But the friends I swore it with are dead
now, so it's time to break that oath
and tell the truth . . .

Nigel Hinton was born and educated in London. He has written sixteen novels, including four prize-winners, and a number of scripts for TV and the cinema. He enjoys swimming, walking, films, reading, watching football and listening to music, especially 50s rock 'n' roll and Bob Dylan.

www.nigelhinton.net

Books by Nigel Hinton

BEAVER TOWERS
BEAVER TOWERS: THE DANGEROUS JOURNEY
BEAVER TOWERS: THE DARK DREAM
BEAVER TOWERS: THE WITCH'S REVENGE
THE FINDERS

For older readers

BUDDY
TIME BOMB

TIME BOMB

NIGEL HINTON

PUFFIN

PUFFIN BOOKS

Published by the Penguin Group
Penguin Books Ltd, 80 Strand, London WC2R ORL, England
Penguin Group (USA), Inc., 375 Hudson Street, New York, New York 10014, USA
Penguin Books Australia Ltd, 250 Camberwell Road, Camberwell, Victoria 3124, Australia
Penguin Books Canada Ltd, 10 Alcorn Avenue, Toronto, Ontario, Canada M4V 3B2
Penguin Books India (P) Ltd, 11 Community Centre, Panchsheel Park, New Delhi – 110 017, India
Penguin Group (NZ), cnr Airborne and Rosedale Roads, Albany, Auckland 1310, New Zealand
Penguin Books (South Africa) (Pty) Ltd, 24 Sturdee Avenue, Rosebank 2196, South Africa

Penguin Books Ltd, Registered Offices: 80 Strand, London WC2R ORL, England

www.penguin.com

First published 2005
3

Set in 11½/15½ pt Monotype Bembo
Typeset by Rowland Phototypesetting Ltd, Bury St Edmunds, Suffolk
Made and printed in England by Clays Ltd, St Ives plc

British Library Cataloguing in Publication Data
A CIP catalogue record for this book is available from the British Library

ISBN 0–141–31833–3

*This story about friends is
dedicated to some good friends of mine:
Iain and Lindi MacWilliam, Roger Sell
and Geoff Baker*

*I would like to thank the following for
help and advice on this book: John Ray,
Peter Prince, Doris Lessing, Wes Stace,
Jonathan Smith and my editor,
Yvonne Hooker*

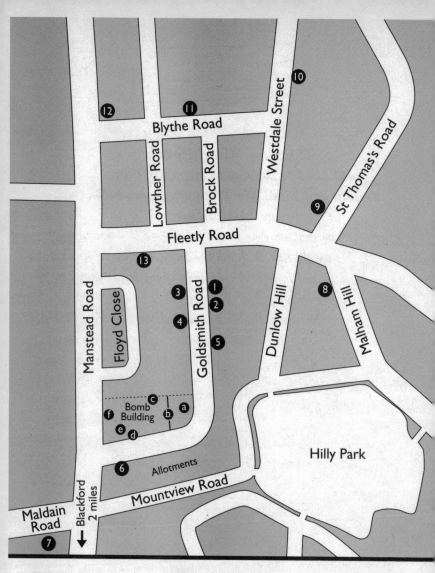

Blythe Road
Lowther Road
Brock Road
Westdale Street
St Thomas's Road
Fleetly Road
Manstead Road
Floyd Close
Goldsmith Road
Dunlow Hill
Malham Hill
Hilly Park
Bomb Building
c
f
a
b
e
d
Allotments
Mountview Road
Maldain Road
Blackford 2 miles

1 Eddie's House
2 Andy's House
3 Manny's House
4 Bob's House
5 Mr Barrington's House
6 The Rabbit Club
7 Maldain Road School

8 The Vicarage
9 St Thomas's Church
10 The Ritzy Cinema
11 Banner's Fish and Chips
12 Bird in Hand Pub
13 Miss Geale's Sweet Shop

Bomb Building

a Site of Big House
b Big Brown 'ill
c Hut/Den
d Side Entrance
e Ruins of Shelter
f Billboards

I've never told this story to anyone because when I was twelve I swore an oath in blood that I would never tell it. But the friends I swore it with are dead now, so it's time to break that oath and tell the truth . . .

It began on our last day at primary school – Friday, 22 July 1949. The weather was wonderful, the worries of the Eleven-plus exams were over, so it ought to have been a really happy day.

Our teacher, Miss Carver, had given us large pieces of paper and asked us to paint something we could keep to remind us of our time at the school.

I wasn't much good at art but I must have been inspired that day. My painting showed the big horse chestnut tree in our playground the way I'd seen it one February afternoon in 1947. It was an incredibly cold winter that year – the snow didn't melt for about six weeks and the whole of Britain almost came to a standstill with the sub-zero temperatures. Anyway, on this particular day some of us stayed behind after school to play on the long, long slide we'd made.

The sun was setting and our slide looked like a thin red mirror across the playground. My knees were bleeding from a couple of falls on the fast ice and the air was so cold that I could feel the blood freezing on my skin. I was standing in line for my go when I happened to look across at the horse chestnut tree. It was black against the fiery sky and a wisp of cloud was passing across the top branches so that the tree looked like a factory steaming in the brittle air.

My heart was throbbing fast and suddenly the ground seemed to be throbbing, too. It was as if I could feel all the energy in the earth. It was waiting there, building up for spring, when it would pulse up through the trunk of the tree and along the branches to produce thousands of leaves. This flash of insight only lasted a few moments and then someone tapped my shoulder – it was my go. I sped off towards that dark mirror of ice and I was skimming down the slide again, the freezing wind making my eyes water.

It was all there in my painting – the black silhouette of the tree, the red sun slipping along the slide, the snow piled up deep along the wall. And I'd used upward sweeps of the paint to make the tree look like a fountain of energy bursting up and spraying out along the branches. I'd even dabbed tiny blobs of pale green paint at the ends of the branches to hint at the budding leaves to come.

Those little blobs were still drying when Miss Carver came up behind me.

'Oh, Andrew – that's absolutely lovely,' she said,

bending towards me so that I caught a whiff of the lavender water she always wore.

Bob Newman, who shared my desk, was on the other side of the classroom chatting with Manny Solomon. Miss Carver said, 'Move up,' and I slid along into Bob's place to make room for her. She had never sat down next to a pupil in the whole year she had been our teacher, so I felt really honoured.

We all loved Miss Carver. She had high cheekbones and beautiful, big, brown, almond-shaped eyes, and I adored the way her long hair swung across her face when she bent her head. She was the prettiest teacher I had ever known and by far the nicest.

Most teachers back then were strict and remote; they called you by your surname and they seemed to be angry and impatient all the time. But Miss Carver was different. She was new to the job and on her first morning with us she picked up the register and started calling out our first names. We were all so surprised we could hardly reply. From that moment on she amazed and delighted us with her friendly openness. She told us stories about her childhood in Bristol. She let us know what scared her – snakes, mice and thunderstorms – and what she liked most: looking at the sea from the top of a cliff on a sunny day. She told us what films she went to see and what books she was reading and what they were about. She was just . . . lovely.

So Miss Carver sat next to me and looked at my painting. She held it out in front of her, shaking her head as if she couldn't believe how wonderful it was.

'You can have it, if you like,' I said, then cleared my throat because my voice had come out husky.

'Oh, Andrew, I can't. It's too beautiful. You must keep it for yourself.'

'I want you to have it,' I insisted. 'It can be like a wedding present for you and Mr Rix.'

The news that Miss Carver was going to get married to our headmaster, Mr Rix, had been a terrible shock to us. She was kind and glamorous and we could hardly believe that she would choose someone as bad-tempered and ugly as him. He didn't have much hair on the top of his head but, in contrast, he had wild black eyebrows and there were hairs bushing out of his nose and his ears. He used to smell awful, too – a mixture of pipe tobacco and stale sweat that clung to the hairy green jacket he wore for the whole time we were at the school. Worst of all, flecks of spit shot out of his mouth when he shouted at us. We just couldn't understand how our princess could fall in love with a stumpy little ogre like him.

'Oh, that's so sweet of you, Andrew,' Miss Carver said, and I can remember the warmth of her hand as she put it on top of mine.

At that very moment there was a rap on the door and Mr Rix breezed into our room. Mr Rix didn't normally breeze anywhere, but it was the end of term and he was seeing his fiancée so he must have been in an unusually good mood. We all leaped to our feet and stood in the aisles next to our desks.

'Well, Miss Carver,' Mr Rix said with a big smile that showed his tobacco-stained teeth. 'I trust these reprobates are making the most of their last day at Maldain Road School.'

'They're doing some painting, Mr Rix. And look what Andrew has done. It's absolutely beautiful.'

She held up my painting and Mr Rix came down the aisle towards us.

'Very nice,' he said taking it from her and giving it a cursory glance. He turned to me and flicked his little finger on the top of my head. His wide gold signet ring cracked on to my skull and I winced.

'Well done, lad,' he said.

Then to show how pleased he was and what a light-hearted joker he could be with small boys, he flicked his ring on to my skull again.

'Sir! Mr Rix!' It was Eddie Williams calling from across the classroom. Eddie was my best friend and the leader of our little gang which consisted of him, Bob Newman, Manny Solomon and me.

'What is it, Williams?'

'There's another smashing painting over here, sir!'

'*Smashing*, Williams? Start again and tell me in English what you are trying to convey.'

'Good, sir. A really good painting, sir. Beautiful, sir. Jackie Gray did it, sir.'

I recognized that tone in Eddie's voice. I'd heard it so many times when he was carried away with excitement and enthusiasm. It was one thing to get excited with us but it was dangerous to get carried away in front of adults, and I had a sudden intuition that he was heading for trouble.

'You've got to look at it. It's you, sir,' Eddie went on. 'Jackie's done a painting of you, sir. And it's just like you, sir. It's got everything just right. The nose. The ears. The hair. And . . .'

We all took a deep breath and Eddie stopped. He replayed what he'd just said and realized how it could be misunderstood.

'Oh, not the hair in your nose and ears,' he said quickly, trying to retrieve the situation, 'I meant the hair on your head.'

Then he stopped again and a blush rose up his throat as he looked at our headmaster's balding scalp. Miss Carver was standing right next to me so I saw the way Mr Rix's eyes darted to her. And I saw how she glanced at his hair and looked away from him, embarrassed.

Mr Rix pointed a shaking finger at Eddie.

'You, Williams . . .' he said, and a fleck of saliva shot out of his mouth and landed on my desk. 'You, Williams . . . You and your . . . jokes . . .'

Who knows? Maybe if he had lost his temper and shouted and screamed at Eddie, even slapped him there and then, things wouldn't have turned out so badly. But as it was, there was a deadly silence as Mr Rix walked to the door and out of the room.

A moment later, the bell rang for mid-morning break and Miss Carver told us to go outside.

2

By the time I got over to his desk, Eddie had already gone. I looked for him in the corridor but he wasn't there. He told us later that he'd gone straight to the boys' lavatory because he had a pain in his guts after his clash with Mr Rix.

I went outside to get my milk. In those days all school children were given a bottle of milk at morning break – it was only small, a third of a pint, but it was supposed to make up for the other food shortages. I got my bottle and strolled across the playground wondering where Eddie was. I reached our usual meeting place, the horse chestnut tree, leaned against the trunk, and used my straw to punch a hole in the silver foil top of the milk bottle. There was a knack to doing this without bending the straw and my friends and I used to take pride in getting it right. I started sipping the lukewarm milk and saw Spencer Eastcott walking towards me.

'Eddie Williams nearly got his goose cooked this morning,' he said.

'Pipe down, Shirley,' I snarled, 'or I'll cook your goose.'

Spencer laughed as if I'd made a terribly witty remark.

Poor kid, his days at Maldain Road School must have been a nightmare. He was desperate to be accepted by us tougher boys but he was a bit of a goody-goody and we didn't like him much. But worse than that, in our very first year at school some thoughtless teacher had said that his long blond curls made him look like the American child film star, Shirley Temple. So he'd had to live with the cruel nickname ever since.

I had just finished my milk when I saw Eddie running across the playground. He was holding his bottle of milk and I noticed that the foil top was missing. He must have had a soft straw that had bent. I got ready to tease him about it but he had more urgent matters on his mind.

'Look!' he shouted, holding the bottle out.

He dashed past Spencer and stopped in front of me. He held the milk bottle up and began to tip it sideways. The milk slowly slid down towards the mouth of the bottle and something small and dark appeared at the bottom of the glass.

'Urrgh, what is it?' I said.

'It looks like a . . . a mouse,' Spencer said.

I looked closer and saw that he was right. It was a tiny, flattened mouse.

'I was drinking my milk,' Eddie said, 'and my straw got blocked and I sucked and nothing came and then I looked and . . .'

It was as if telling us made the whole thing more real for him, because Eddie's face suddenly changed. He leaned forward and a gush of milk spewed from his mouth and splattered against the trunk of the tree. A moment later he jerked forward again and heaved as if he was about to empty the whole contents of his stomach. Spencer and I backed away but nothing came out. Eddie stood up straight, pulled a grey hanky from his pocket, and wiped his mouth.

'You all right?' I asked.

He nodded and put his hanky away.

'Who's on duty?' he asked, looking across to the main door where the duty teachers stood on the steps to survey the playground. Miss Carver was there, talking to Mr Wooding.

'I'm going to show it to Miss,' Eddie said.

'No, don't,' I said, remembering the embarrassed look she'd given Mr Rix. 'She's fed up with you.'

But Eddie was already on his way across the playground. Heading to disaster. We ran after him.

'Miss, please, Miss,' Eddie called up the steps.

Miss Carver looked down at him and frowned, 'Go away, Eddie, I don't want to speak to you.'

She turned back to talk to Mr Wooding. I took hold of Eddie's arm and tried to pull him away but he glared at me and I let go.

'Miss, please – it's important!'

'Williams, you heard Miss Carver. We're talking. Stop interrupting and go away,' Mr Wooding said.

'Look, Miss – look what I found,' Eddie insisted, and tipped the bottle up and slowly poured the milk out on to the ground.

'What on earth . . .?' Miss Carver said and came down the four steps to look at the bottle.

Eddie held it up for her to see. She leaned forward and then, as she realized what it was, staggered back and bumped into Mr Wooding.

'It's a mouse, Miss,' Eddie said, moving towards her.

'Take it away! Take it away!' Miss Carver shrieked, dodging round Mr Wooding and running up the steps.

Her reaction was like something from a comedy film and I couldn't help giggling. And my giggle set off Spencer. And once we'd started, we couldn't stop.

Miss Carver disappeared through the door, slamming it behind her. Mr Wooding watched her go and then swung round to us.

'So, you find it funny, do you?' he barked. 'Well, I can play jokes on people, too. Turn round and face the wall. Go on, jump to it.'

We turned round as quickly as we could. Mr Wooding was notoriously short-tempered and he had a long, thick ruler which he called George. A hard blow from George could make your hand ache for the rest of the day.

As we stood there, waiting for the end of break, I glanced at the others. Eddie was staring straight at the red bricks of the wall, the milk bottle held tightly in his hand. He seemed calm, as if lost in thoughts of faraway places. Spencer, on the other hand, had tears in his eyes and I could see him trembling. This was probably the first time in his whole school career that he'd been in trouble.

We heard the whistle for the end of break then the sound of shuffling feet as everybody got into line and began to file inside. I peeked sideways as our class went past and Bob Newman gave me a wink and a V for Victory sign.

'Newman!' Mr Wooding shouted.

'S–S–S–Sir?' Bob said, jerking his head to stop his stutter and complete the word.

'Do you want to join your friends here?'

Bob shook his head and followed the last of the class into the building.

'Right, gentlemen, follow me,' Mr Wooding ordered.

He walked round the side of the building towards his classroom door. He opened the door and his class fell silent. He pointed to some maths problems written on the blackboard.

'Get on with those. If I hear so much as a whisper, you'll be sorry.' Then he opened the drawer of his desk and pulled out his ruler. 'You three, in here.'

We followed him through another door into a little side room which he used as a stock cupboard and utility room. He put George down on the draining board next to some paintbrushes.

'Well,' Mr Wooding said, turning towards us. 'Three little jokers who thought they would have some fun at Miss Carver's expense.'

'No, sir,' Eddie said. 'It wasn't a joke, sir. I can explain it all. And it's just me, sir – they didn't do anything.'

'Oh, I have no doubt that you are our principal joker, Williams; you always are. But all great comedians need an audience and these two certainly provided that.'

He picked up George and pointed it at Spencer. 'You found it very amusing, didn't you? Laughed like a drain at Miss Carver's distress, didn't you?'

Spencer swallowed hard and nodded.

'Yes,' Mr Wooding said. 'Hold your hand out!'

'Sir, it's not his fault!' Eddie protested.

'Don't say another word until I tell you to, Williams!' Mr Wooding growled, then pointed again at Spencer. 'Hand out.'

Spencer held out his left hand and closed his eyes. I noticed that his thumb was raised higher than his palm – a bad mistake. I knew from experience that the bone of his thumb would be badly bruised.

Mr Wooding raised the thick ruler high and brought it crashing down across Spencer's hand. Spencer let out a whimper and his feet did a little tiptoe dance as he wrung his hand in agony then tucked it into his right armpit as if hiding it from any more pain. Tears sprang to his eyes and he bit his lip to try to stop them falling.

Mr Wooding turned to me and I held out my hand even before he told me. I tucked my thumb well below the level of the palm, and arched my hand so that he could only hit the fleshiest part of it.

He raised George above his head. He held it there for a teasingly long time, then it came whistling down and hit me. The pain exploded across my palm but I forced myself not to draw my hand away. I held it out in front of me, rock steady, as if the burning and throbbing didn't exist. I wanted him to think that I didn't care, that it hadn't hurt me. It was a stupid thing to do because he could so easily have hit me again. But, luckily, he didn't. After a long moment I slowly lowered my hand to my side. It wasn't much of a victory and it didn't stop the pain, but I knew he was disappointed by my lack of reaction.

'Well, the audience seems to have stopped laughing,' Mr Wooding said. 'And now it's time for the star of the show to face the music.'

'Sir, it isn't fair,' Eddie said. 'I found the mouse in the bottle and I wanted to show someone, sir. I forgot Miss Carver was scared of them, sir.'

'*Found* the mouse in the bottle?'

'Yes, sir.'

'Didn't *put* the mouse in the bottle?'

'No, sir.' Eddie's voice was husky as he tried not to show how nervous he was.

Mr Wooding reached out and took the bottle from Eddie. He held it up and swirled it round so that the tiny dead mouse sloshed about in the shallow pool of milk at the bottom.

'Now, how does a mouse get into a bottle of milk?' he asked, like Sherlock Holmes trying to solve a mystery. 'It runs in there of its own accord? Perhaps it's fed up and wants to drown itself? On the other hand, this mouse looks rather flat. Squashed. As if it had been caught in a trap. Now, how would a dead mouse get into a bottle of milk?'

'I don't know, sir,' Eddie said when Mr Wooding looked at him for an answer.

Mr Wooding gave the mouse and the milk another swirl, then looked closely at the top of the bottle.

'Where's the foil top, Williams?' he asked quietly. 'Correct me if I'm wrong, but you and your friends usually poke the straw through the top, don't you?'

'Yes, sir,' Eddie said.

'So why did you take the foil off today?'

'I tried to poke the straw in but it bent,' Eddie said, his voice cracking as he saw where this was leading.

'I see,' Mr Wooding said, turning back to Eddie. 'Today, of all days, the straw won't go in. So you take the foil off and suddenly – what a coincidence – there's nothing to stop you putting a small dead mouse into the bottle.'

Mr Wooding put the bottle on the draining board and pointed George at Eddie.

'Hold your hand out.'

Eddie shook his head.

I thought Mr Wooding would explode but, instead, he spoke almost gently.

'Williams, I know what this was: a silly end-of-term prank that went too far. Now, what's it to be – a couple of quick strokes from George or do I send you to Mr Rix, who will doubtless prove less understanding than I? It's up to you.'

Mr Wooding waited. As far as I was concerned there was only one option. Accept the two strokes from George. But Eddie's sense of honour, or his trust in justice, was greater than mine. When Mr Wooding broke the silence and told him to hold out his hand, Eddie refused again.

Still Mr Wooding remained calm. He unclipped his pen and wrote a long note on the top sheet of a pile of paper on one of the shelves. We stood watching him, listening to the scratch of his nib against the paper.

'You two, back to Miss Carver's class and apologize for being late,' he said to me and Spencer as he folded the note. Then he handed it to Eddie. 'And you, my silly young friend, can take this note and your bottle to Mr Rix – and may God have mercy on your soul.'

He opened the door and the three of us walked through the classroom and out into the corridor.

'Where you going?' I called as Eddie hurried away in the opposite direction to Mr Rix's study.

'Miss Carver,' he said.

And my heart lifted as I ran after him. Of course, he was right. Miss Carver wasn't like Mr Wooding. She would understand. She knew us better than the other teachers. She might have been upset by what Eddie had said about Mr Rix but she knew he wouldn't lie. She'd sort everything out.

We reached our classroom door and Eddie paused. He bent down and put the milk bottle on the floor.

'Don't want to scare her again,' he said as he stood up. He looked carefully at us. 'We just tell her the truth. She'll believe us. OK?'

We nodded and he gave us an encouraging wink, then he knocked on the door and opened it.

3

There was complete silence in the classroom and every-body had their heads bent over their exercise books. The three of us stood for a full minute next to Miss Carver's desk, waiting for her to look up from her marking; then Eddie broke the silence.

'Miss,' he whispered.

Miss Carver continued reading, then she finally came to the end of the page, ticked it, and lifted her eyes.

'Yes?' she said coldly.

'We're sorry we're late, Miss,' I said, trying to break through to her. 'And I'm sorry I laughed.'

'So am I,' Spencer mumbled.

'And I'm sorry I scared you, Miss. I didn't mean it, honest,' Eddie said.

We stood there, desperate to make things right again and she just looked through us.

'I suppose you'd better sit down then,' she said flatly.

'Mr Wooding, Miss . . .' Eddie began.

'What about Mr Wooding?'

'He didn't believe us, Miss. He gave Andy and Spencer

the ruler. And he's given me a note and I've got to go and see Mr Rix.'

The whole class still had their pens in their hands and their heads lowered to their books, but nobody was writing.

'Well, you'd better go then, hadn't you?' Miss Carver said.

'Will you come with me, Miss?'

For an instant Miss Carver looked surprised.

'What on earth for?'

'You can tell him, Miss. Tell him I didn't put the mouse in the bottle. Tell him I found it there. And it's not my fault. And Mr Wooding shouldn't have hit Andy and Spencer because they didn't do anything.'

'I'll do no such thing!'

'You've got to, Miss. You're the only one. Please! He'll believe you because you're his – Oh please, Miss.'

Eddie had been becoming more and more frantic, but now he held his hands out to her in one last appeal.

'You *know* me, Miss.'

He was throwing himself on her mercy. Asking her to remember what he'd been like for a whole year. Yes, a bit cheeky; yes, too talkative; and yes, lots of small faults. But honest, loyal, enthusiastic, thoughtful, honourable. *You know me, Miss.* It was a simple statement to remind her of the truth, but she threw it back at him.

'I thought I did know you,' Miss Carver said. 'But I was wrong. Go and see Mr Rix.'

I saw the hurt in Eddie's eyes. He had trusted her, opened his heart to her. And she had betrayed him.

He turned and walked to the door.

'Miss, you can't let him go,' I said as he opened the door.

Her face was blank and unyielding.

I heard the door close and, when I looked, Eddie had gone.

I went to my desk and Bob Newman silently showed me what Miss Carver had given us to do. It was stupid, pointless, word-for-word copying of a whole chapter from our geography book into our exercise books. It wasn't work, it was bad-tempered punishment and it was unworthy of Miss Carver; another betrayal, this time, of all the pleasure we'd got from learning during the year. I sat there doing the mindless task but my ears were straining to hear what was happening at the other end of the corridor.

Twenty minutes went by and still Eddie didn't come back. The tension was awful. Finally I couldn't wait any longer so I put up my hand.

'Please, Miss, may I be excused?'

She wanted to refuse but I fidgeted and made a pained face as if it was urgent so she gave me a curt nod.

I hurried along the corridor, past the boys' lavatories, and peered round the corner. Eddie was standing outside Mr Rix's door, holding the note in one hand and the bottle in the other. I checked that no one was coming, then tiptoed over to him. I pointed my thumb at the door.

'He's not there,' Eddie whispered. 'I think he's in the Infants' block.'

I heard a distant door slam and footsteps echoing down

the corridor. I gave Eddie a quick look of sympathy then hurried round the corner towards the boys' lavatories. Mr Rix was walking fast down the corridor.

'Out of your class?' he shouted.

'Toilet, sir,' I said.

'Quick about it,' he said as he drew level with me.

'Sir,' I said, pushing the door to the lavatories.

I got inside and heard his footsteps stop at the end of the corridor.

'You again?' I heard him roar. 'What are you doing here?'

Eddie must have said something about Mr Wooding's note because Mr Rix said, 'Let me read it.'

There was a pause.

'You did what?' Mr Rix shouted. 'Where is this bottle? Give it to me! Why, you disgusting little … Get into my office, now!'

I could hear Eddie's voice but I couldn't make out his words.

'Don't you lie to me!' Mr Rix screamed. 'We're living in a time of shortage. The public pays for you to have milk every day to help you grow and all you can do is abuse the privilege! You wretched ingrate. Get in there!'

I heard the door to his office slam.

I stood for a moment, aware of the blood pulsing in my neck, then I opened the door and ran as quietly as I could up the corridor. I had to know what was happening. I turned the corner and tiptoed towards Mr Rix's office.

'I'm warning you!' Mr Rix bellowed from inside the room. 'I will – not – be – lied – to – in – this – way!' The staccato pauses sounded as if he was shaking Eddie for emphasis.

Eddie's voice, with only two words clear, cried '– can't make –'

'Don't you dare speak to me like that!' Mr Rix thundered.

I heard a faint scuffle and then the whistle of a cane. The whistle ended in a *thw-op* sound. Eddie had lost. The worst was happening. A furious Mr Rix was caning him on his bottom: that noise was unmistakably different from the *thwack* of a cane across the hand. I'd had the cane twice on my bottom and the pain and humiliation had been much worse than the other times when I'd been hit on my hand. I imagined Eddie, bent over Mr Rix's desk, his hands gripping the sides.

The *thw-op* came again. A shiver ran down my back and I held my breath. For some strange reason, Mr Rix's beatings never stopped at three. It was either one stroke, two strokes or four strokes. If there was a third, it meant … *Thw-op*. Eddie was getting four.

I heard the fourth and got ready to race away before the door opened. Then, to my horror, I heard a fifth. Was Eddie going to get six? Only once in my whole time at Maldain Road had anyone had six. It was when I was in the second year and a boy in the top class had been caught trying to set fire to his classroom after school.

The terrible sound of the cane came again. Six! My face was crawling with a strange tingling and I felt a bead of sweat run down my side from my armpit. But when there was a seventh *thw-op* my whole body jerked in shock.

Seven? Nobody ever got seven. Had Mr Rix lost count? Had he gone crazy? Was he going to keep hitting Eddie until he begged for mercy?

I was so shocked that I almost didn't hear Mr Rix's voice. I caught the word 'up', and then heard him repeat the phrase. 'Stand up.'

He'd finished. And now I fled away down the corridor. I burst into our classroom without knocking and Miss Carver started to speak, then stopped. She must have guessed where I'd been and the expression on my face must have given her the first indication that she had been involved in something that she was going to regret.

'Sit down, Andy,' she said, smiling, trying to make things better. But it was too late, she could never make things better.

I sat down, nudged Bob, and wrote on the back page of my geography book: EDDIE GOT 7.

I underlined the number seven.

Bob's mouth fell open and he looked at me to check I wasn't lying. I nodded to confirm that it was the truth. He immediately took my book and passed it to Angela Edwards in the desk next to us. Angela read it and passed it on.

Within five minutes the exercise book had been round the class and was back with me. Whispered discussions were taking place everywhere. Miss Carver cleared her throat meaningfully and the conversations died down, though people kept looking at the door expecting Eddie's return. Five minutes went by and he still didn't come in. The whispers began again.

Finally the bell rang for lunch and we straightened up in our desks.

'Well, I'll see you at the assembly, of course,' Miss Carver said with desperate brightness, 'but I suppose this is the last time we'll all be together.'

Everyone's eyes shot to Eddie's empty desk and Miss Carver realized her mistake – we weren't all there.

If the morning had gone differently, this would have been the moment when one of us would have leaped to our feet and shouted, 'Three cheers for Miss Carver!' and Manny Solomon, who had it ready in his desk, would have given her the card we had all signed. As it was, we sat stony-faced, staring at her, our eyes filled with hatred. She must have thought it was terribly unfair – a whole year of good feeling wiped out by one morning of bad temper. But it was precisely because we had liked her so much that we felt so let down. Our fairy princess had turned out to be the wicked witch after all.

'Well, you'd better go to lunch,' she said.

We filed out in silence and nobody looked at her or said a word.

Out in the corridor, everybody began talking at once as they walked towards the dining room. I ran in the other direction, guessing where Eddie was – the place I always went to after I'd been caned. I burst into the boys' lavatories and saw a pair of feet behind one of the cubicle doors.

'Eddie?'

There was a long sniffing noise and then the sound of the bolt being drawn back. The door swung open. Eddie looked terrible. His hair was matted with sweat and standing up straight as if he – or someone – had pulled it. His face was drawn and pale and his eyes were red from crying. He had been rubbing his face with grimy hands and his cheeks had dirty patches on them. He opened his mouth to speak but his eyes brimmed with tears which overflowed and ran down, leaving clean lines in the patches of grime. He wiped the tears away, leaving new smears of dirt.

'It hurts. It bloomin' hurts,' he managed to say before his face creased up and his shoulders heaved with a sob.

He stepped back into the cubicle and closed the door. I heard the bolt slide into place.

'Eddie . . .'

'Go away!' he said, choking with sobs.

I went.

I walked slowly down the corridor and glanced into the dining room at the chattering people stuffing food into their mouths. I felt sick and hurried out into the fresh air. I leaned against the trunk of the horse chestnut and looked through the wire fence at the infants running around their playground. They were laughing and shouting and happy and I can remember thinking, 'That won't last. They'll learn.'

Gradually people from my class drifted out from the dining room but I waved them away impatiently when they tried to ask me what had happened. Then Bob Newman came running out to join me under the tree.

'W-W-W-Where's, E-Ed?'

'In the bogs.'

23

'Is he all r–r–right?'

'What d'you think? What are we going to do, Bob? We've got to do something. You should see him. I mean, seven. Nobody gets seven. It's wrong.'

'W–W–W–What can we do? N–N–N–Nothing.'

I looked at Bob and I knew he was right: there was nothing we could do. We shrugged our shoulders at the hopelessness of it all. A moment later someone started a kick-around in the playground and we ran to join in.

There was no sign of Eddie as we filed into the hall that afternoon for the final assembly and I wondered if he was still in the lavatory or if he'd gone home. We sang a hymn, then Mr Rix began his end-of-term speech. He had been speaking for five minutes when the door at the back of the hall creaked open. Everybody turned to look.

It was Eddie. He had flattened his hair and washed his face but he was terribly pale and his eyes were still red. I was sitting at the end of the second row and when he got level with me I squeezed up to make room for him. He sat down, putting his fists under the backs of his thighs so that his bottom didn't touch the bench. Even so, he grimaced with pain.

Mr Rix got to the end of his speech and handed out some prizes. Then he asked the pupils in the front row to come up on to the stage. It was a tradition of the school that, at the final assembly, every leaver was given a small Bible with the pupil's name and the headmaster's signature on the inside cover. One after the other, our classmates shuffled forward to receive their Bible from Mr Rix. When the front row had all sat down again, he signalled the second row to come up and, with Eddie in the lead, we climbed the stairs on to the stage.

I was just behind Eddie. I saw Mr Rix hold out a Bible and offer his hand for a handshake. Eddie reached for the Bible but deliberately put his other hand behind his back.

'Come on, lad, shake hands like a man. No hard feelings,' Mr Rix said quietly so that no one in the hall would hear.

Eddie reached forward and took hold of his Bible but Mr Rix pulled it out of his grasp.

'Shake hands,' Mr Rix insisted, his voice beginning to rise slightly. 'Come on, let's shake on it and forget the whole sorry incident.'

'No,' Eddie said.

'Right then – no Bible.' Mr Rix's voice was loud enough for everyone in the hall to hear. 'Get off this stage. Collect your things from your room and leave these premises. You are no longer a pupil at this school.'

In total silence Eddie walked across the stage, down the stairs, past the rows of gawping pupils and out of the door.

Then Mr Rix turned back to me. He held out my Bible. For an instant I thought about refusing to shake his hand but then I saw that he wasn't offering it. I took my Bible and went back to my place.

There was a closing prayer and we were dismissed. We hurried to the classroom for our belongings, then walked across the playground for the last time and out through the school gates on to the hot streets.

Bob and Manny stood next to me at the main road waiting for a gap in the traffic. Two trams rattled by in opposite directions, then we ran across the road, jumping the tramlines because someone had said you could get your foot trapped in them. We looked back at the school and Bob shot a big gob of spit on to the pavement. It seemed like a good final gesture so Manny and I copied him. The end of school and the end of a bad day.

But it wasn't the end. It was only the beginning. Other things happened that summer – a whole chain of events, one thing adding to another and another, and we all got caught up in such anger and bitterness until . . .

When Bob and Manny and I turned into Goldsmith Road on that last afternoon of school, Eddie was waiting for us, leaning against the wall of the Rabbit Club storerooms.

During the war and well into the 1950s, meat was rationed and a lot of people kept rabbits and chickens for the table. My own family had three rabbit hutches and a chicken coop in the backyard of our house. The Rabbit Club was where everyone bought the feed and straw for the animals and it was also a social centre where the men met to talk and drink.

'Wotcha, Eddie,' Manny said when we got up to him.

Eddie was still pale and tight-lipped. He nodded curtly at us, then crossed the road and started up the hill towards the side entrance of the bomb site. We followed in silence. The sun beat down on us and a warm wind sent spirals of dust whirling in the gutter. It hadn't rained for over a month and there were rumours that water might soon have to be rationed.

We pushed aside the loose boards of the fence and ducked through the gap into what we always called the Bomb Building.

This bomb site had been created one night in March 1941 when a German bomber had dropped a landmine on the big Victorian house at the top of the hill. The huge explosion had blown the house apart and no one had ever found the bodies of the two old ladies and their brother who lived there. Then about five minutes after the first raid, another bomber had spotted the burning ruins and come in low, dropping his load of 50-kilo bombs. Some of them had landed in the garden of the big house, obliterating a small orchard and some huge greenhouses; one had buried itself in the thick clay next to the greenhouses and failed to explode; two others had destroyed a smaller house near the bottom of the hill and another one had fallen on the air-raid shelter where the family of that house were hiding. The entrance to the shelter was down four steps and the bomb had hit the bottom step and blown the door off its hinges. The parents and their three children had been lifted up by the blast, thrown against the concrete wall, and killed instantly.

When we were little kids we were terrified of the area. Eight people had died there and we thought it was haunted. We didn't even like walking past it on the way to school so we used to cross over to the other side of the road. But when we were about nine we dared each other to go in there and discovered our own private adventure playground.

It was a jungle of wild flowers, weeds, brambles and nettles, where wildlife flourished unchecked. Foxes and feral cats skulked in the undergrowth; birds sang and built nests there; slow-worms and grass snakes slithered through the thick grass; the air buzzed with a multitude of insects, and enormous stag beetles nipped our fingers with their huge black pincers when we tried to catch them and put them in matchboxes.

It was a wonderful place. But it was full of dangers, too, and we were always cutting ourselves on glass or falling into holes or grazing ourselves on piles of bricks. But the danger was part of the attraction. And best of all, right in the middle of the area, was the Big Brown 'ill.

My mum used to say, 'It's not 'ill, it's *H*ill. Big Brown *H*ill. And, anyway, I don't like you playing there: it's a death trap. Someone's going to get themselves killed there one day.'

She was right. It really was dangerous. It had always been a steep slope but the bombs had ripped huge craters at the bottom, so now the hill was about fifteen metres high and a sheer slope of clay. We used to shoot down it on our bikes and it was like going over a cliff. And trying to brake only made it more dangerous. You just had to let go and hope.

The Bomb Building seemed to bring out a savage, primitive streak in us. Sometimes we'd even strip to the waist and smear clay across our chests as camouflage, and we invented all sorts of rituals and superstitions: before you rode down the Big Brown 'ill you had to put your foot on a piece of concrete that stood at the top of the slope; you had to honour the memory of the dead old ladies and their brother by crossing yourself whenever you walked over the large flagstones which were all that remained of the Big House, and no one was ever allowed to hide or play in the ruins of the bomb shelter where the family had been killed.

There was something powerful, almost frightening, about the Bomb Building and we never went there alone and we never stayed when it got dark. Even on a bright day it only took a sudden shiver of wind through the bushes to give us the creeps, as if something menacing was hiding there.

As soon as we climbed through the fence that afternoon Eddie pulled a penknife from his pocket and cut a sapling growing by the path. He ripped the leaves off and went ahead of us, slashing at the bushes and brambles on either side. The whistling noise was like the swish of a cane.

'Did you really get seven, Ed?' Manny asked.

'Yep,' Eddie said, aiming a vicious swipe at a tall thistle.

'Blimey,' was all Manny could say.

We came out of the thicket on to the open space below the Big Brown 'ill. The hot weather had baked the clay into a light gold colour and the surface was cracking up into large diamond shapes, which were useful toe-holds, but it was still a hard climb and we were panting by the time we got to the top. Bob and I immediately sat down, our legs hanging over the edge. Eddie didn't want to place weight on his bottom so he squatted on his haunches next to us.

'Gotta go,' Manny said, wiping sweat off his upper lip. 'Toodle-oo.'

'T'ra,' we called as he ambled off towards the top exit.

Manny was always the first one to leave. His sister,

Esther, had died from diphtheria at the age of two, so his mum was terribly protective of him and was only really happy when he was safe at home.

In some ways I quite envied Manny. His father didn't earn much money from his job as a Trades Union official in the Seamen's Union, but his mother's parents were rich so he always had far more toys and comics and books and sweets than the rest of us. I also quite envied the fact that he missed school at the slightest sign of a tummy upset or a cold and was fussed over and coddled by his mother.

But in almost every other respect Manny's life seemed awful. For a start, his mum had filled him with fears about germs and illness and he was forced to wear warm clothes even when it was baking hot. He was also spectacularly unattractive with a pale, flabby body and a big, round face with a large hooked nose. He wore very thick glasses and his hair, which waved as if it had been tightly permed, was the colour of ox-blood shoe polish. On top of all that, he was a Jew.

Kids got called lots of cruel names at school: 'blubber', 'four eyes', 'big ears', but when someone called Manny 'Jewboy' or 'Yid' it was much worse. It was only a few years since the Nazis had killed millions of his people in the concentration camps, so every insult must have seemed like a reminder and a threat.

We watched as Manny made his way out of the Bomb Building, then Eddie sucked a breath in through his teeth and sank forward on to his knees.

'Blimey, my bum hurts like hell,' he said, undoing his snake-buckle belt. 'Is it bleeding, Andy?'

31

I pulled open the elastic top of his shorts and took a quick look at his buttocks. I could only see down as far as the top two wheals which were still raised in purple ridges across his cheeks.

'I don't think so but it isn't half bruised. God, he's a tosspot, that Rix.'

'He's not a t-toss-pot, he's a s-snot-p-pot!' Bob said. Perhaps it was the timing that the stutter gave to his jokes, but Bob could make us laugh more than anyone and this silly rhyme sent us into fits of giggles.

Finally, Eddie stood up and buckled his belt. 'I'm gonna have to hide the bruises,' he said, half to himself.

Eddie's house, like mine, had three bedrooms. His seventeen-year-old twin sisters slept in one of them and his twenty-one-year-old sister slept in another. Eddie had to share the third bedroom with his mother and his stepfather, so they were likely to see his bruises while he was getting dressed or undressed.

'I'll have to put my pyjamas on in the lav,' he said and his face was grim as he thought of all the problems that his beating was going to cause.

Bob and I stood up and looked at him, feeling awkward. A pigeon swooped in low over the Big Brown 'ill then banked and swept away towards the allotments.

We walked down the road and Bob and I sat on the garden wall of number thirty-one, Mr Barrington's house, while Eddie stood next to us. There was shade from the hot sun under the big lime tree that grew at the edge of the garden and Mr Barrington, unlike many others, never banged on his window or shouted if you sat on his wall.

Eddie pulled down a low hanging leaf from the tree and rolled it into a tube.

'You gonna be able to sit down for tea?' I asked.

'Have to,' Eddie replied, biting a chunk out of the leaf tube and chewing it.

'Is it still burning?'

'No, that's gone. It's the achy and sore bit now. And my bum crack's all sweaty.'

I nodded, remembering all the stages of pain after a caning, although I couldn't really imagine what seven would be like in comparison to my worst: four.

'That Rix,' Eddie said bitterly, spitting a wad of chewed leaf on to the pavement. 'I hope he dies. And her as well. I hope their car crashes and they get killed when they're going to be married.'

Bob and I looked at him in shock. Wishing someone dead was terrible because it might happen.

'Oh God!' Eddie suddenly said. 'Mum'll want to know where my Bible is. I can't tell her I didn't get it; she'll want to know why and everything.'

'You could say someone nicked it,' I offered.

'Oh yeah, some yob with a cosh robbed my Bible!' Eddie snapped.

'You c–c–can h–h–have m–mi–mine,' Bob said.

'Thanks, Bob,' Eddie said, and I wished that I'd made the offer instead of my stupid suggestion about lying, 'but your parents'll want to see it.'

'They wo–won't even a–a–ask. I know.'

'Anyway, it's got your name in it.'

'You c–c–can t–t–tear it out. I don't m–m–mind, honest.'

Eddie thought for a moment and then shook his head, 'My mum'd notice. But, you're a pal.'

He smiled at Bob and put his hand on his shoulder. Bob was so much shorter and slighter than Eddie that a stranger would have thought that the little curly-haired boy was at least two years younger than his friend.

'I'll just have to keep my mouth shut and hope CL doesn't find out what happened – he'd kill me,' Eddie said.

CL was what he called his stepfather, Chris Lang. His real father had been killed when Eddie was two. He was a docker and he'd fallen into the Thames while he was working and had been crushed between a ship and the dock. Eddie's mother had used the small union compensation to move herself and her four children from Deptford, where they had been living, into the house next door to us. So I couldn't remember a time when Eddie wasn't my best friend. When Eddie was seven his mother had met Chris Lang, a print worker, and a year later they had got married.

Eddie's three sisters adored their new stepfather and Eddie liked him too, but CL was very strict with him: any trouble at school or in the road meant, at the very least, a row and often worse.

'Oh well, better go,' Eddie said.

We walked down the road and Bob peeled off into his garden.

'Now is the hour when we must say goodbye,' he sang as he closed the gate.

I think if he had been allowed, Bob would have sung

everything that he wanted to say, because it was the only time he didn't stutter. That's why he loved being in the church choir.

Eddie and I crossed over the road and I opened my gate.

'Do you want to come in my place?' I asked, wanting to do something to show that I was his best friend.

'No, better go in,' he said, opening his gate.

'OK. Ta-ta for now.'

'TTFN.'

I walked up the short path and climbed the three steps to my front door. I rang the bell. Eddie was at his front door doing the same thing. We winked at each other. Then I heard feet clumping down the stairs. The front door opened and my sister, Kate, was there.

'It's only Andy,' she yelled then ran back up the stairs.

I went inside and closed the door.

5

I walked along the dark hallway and down the step into the kitchen. My tea was already on the table. I dumped my satchel on the easy chair and went through to the scullery where my mother was ironing one of Kate's blouses at the table next to the open back door.

'Hello, dear,' she said, briefly turning round and smiling.

I felt a rush of affection for her and I went up and put my arms round her waist. She felt hot and the back of her blouse was damp with sweat but I gave her a hug and kissed her shoulder, noticing that I would soon be as tall as she was.

'That's nice,' she laughed. 'What are you after?'

'Nothing,' I said, letting go and going back to the kitchen.

I sat at the table and checked my two sandwiches: fish paste and thin rounds of tomato.

'Has Kate had her tea?' I called.

'She's not having any, she's going to the leaving party tonight.'

Friday, 22 July 1949 was Kate's last day at school and

the next day she was going up to Nottingham. She had always wanted to be a nurse and she was going there for the summer to get some experience working with our Auntie June who ran a private nursing home.

I finished my sandwiches, gulped my lemon barley squash and then got my Leaver's Bible from my satchel.

'Look, Mum.'

'Oh, your Bible,' she said, standing the iron on its end. 'Let me look. "Maldain Road School. Andrew Adamson. Class Six. 1949. S. G. Rix. Headmaster." It's lovely, dear. Keep it safe.'

'What time's Dad home?' I asked, taking the Bible back from her.

'No use asking me. He gets later and later. He'll turn up when it suits him,' she said, banging the iron down hard on one of my shirts. '*And* expect his meal when he does.'

I went upstairs. Kate was in the bathroom, brushing her hair in front of the mirror.

'Hello, schoolkid!' she mocked.

I stuck my tongue out at her and then held up my Bible.

'Whoopee!' she said.

I sat on the edge of the bath and watched as she began to put her lipstick on.

'Is Mum wild with Dad?' I asked.

'Search me. Why?'

'Dunno.'

She dabbed at her lips with her hanky.

'Right, you, out of my boudoir.'

'It's the bathroom, not your boudoir.'

37

'Out!' she said, raising her hand as if to clip me.

I knew that she wouldn't but I stuck my tongue out and went anyway. She slammed the door behind me.

I lay on my bed. The window was open and there was a bit of a breeze blowing the net curtains. I searched through the pile of old comics next to the bed and chose my favourite, *Film Fun*. Kate went past my room and down the stairs and I could hear her talking to Mum. It would be strange when she went tomorrow. For the first time ever, I would be the only one in the house.

I looked across at Michael's bed. My twenty-year-old brother was doing his national service in Malaya. My mother worried about him all the time but, as far as I was concerned, he could stay there forever. I'd idolized him when I was younger but by his mid-teens he hated having to share his bedroom with me. He nagged me and bullied me with sly punches and Chinese burns, so I had been really pleased when he had been called up to the army at eighteen. The only time I even thought about him was when they showed bits about what they called 'the emergency in Malaya' on the cinema newsreels and I hoped that I might see him on screen.

I heard Kate call goodbye to Mum and then the front door banged. I got up and went to my window. I pulled the curtain aside and looked out beyond our backyard to Eddie's house. I wondered if his mum had asked about his Bible yet. I leaned out and softly whistled our special whistle in case Eddie could hear me. I waited, but there was no sign of him. Then an idea struck me and I ran downstairs.

'Mum?'

'What?'

'Can Eddie come and sleep here during the holidays? He could have Mike's bed tonight and then Kate's after tonight. Or stay in Mike's bed if you don't want Kate's room messed up.'

'Don't be silly, dear. He's got his own bed. Why would he want to sleep here?'

I could hardly explain about him having to hide his bruises, so I just said, 'Oh, go on!'

'No.'

Her eyes looked past me and I heard a footstep but, before I could turn, an arm came round my chest and pulled me backwards and a hot hand covered my eyes.

'Guess who,' my dad said, putting on a high squeaky voice.

'I dunno. Humphrey Bogart,' I said, breathing in the familiar smell of my father: a mixture of Woodbine cigarettes, beer and tangy sweat.

'Humpty Go-Cart,' my dad said in a bad imitation of the film star. 'Cor-rect. First prize to the ex-Maldain Road Schoolboy in the green dress.'

He let go of me and stepped past me to kiss my mum.

'Hello, Peg love.'

'What time do you call this?' she said after their cheeks had brushed.

My dad made an elaborate show of looking at his watch.

'Gee, Officer, don't arrest me,' he said in his Humphrey

Bogart voice, 'I call it ... six forty-three. Hey no, make that six forty-four.'

'Oh, *Dick Barton*!' I said and ran towards the front room. I wanted to hear the programme – my favourite on radio – but I also wanted to get away from my parents in case they started having a row. It wasn't something they did often but I hated it when it happened.

I switched on the radio and sat down close to the speaker so that I could get completely caught up in the story and not hear anything from the kitchen. At the end of the episode I left the radio on for a few minutes just in case, then switched it off and listened. There was no sound of raised voices.

As I stood up and walked to the door a sudden dread swept through me about going to the new school in September. All the comfort of the familiar would be gone. What would it be like? Everybody kept telling me that it was a time of big changes and that I would have to be more grown-up. Would I still be allowed to listen to *Dick Barton* and read *Film Fun*?

When I got to the kitchen I was glad to find that the danger of a row had retreated. My dad was at the table eating and my mum was out in the scullery, humming while she folded Kate's clothes and put them in a suitcase.

'Don't tell me,' my dad said, 'Dick Bathbun got killed by the baddie.'

'No!' I laughed.

'Phew, it's hot,' he said, wiping his forehead. 'Open the cellar door and get a bit of draught going.'

I opened the door and a current of cool damp air

wafted up, smelling of the coal we kept down there. I leaned against the door and watched my father eating.

'What's the liver like?' my mother called.

'Delicious. Small. But delish.'

'The butcher kept it for me specially.'

'I don't understand you, Peg, I really don't. Why won't you let me get a bit of extra meat from one of my contacts?'

'Because it's black market.'

'What's the difference between that and someone keeping it specially for you?'

'A lot. One's a little bit that the butcher has got left over from his legal ration and the other's just plain criminal.'

'Right, you won't be interested in the little something I've got, then.'

My dad pointed at his briefcase and signalled me to bring it. I picked it up and took it to him.

'A little something from the U S of A!' he teased, winking at me. 'A little something to wear. A little something you can't buy in shops over here.'

'Oh, not nylon stockings, Harry,' my mother said, coming into the kitchen with an excited smile on her face.

'Cor-rect!'

'Oh, just in time. My others are all laddered.'

'Yes, but you don't want these. They're nasty old black-market nylons,' he said taking some from the briefcase.

'It's not the same, Harry, and you know it,' she said, grabbing them out of his hands. 'You haven't got a pair for Kate, have you? For Nottingham?'

He pulled another pair from the case and handed them over.

'How many have you got in there?'

'Forty pairs. A pal of mine came to the stadium today and asked if I could shift them. I'll go up to the Rabbit Club later – get rid of them up there.'

'What are you going to do with the money?'

'It's my mate's, isn't it.'

'And you'll get a cut of it and put it all on the horses or the dogs.'

'Cor, is she ungrateful or what? I give her nylons and she moans!' He handed his empty plate to her, then brushed his hand across her arm and smiled. 'It was lovely. Ta.'

My mum went back to the scullery and my dad lit one of his Woodbine cigarettes and stretched out in his chair looking through the window at the sky above Eddie's roof. He took a puff and blew a perfect smoke ring. He put a finger through the centre of the ring, then quickly pulled it back and watched the draught disperse the smoke. He checked his watch and stood up.

'Well, I'll just nip up to the Rabbit Club, get rid of these.'

'Can I come?' I asked.

There was a hesitation, almost a flicker of irritation, and I thought he was going to say no, but he looked towards the scullery, then back at me.

'Okey-doke,' he said. 'Andy's coming with me, Peg.'

My mum murmured something to herself but we were already on our way towards the front door.

Dark clouds had rolled in to hide the sun, but the air seemed hotter and stuffier than before. We were both sweating by the time we were halfway up the hill.

'Here, I read they've got a new Tarzan for the next film,' my dad said, panting slightly. 'Bloke called Lex Barker.'

'What's happened to Johnny Weissmuller?'

'Eaten by crocodiles, it said.'

'No, really.'

'Dunno. Too old? Pity, I liked him. Anything good on the flicks next week?'

My dad relied on me to pick the films we went to see. And in those days there was an amazing choice. There were eleven cinemas within a ten-minute tram ride of our house, few of them showing the same film, many of them changing programmes twice a week, plus a different programme on Sundays. And I knew all the details: the films, the actors, the directors, the times. I also took my selecting responsibility seriously, trying to pick films that we'd both like.

'There's *Whispering Smith* at the Rivoli. It's got Alan Ladd in it,' I suggested, knowing that my dad liked Alan Ladd. 'Or there's *Passport To Pimlico* at the Astoria, Thursday to Saturday. It's funny.'

'We can do them both, can't we? Now you're on holiday.'

'Spiff!'

We climbed the last part of the hill and, as we got level with the Bomb Building, Dad stopped and pulled out his cigarettes.

43

'I hear they're finally getting round to doing something there,' he said, nodding to the bomb site. 'Going to clear it for houses.'

'Clear it?'

'About time, too,' he said, lighting his Woodbine.

'When?'

'Start in three weeks' time, I heard.'

I stood speechless with shock as he walked away.

'Come on,' he called.

I caught up with him and we turned right and headed down the hill past the allotments towards the Rabbit Club. The windows were open and we could hear music and men's laughter as we got closer.

'Right, I'll go and flog this lot,' Dad said, when we got to the door. 'You might as well pop off home.'

'It's OK, I'll wait.'

'I'll be ages.'

'It's OK.'

'Suit yourself,' he said sharply, then pushed open the door and went in.

I leaned against the wall and looked over at the tree-tops of the Bomb Building. It seemed impossible that soon there would be houses there. Where would we play?

Maldain Road School was finished forever. Kate was going away. The Bomb Building was going to disappear. Everything was changing. My heart suddenly filled with all this loss, and tears welled up in my eyes. It wasn't fair. Why did things have to change?

There was a burst of noise as the door opened. It was

my dad. I wanted to throw myself against him and cry and cry like I'd done when I was little. I wanted him to hold me and tell me everything was all right.

'What's the matter with you?' he asked, looking at my brimming eyes.

'Nothing,' I said, turning away.

'Listen, I'm going to be here a while. So you'd better get off home.'

'It's OK.'

'Don't argue; go home,' he snapped. 'Tell your mum I've got caught up with the blokes for half an hour.'

I didn't dare turn round to him in case the tears spilled down my face.

'Do you hear me?'

I nodded and started walking fast.

'Andy.'

I kept walking.

'See you later, all right? Tell your mum.'

I crossed the road and walked fast up the hill. The noise of the Rabbit Club subsided as the door closed and I ducked through the break in the fence and into the bomb site. The heavy cloud cover seemed to be coming lower and lower and the light was fading fast. I was scared at being here alone but I wanted to cry and I didn't want anyone to see me. I leaned against the fence and felt my face crumple up as a sob shook me. But it was no good, the misery wasn't going to come out in one big relieving burst. It was stuck there inside me.

I didn't fancy walking home through the Bomb Building in the rapidly thickening gloom so I wiped my blurry eyes and bent to climb back through the fence. At that moment the noise from the Rabbit Club increased as the front door opened again. I froze.

Through the gap in the fence I saw my dad come out of the door and glance rapidly up the road – and I knew that he was checking to make sure that I'd gone. He crossed the road and strode away towards Manstead Road. I saw him turn the corner.

For a moment I hesitated. Then I ran after him.

When I got to the corner I peered round it and saw him in the phone box along the road, dialling a number. There was a pause then he pushed a coin into the slot and started speaking. He spoke for a long time. He fumbled in his pocket, took out another coin and put it into the slot. He turned his back and I couldn't tell if he was talking or listening.

My heart was thumping hard and I fled away in case he suddenly finished and saw me. I reached the broken bit of fence and jumped into the Bomb Building. I peeped out; the road was empty. I waited and waited while my heart calmed down and then he came round the corner and went back into the Rabbit Club.

I counted to ten then dashed home. The air was thick and hot and the sweat was pouring off me by the time I got there. I pulled the end of my shirt out of my shorts and wiped my face, then walked into the dark house. It was silent, and a shiver ran through me as if the ghosts of the Bomb Building had followed me down here to my very house.

'Mum?' I called softly.

'I'm in the kitchen.'

She was sitting in the easy chair and the light was so gloomy in the corner that I could barely make out her face.

'I think it's going to thunder,' she said. 'It's so close, you can hardly breathe. Where's your dad?'

I tried to remember the exact words he had used. If I got it right, maybe she wouldn't know it was a lie. 'He got caught up with the blokes for half an hour.'

It sounded so clumsy and untrue that my tongue felt thick as I said it. I was angry with him for making me do this.

'I expected as much,' my mother said. 'They're all the same when they get together.'

I sat on the floor next to the chair. I wanted to tell her about the phone call. I wanted to tell her that I was scared he was arranging another black-market deal and that he might get caught by the police. There were stories every week in the local paper about people being sent to prison for selling things on the black market. But I couldn't find the words. They all sounded too dramatic, like an episode of *Dick Barton*.

'Goodness knows what's been going on next door,' she said suddenly, nodding towards Eddie's house. 'Shouting and banging and crying; a right do.'

We sat in silence then she put her hand on my head.

'Gosh, your hair's all sweaty,' she said, but she didn't take her hand away. And after a moment she began stroking my hair, running her hand from the crown of my head to the back of my neck.

47

For the second time that evening, tears sprang into my eyes.

'I'm tired,' I said, getting up.

'I bet. Night-night,' she said, taking my hand and giving it a squeeze.

'Night.'

I went upstairs to my bedroom, closed the door, peeled off my sticky clothes and pulled on my pyjamas. I leaned out of my window and tried to see the one parallel to mine, the window of Eddie and his parents' bedroom. It was open.

'Eddie,' I whispered, as loudly as I dared. No reply.

My chest was pressed against the window sill and I could feel my heart thudding, shaking me so that the whole world seemed to tremble. Lightning lit up the clouds in the distance. I waited for the thunder, but none came and I went to bed.

6

My dad had already left for work when I got up the next morning. He was the assistant manager of Blackford Greyhound Stadium, so Saturdays and Wednesdays were his busiest days because of the race meetings. Sometimes he left at seven in the morning and didn't get home until well after midnight.

I hung around the house all morning waiting to say goodbye to Kate, but when the moment came, I couldn't face it. Just before eleven, when she was going to leave, I went downstairs and locked myself in the outside lavatory. I sat there and refused to open the door when Kate knocked on it to say goodbye.

'Come on, Andy, give me a kiss!' she said.

'No!'

'Oh, just leave him, dear – we're going to be late,' my mother said.

'Come out, please,' Kate called.

'Go away, I'm on the lav,' I shouted.

'There's no need to tell the world,' my mother said in a low voice.

I heard Kate run upstairs and then come down again

about a minute later. I heard some chatter between her and Mum, then the front door closed.

I stayed there listening to the silence from the house, smelling the mixture of Sanilav and the distemper on the brick wall, and looking up at the dark net of spiders' webs in the corner above the door. A silverfish glided along the base of the wall and, partly because they revolted me and partly because I felt angry with myself, I crushed it with the side of my sandal. Then I unlocked the door and ran upstairs to Kate's room. Everything looked far too tidy and the room already felt unlived in.

I went to my room and found a big note on my pillow: 'Have a good holiday. I'll miss you like mad. Love Kate.'

I raced down the stairs and out on to the pavement. She'd gone.

It was warm again outside but none of my friends was on the street yet. I walked down to Fleetly Road and turned left in order to take a quick look at Miss Geale's sweet shop. Sweets had come off the ration in April but supplies had been so limited that most shops had soon run out and rationing had been reintroduced. Every day I checked to see if there was a sign saying that coupons weren't needed any more. Nothing. I looked at the boxes in the window – all empty, I knew – and repeated the names to myself: Squirrel Floral Tips, Sun Pat Chocolate-Covered Nuts and Raisins, Meltis Turkish Delight, Clarnico Mints.

I strolled back up Goldsmith Road and along the front of Eddie's house, looking for any sign of life in the window of the front room. Nothing moved. I sensed that

I ought not to, but I went up the path and rang the bell.

One of Eddie's twin sisters opened the door. Margot and Gwen were so alike that it was hard to tell them apart, and they didn't help by insisting on wearing identical clothes.

'Hello . . .'

'Margot,' she said, used to filling the uncertain gap that everyone left.

'Is Eddie in?'

'He can't come out.'

'Why?'

Margot glanced back into the house, then walked down the steps and across the garden, pulling me with her.

'He's in dead trouble. What's got into him?'

'What?'

'Why didn't he get his Leaver's Bible?'

'I don't know,' I lied.

'Mum kept asking him but he wouldn't tell her. In the end she got all upset and CL threatened to hit him for making her cry. Well, Eddie just went mad.'

'What happened?'

'He only jumped on CL and tried to punch him, that's what. Then CL went to push him away and Eddie bit him. Right on his arm. That was it, wasn't it. You know what CL's like. Off with his belt and he gives him a right walloping.'

'He didn't!'

'Blimey, Eddie bit him – there was blood, teethmarks, everything. So now he's got to stay in his room until he says he's sorry.'

'Who, CL?' I said bitterly.

'Ha, ha, very funny, I'm sure. Anyway, you won't be seeing Eddie today, I can tell you that.'

She started back towards the house.

'Margot . . . can you tell him I came round?'

'Fat chance,' she said, going in and closing the door.

I spent the next hour out in our backyard. I whistled songs and talked loudly to the rabbits to let Eddie know I was there, but every time I looked up at his bedroom window it was empty.

I was desperate to talk to someone about it, but Bob was out and Manny always stayed indoors on the Jewish Sabbath. Then, finally, at nearly half past seven I looked out of the window and saw Bob sitting on his garden wall.

'Where've you been?' I complained when I ran out to meet him.

'D-D-Dad was p-p-playing cricket and we had to go and w-w-watch him. It was d-d-dead b-boring.'

We walked up the road as I told him the news about Eddie.

'Bli-imey, he m-m-must be b-b-black and b-blue. Poor Ed.'

'It's not fair, hitting him after he already got seven. Someone ought to tell that CL.'

'B-B-Bagsy it's you.'

We walked into the Bomb Building, brooding over the injustice of it all, and sat down at the top of the Big Brown 'ill. Below us, the bushes were swaying in the wind that had sprung up. It felt colder and the sky was solid grey.

'They're going to build houses here!' I said, suddenly remembering. 'My dad told me. They're going to get rid of everything. There'll be nothing left.'

'You're j–j–j–j–j–j–j–j–'

Most of the time Bob managed to get his sentences out with only a few stutters, but when he was excited or upset or afraid it could become really chronic.

'You're j–j–j–j–j–j–j–j–' he tried again.

'I'm not joking,' I said.

Bob hated that. Even when his tongue was totally tied and he couldn't force the word out, he never wanted you to help him.

'D–D–D–D–D–D–D–D–D–D–D–D–' he said, his tongue hitting the roof of his mouth in a frenzy. 'D–D–D–D–D–Don't do that!'

He glared at me, breathing hard from the effort of wrestling with the stutter.

Bob hadn't always stuttered. It had started when he was four. He had been sent to live with his grandmother in Exeter to get away from the bombing in London. She adored Bob so, just in case, she bought a Morrison shelter to protect him. These shelters looked a bit like cages; they had steel plates on the top and bottom and the sides were made of criss-crossing steel mesh. Bob's grandmother had heard that they gave even more protection if they were under a table so she put hers under the solid pine table in the kitchen. And each night she tucked Bob up in his shelter and went upstairs to her bedroom to be with her six cats and her parrot.

She didn't bother to shelter herself because, like most

people, she didn't really think that Exeter would ever be a target. But in March 1942 the RAF destroyed a large number of historic buildings during their bombing raids on Rostock and Lübeck. In retaliation, Hitler ordered the Luftwaffe to bomb historic cathedral cities in England. Exeter was one of them.

On 3 May thousands of bombs fell on the city. Two of them fell on either side of Bob's grandmother's house. She and her pets were killed instantly as the building collapsed and Bob was buried under tons of rubble. The table was crushed but the steel cage of the Morrison shelter held and Bob was trapped there, alone, for thirty-two hours before the rescue services found him.

When he was dug out, he was totally white, his hair and clothes covered in plaster dust. The only colour was the blood round his mouth where he had gnawed his lip in terror. He was curled into a ball and it seemed as if he was frozen in that position. They opened the cage and lifted him out, still curled up. They got him on to a stretcher and tried to ease his legs straight but his limbs were locked.

The nurses at the hospital cut the clothes off him and lowered him into a warm bath. At last he began to uncurl. They washed him gently and rubbed his body with oil and put him to bed. It was another whole day before someone located his parents. Bob simply stared at them when they arrived and he seemed unable to talk. Despite all his mother's patient coaxing, he didn't say a single word until four months later when, slowly, he began to speak again – but with an excruciating stutter.

During our time at Maldain Road School, Bob's stutter grew less as he grew more confident. And, surprisingly, no one ever teased him about his speech impediment. He was by far the smallest boy in the class and occasionally someone called him 'Half-pint' or 'Shrimp' but nobody was really cruel to Bob. His size and stutter seemed to bring out a protective instinct even among the tough kids.

Not that he really needed protection. Most of the time he seemed to ignore his stutter and he was generally a happy kid. He loved laughing and making other people laugh and, despite his size, he was a fearless and brave player of games. But he had another, less obvious, kind of courage, too; one that allowed him to take control of his life in a way that I found impossible. I was swept along by things, but Bob made big decisions and acted on them.

His most recent big decision was to fail the Eleven-plus exam deliberately so that he wouldn't be accepted at Wolfe's College. Wolfe's was a highly rated grammar school and the rest of us had worked hard to try to get in, but Bob didn't want to go because his father was the PE and Sports Master there.

Mr Newman was a big, muscular man who hated weakness. He was naturally gifted at all sports and his nickname at Wolfe's was 'Slipperman' because he thought that a couple of stinging swipes on the buttocks with a slipper would make even the most hopeless boy perform better in the gym or on the playing fields.

Bob sensed that, deep down, his father regarded his stutter as a kind of weakness. Perhaps, at some even deeper level, Bob shared this feeling. So, in his Eleven-plus exam he left questions unanswered and generally made a mess of his papers to ensure that he failed.

His three best friends – Eddie, Manny and I – were going to Wolfe's, and the school he was going to, Croxley County Secondary School for Boys, had a reputation as a tough, violent place, but none of that stopped Bob. He had a resolute and stubborn streak. Which was why he was so angry with me that day for completing his sentence. He didn't want help – he could look after himself.

'D-D-Don't f-finish f-for me,' he repeated, his stutter back under control.

I placed two fingers to my forehead and pulled the trigger. The anger in his eyes faded and he smiled at my mimed apology.

'Anyway, it's true, they're going to build flipping houses here,' I said.

We gazed down at our threatened wilderness for a while, then walked home in silence.

Bob and I rang the Langs' bell at 10.15 on Sunday morning and Eddie's mother answered.

'Is Eddie coming to choir, Mrs Lang?' I asked.

'Edward is in disgrace,' she said abruptly and closed the door.

The Rev. Peter Maddox was standing outside the vestry door when we arrived.

'Morning, lads,' he said, catching us under the chin and raising our heads to look at him. 'Both in good voice this morning, I hope.'

'Yes, Vicar,' we said.

'That's the spirit! Sing your hearts out and wake everyone up if they fall asleep in my sermon!'

We both laughed.

We had liked the Rev. Maddox from the moment he'd arrived at St Thomas's Church the previous year. We called him Parachute Pete because he'd been a padre with the commandos during the war and had parachuted into a number of war zones with the troops. He'd altered our whole idea of church-going. Not only was he young and a war hero, he made jokes in his sermons.

'Well, nearly zero hour, better go and get togged up,' he said, checking his watch.

There were no jokes in Parachute Pete's sermon that morning. He reminded us that he had been among the first soldiers to go into the concentration camp at Belsen and had seen huge piles of dead bodies, and how even the survivors looked like walking skeletons. Then he told us that many Germans were now claiming they couldn't be held responsible for what the Nazis had done.

'But they are wrong. Remember, we can be guilty in thought, word and deed,' he said, and he looked straight at me. 'We call those the Sins of Commission. But what about the Sins of Omission? The sin of doing nothing or saying nothing when we see something wrong.

'Remember the parable of the Good Samaritan. Think of those people who passed by on the other side when they saw the man who had been robbed. They were all guilty of the Sin of Omission. Like the people who knew about Belsen and did nothing. The Nazis who perpetrated those monstrosities – they were guilty of terrible, terrible Sins of Commission. But those who saw the evil and did nothing to stop it – they, they were guilty of the Sin of Omission.'

He paused here, for emphasis. Then he slapped his hand on the edge of the pulpit, with each word, 'And the Sin of Omission is as evil as the Sin of Commission.'

The sermon worried me: there were so many ways to sin.

*

Without Eddie it didn't feel as if the holidays had started properly. Bob and Manny and I spent the first couple of days at the Bomb Building constructing a den in the bushes below the Big Brown 'ill. There was plenty of wood and other building material lying around in the rubble so we quickly managed to put together a solid little construction.

We sank four corner posts deep into the clay and nailed planks to them. We covered the plank roof with bits of slate to keep the rain out and we even had a proper door with long hinges that Bob nicked from his dad's tool shed. Then we made a couple of benches out of planks and bricks and we sat inside talking and admiring our work.

But once the hut was completed, we felt aimless and we missed Eddie's talent for inventing exciting things to do. And, over everything, hung the threat that soon the builders would move in to smash the den and flatten the bushes and knock down the trees and take away the only place that felt like ours.

It was a disappointing week, that first week of the holidays. Even the trip to the Rivoli to see *Whispering Smith* wasn't as enjoyable as I'd hoped. My dad was in a good mood because he'd won over twenty pounds at the dog races earlier that week.

'Don't say anything to your mum,' he said as we walked to the cinema. 'She'll only get the hump if she knows I've been having a flutter.'

We sat in the front row downstairs – our favourite place because there was no one between you and the screen – and I was enjoying the film until Whispering Smith discovered that his best friend was mixed up with crooks. I suddenly thought about my dad and the black market and I became worried about him.

'You know those nylons,' I plucked up courage to say on the way home through the wet, glistening streets.

'Want some for your girlfriend?' he asked.

'No!' I laughed. 'It's just . . .'

'What?'

'They won't catch you, will they? There's always stuff in the papers –'

'Oh, come off it,' he said in irritation, and I didn't go on.

On Saturday morning, Bob and I went to the ABC Minors. Manny could never come to these weekly film shows for kids because, as Bob put it, 'S-S-Saturdays are S-S-Sundays for Je-Jews.'

The films were usually hopeless at these shows, but the serials were good fun and we always liked the sing-song at the start. But best of all was the total anarchy in the dark cinema. There was continuous shouting and screaming and whistling and throwing of things, and the attendants couldn't stop it, no matter how much they shone their torches trying to catch the culprits.

Eddie came to church the following Sunday but his mother made him sit with her rather than with the choir. He looked pale and thin but he winked at me when we processed out at the end of the service.

That evening I added a request to my nightly prayers:

'Please let Eddie be able to come out. Your will be done forever and ever, Amen.'

The next day it seemed as if my prayer had been answered. Eddie was released from his prison.

It was also the day when Bob made the first of his two discoveries at the Bomb Building.

I was just finishing breakfast when my dad came down-stairs. He sat opposite me and yawned, then leaned across and ruffled my hair. He picked up the paper and began to read it, waiting for my mum to bring his breakfast.

'What are we going to see at the flicks tonight?' I asked, ready to give him the programme times of the possible films I'd chosen.

'Can't make it tonight, Andy,' he replied.

'Can't make what?' my mum asked, bringing him his bowl of porridge.

'The cinema,' my dad said. 'I'm working late.'

'Oh?' my mum retorted. 'That's nice, not telling me.'

'Very nicely, I'm telling you I'm working late tonight. All right?'

My mum banged down the bowl of porridge and went back into the scullery. My dad shook his head as she walked away. He took a mouthful of porridge, then looked at me.

'Sorry, mate, we'll go on Friday – all right?'

I shrugged a yes and got out of the house as quickly as

I could. As I opened the gate on to the pavement someone leaped out from behind the wall.

'Bloomin' hell!' I squawked.

'Gotcha!'

'Ed!'

'Cor, he almost wet his nappy,' Eddie laughed.

'How'd you get out?' I asked, glancing at his house as if
CL might emerge to drag him back inside.

'Dick Barton, Special Agent, escapes again!' Eddie said,
and then hummed the theme tune of the programme.

'Escaped?'

'My mum let me out. CL's doing his nut. Serves him
right,' Eddie explained as he guided me across the road,
away from the house.

'What happened?' I asked.

'It was a laugh! Mum thought I was going to die.'

'What?'

'I went on hunger strike! Didn't eat anything for three
days. Well, I did: the twins brought me some biscuits
every day, but Mum didn't know. She only took me to
church yesterday cos she hoped it would make me eat.'

'Weren't you hungry?'

'Starving! She didn't half give me a good breakfast
this morning, though: egg, bacon, toast, tomatoes, beans.
I reckon that's why CL's so fed up – I got his egg ration
for the week! Hope he chokes; I hate his guts.'

'Eddie!' Bob shouted, running out of his house with a
big grin on his face. 'I saw you from the w-w-window.'

'He's been on hunger strike,' I said. 'Three days.'

'Blimey! D-D-Didn't you eat a-a-anything?'

'Picked my nose and ate my bogeys!' Eddie laughed.

'Three d-days! What di-did your m-m-mum say?'

'It put the wind up her, I can tell you. Serve her right!'

Eddie was still telling us about his time locked in the bedroom when Manny came out of his garden riding a bike. It was a sparkling new Raleigh that he'd been given as a reward for passing his Eleven-plus. The rest of us had old bikes, mine being the worst: a big, heavy, rusty thing that my dad had bought second-hand in 1932 and then passed on to Michael who, in turn, had passed it on to me.

'Hey, that's an idea,' Eddie said. 'Let's go up the Bomb Building and play Bike It.'

The rules for Bike It were simple: someone was It and had to catch one of the others who then became It in his turn. It was a high-speed game of chase on our bikes along the paths, around the bushes, and up and down the hill. There was only one safe Home – the concrete block at the top of the Big Brown 'ill – and trying to drag your bike up the hill pursued by It could be heart-stoppingly tense. There was another, gentler slope at the side of the main hill but that was less exciting. The only one who took that path was Manny.

Manny was completely useless at Bike It. He was overweight and worried about hurting himself, so he was far too easy to catch. Despite that, he loved the game. It was probably the most dangerous thing he ever did and he used to trundle slowly round the Bomb Building squealing with excitement when It was near him. There was even a famous time when he'd actually wet his pants while he was being chased up the hill.

The game of Bike It on the morning of 1 August 1949 was the last we ever played in the Bomb Building and it was memorable because of Eddie's daredevil bike-riding. It was as if the week of being locked up had filled him with mad, reckless energy and he took the most outrageous risks: leaping potholes, scooting up and over piles of bricks, crashing through bushes and diving headlong down the Big Brown 'ill. Finally Bob and Manny and I combined to try to catch him, but even three against one didn't work and we tired of the game.

'Come and get me!' Eddie taunted, coming teasingly near to us as we stood next to the concrete block.

'We're too puffed,' Manny said, laying his bike down.

'Bunch of sissies!' Eddie jeered, then pedalled forward to the top of the slope. He looked over the edge and smiled. 'Right – out of the way. I need a clear run.'

He wheeled away towards the remains of the Big House then turned and faced us. It was obvious what he was planning to do.

'Don't be daft, Ed!' I warned.

'Get out of my way or I'll knock you over.'

We knew he was crazy enough to do it, so we stepped aside. He stood up straight on his pedals and drove the bike forward. He shot past us and his bike left the earth. Bob and Manny and I gasped. He sailed straight out, as if suspended above the hill, then he began to drop.

When his back wheel landed he immediately leaned

forward to bring the front wheel down, but he was too near the bottom of the slope and there wasn't enough time to adjust his weight. The bike hit the level ground, tipped forward, and Eddie flew over the handlebars. He crashed down with a terrible thump and lay still.

'Ed?' I called.

He didn't move and we started slowly down the hill, dreading what we would find. His head was twisted away from us and I was sure that he had broken his neck. I bent down and touched his shoulder.

'Waarrrgh!' Eddie shrieked, sitting up straight. His laugh was cut short as blood sprayed out of his mouth. 'Oh God, I've bitten my tongue off!'

He spat out a big gob of blood then poked his tongue out. A huge drop of blood swelled and plopped to the ground.

'It's only a l-l-l-little b-b-bit at the end,' Bob said, peering closely.

Eddie stood up and grinned.

'You jammy beggar!' I laughed. 'We thought you were dead.'

A thin rain had started to fall so we went and sat in our new den and watched while Eddie squeezed the end of his tongue to try to stop it bleeding.

'Urgh, you're making it worse,' Manny said as another big drop of blood hit the ground. 'Shut your mouth and swallow.'

'I'm Dracula!' Eddie said, letting blood run down his chin.

'Urrgh, you mucky pup!' Manny said, holding his

tummy. 'We might catch something off your rotten blood.'

Eddie laughed and bared his bloody teeth. Then he looked around at the inside of the den, 'Hey, it's not bad, this place. How long did it take you to build?'

'C–C–Couple of d–days. D'you like the d–door?'

'Yeah, it's good. We ought to block up those gaps in the walls, though. We could use clay.'

'What's the p–p–p–point? They're g–going to kno-knock it d–down,' Bob said, stabbing a pointed stick into the earth and levering it to break up the surface.

'Who?' Eddie asked, and I told him the bad news about the planned development.

'Yeah, they would, wouldn't they? They're all against us,' Eddie muttered when I finished.

'There's s–s–something d–down here,' Bob said, poking at the earth again. He got down on his knees and brushed away the clods of clay. 'It's m–m–metal.'

'Probably a water pipe,' Manny offered. 'My dad told me there used to be loads of greenhouses down here.'

A drop of rain landed on my head.

'Strewth, the roof's leaking,' I said. 'I'm going for lunch.'

'Me too,' Manny said, following. 'Come on, Bob.'

'OK,' Bob said, getting up reluctantly.

It had stopped raining by the time I finished lunch. My mum asked me to feed the chickens and clean out the rabbit hutches, so it was nearly three o'clock before I got back to the Bomb Building. Manny and Bob were down on their knees in the den, scraping away at the floor with pieces of slate. They had unearthed a small triangle of metal like the blade of a rusty spade.

'Look at you two. What you doing?'

'Wiping our b-b-bums. Wh-Wh-What's it look like?'

'Ed not here?' I asked.

'Somewhere,' Manny replied without looking up from his work. 'He's in a right hump.'

I made my way down the path and found Eddie at the bottom of the site, slumped on the ground with his back against the billboards.

'Wotcha,' I said.

The wild energy of the morning had gone and he didn't even glance at me as I squatted next to him. We sat in silence for a long, long time, staring at the bushes and the distant top of the Big Brown 'ill.

'They can do what they want. And we can't do anything,' Eddie finally said in a low, dull voice.

'Who?'

'All of them. Rix. CL. The pigs who're gonna mess this place up. What can we do? Nothing.'

I looked at him helplessly, then, as another long silence fell, I started picking at the grass next to me for something to do.

'One day when I'm bigger, I'm going to walk in there and . . . kill Rix.'

I nodded, but Eddie's level of anger and hatred was beyond me. Would he really do that? There was a long pause again.

'You like your dad, don't you?' he asked at last.

'Course I do,' I said.

His eyes met mine and I knew he was thinking about CL. A jerky sigh escaped through his nose and he leaned forward and laid his head on his raised knees.

'Andy! Eddie! Quick! Quick!'

The urgency in Bob's voice shot us to our feet and we ran in the direction of the den. Bob and Manny were waiting on the main path.

'What is it?' I asked.

Bob beckoned and started walking slowly through the undergrowth towards the den.

'You're not going in there, are you? You're nuts!' Manny said as we followed Bob into the bushes, but he fell into step behind us.

Bob tiptoed up to the hut and gingerly opened the door. Eddie and I leaned forward to look. Where Bob and Manny had scraped the earth away, there were four rusty-red triangles poking above the lip of the hole they had made.

I saw everything with startling clarity.

I saw the pieces of slate that Manny and Bob had been using to dig round the triangles. The pieces of slate they had dropped as they had suddenly realized what they were looking at. I saw the four triangles. I saw a curve of metal and the intricate detail of the smeared and bobbly weld lines that joined the triangles on to it. Then my brain put the various shapes together, just as Bob and Manny's brains had suddenly put them together, and I understood what I was looking at. They had unearthed an unexploded bomb.

Even four years after the war, bombs were still part of our world. Every month or so, newspapers had stories of mines washed up on beaches, or bombs found on building sites. In June that year, for instance, a cross-Channel ferry called *The Princess Astrid* had struck a mine off Dunkirk. The explosion ripped a huge hole in her side and five passengers were killed.

So, as soon as we saw the fins of this bomb, we knew what we were looking at.

At that very second a gust of warm wind ran through the bushes, snatching the door out of Bob's hand and slamming it against the hut wall so that the whole wobbly construction shook.

We turned and exploded along the narrow path, bumping into each other in panic. Manny was in the lead, bleating with terror, and when my foot caught his heel he tripped and we all tumbled on to him. We scrambled up and bolted along the base of the Big Brown 'ill towards the nearest exit: the hole in the fence. We jostled and pushed our way through the narrow gap and ran down the road before stopping, panting, outside the Rabbit Club.

Manny was bent over, coughing for a while, but he was the first one to speak. 'It could've blown up. We ... we ... could've been killed.'

'What we gonna do?' I asked.

The others looked at me blankly as if they didn't understand the question. I was just about to repeat it when the door of the Rabbit Club opened and two men came out. They glared at us blocking the entrance and we moved away hurriedly, following Eddie up the hill. He didn't stop until we'd rounded the corner. He sat down on the kerb and we joined him, silently gazing across the road towards the Bomb Building.

'I'm never going there again,' Manny said after a moment.

'Nor me,' I said, and Bob shook his head in silent agreement.

We looked at Eddie, but his eyes were staring, far beyond the Bomb Building, into his secret thoughts. A long silence passed, then he stood up and started across the road. We got to our feet and followed. He headed straight for the entrance and stepped inside.

'No,' Manny said. 'Ed, you can't! There's a bo–!'

'Sssh!' Eddie hissed, turning with a look of such fury that the word froze on Manny's tongue.

He slipped between the brick gatepost and the corrugated iron fence and, after a moment's hesitation, we went in after him. He stopped near the edge of the flagstones of the Big House.

'We're safe here, aren't we, Ed?' I asked, hoping for reassurance.

'Yes. It's only a 50-kilo,' he said with authority.

I nodded, calmed by the technical detail and recognizing at once that he was right. This was too small to be a 100- or 250-kilo bomb and far too large to be a 1-kilo incendiary device. There was no doubt, Bob and Manny had unearthed a 50-kilo bomb. The blast from a bomb like this would pulverize our den and anybody in the immediate vicinity but, at our distance and protected by the slope of the Big Brown 'ill, it was unlikely to harm us.

From where we were, the top branches of the elm tree and the tops of the bushes down near the billboards were all we could see beyond the lip of the Big Brown 'ill.

'Do you think it would blow up the elm?' I asked.

'Make a mess of it,' Eddie said after consideration. 'Probably a dud, though.'

'Bet it's not,' Bob said quickly, wanting to hold on to the thrill.

'Didn't go off, did it? Not when it landed. Not even when you and Manny were knocking it about,' Eddie pointed out.

'We w-weren't knocking it about,' Bob said, offended. 'We were d-d-dead c-careful.'

'Oh, come on, Bob, we've walked on it and every-thing. It's a dud,' I said.

'Oh yeah? Well, why don't you g-g-g-go and k-k-kick it, if you're so s-sure,' Bob challenged.

I had no intention of doing any such thing, but it was the kind of dare that couldn't be ignored. I started walking towards the edge of the Big Brown 'ill, praying that somebody would stop me.

'Don't be stupid, Andy!' Manny shouted just as my nerve was about to fail.

'All right then, scaredy-cat,' I said.

Then, to prove my fearlessness, I stayed where I was near the lip of the slope. A minute later the others crept forward and joined me. From there we could look down to the clump of bushes that hid our den and the bomb.

During the next half-hour we moved ever closer, led

by Eddie who seemed lured by an irresistible force. First we went to the edge of the Big Brown 'ill. Then we ventured on to the actual slope and began the slow descent with our leg muscles trembling from the tension and the strain of not slipping. Manny, in particular, was sweating profusely from the effort and his blue Aertex shirt had dark, wet patches under his arms and on his back.

When we finally got to the bottom of the slope, Manny sat down, exhausted, letting out a long squeaky fart in the process. We all giggled helplessly, holding our hands over our mouths for fear that a loud noise might set off the bomb.

Slowly, compulsively, we were drawn down the main path and up the side track, nearer and nearer, until we were standing next to the hut.

'No!' Manny gasped as Eddie stretched out his hand to the door.

Eddie hesitated, then leaned forward again.

'No!' Manny squealed, and his nerve broke. He barged past me and away down the path.

'Silly clot,' Eddie said, glancing over his shoulder.

Then he reached forward again. I saw his hand trembling, but he grasped the door and pulled. I closed my eyes and when I opened them, Eddie had already disappeared into the den.

A series of thoughts swept through me: the bomb wasn't going to explode and kill me, and even if it did, I didn't care. I brushed past Bob and went into the hut. Eddie grinned as I stood next to him. I lowered my gaze to the bomb and was aware that my heart was thudding so hard that my shirt was shaking. There was a loose, burning feeling in my bowels.

'Come on, Ed, let's go,' I whispered after staring at the bomb for a minute. I felt that I'd proved my courage and loyalty to my friend.

'It's great,' Ed breathed, in awe. 'Look at it. Just think . . . it could . . .'

A shiver ran across my shoulders and I clenched my buttocks as I felt my guts gurgle and cramp.

'We mustn't let anyone else find it,' Eddie said. 'Gotta cover it.'

He bent down and took a handful of earth.

'Don't, Ed. Might go off.'

Eddie looked at me, then down at the bomb. He nodded.

'You're right,' he said. 'You go up the hill with Bob and wait.'

'Ed –' I began.

'I'll count to thirty before I start.'

'Ed, you can't.'

'One . . . two . . .' he intoned meaningfully. 'Three . . . four . . .'

I backed out of the hut and closed the door gently.

'Five . . . six . . . seven . . .' I heard Eddie count as I signalled to Bob and we made our way quickly along the path. I took up the count in my head.

At twenty-five we reached the top of the Big Brown 'ill and found Manny waiting for us. I looked down at the bushes while I counted the last five.

'Thirty,' I said out loud.

A very high cloud layer had obscured the setting sun. The sky had turned a strange yellowy-green colour and, as the seconds ticked by, I became convinced that it was an ominous sign. It was a death sky.

I fixed my eyes on the bushes and felt certain that Eddie was going to die. I pictured the blast. The tearing of the bushes. The shower of earth and fragments of wood. The crater. The traces of blood and shreds of flesh.

Long minutes went by and the tension became unbearable. Surely it couldn't take all this time to push the earth back on to the bomb?

'Come on, Ed!' I shouted.

'Shut up!' Manny squeaked, covering his ears as if expecting an explosion.

There was a bang as the door of the den slammed and a moment later Eddie ran out of the bushes and up the hill. My relief turned to panic as he reached the top of the hill and ran straight past us. I turned and ran after him, followed by Bob and Manny. Past the flagstones, out on to the street and down the hill until Eddie finally stopped and leaned against Mr Barrington's wall. Sweat was glistening on his face and his eyes were wild.

'Oh God,' he panted when he finally got a bit of breath back.

'What?' Bob asked.

'A click,' Eddie said. 'I was just patting the earth down a bit and there was this click. I don't know if it was the bomb or what, but I thought I'd had it.'

'We're going to have to tell someone,' Manny said. 'The police or something.'

Bob and I nodded, but that faraway look had come into Eddie's eyes again.

'Don't be daft,' he said mildly. 'It's ours. We're going to keep it.'

We were dumbstruck. This was a shocking suggestion and Eddie's calm, reasonable tone made it even more chilling.

'Manny!' came a high-pitched cry.

'Just a minute,' Manny called to his mother who was standing at their front door.

'Now! It's getting chilly and I don't want you catching your death,' she yelled, heading back into the house.

Manny stood up to go. Eddie grabbed his arm.

'Don't say a word. If you tell anybody, I'll beat you up. I mean it.'

'Ed!' I gasped, shocked by the threat and seeing the way his fingers were digging into Manny's arm.

'Understand?' Eddie insisted, ignoring me.

Manny nodded and then rubbed his arm when Eddie let go of him.

'And the same goes for you two,' Eddie said, glaring at me and Bob.

'OK, OK,' I said, trying to calm things down.

'It's important,' Eddie said.

His green eyes pleaded with me to be on his side, to understand. I shrugged. He looked at the others for help. They shrugged. He was alone; he was further down that dark road of hurt and anger and the need for revenge. We weren't ready yet.

'I trust you,' Eddie said, then he walked away and into his house.

He had said the one thing that would ensure our silence.

9

Bob and Manny refused to come down to the den the next morning. I wished I could stay with them, safe at the top of the Big Brown 'ill, but stubborn pride wouldn't let me, so I abandoned myself to my fate and numbly followed Eddie.

'You're cracked!' Manny called as we started down the slope.

'It's a dud, you chickens,' Eddie called back.

He went straight into the hut but I stood at the door and watched as he squatted down and peered intensely at the pile of loose clay, as if he could see the bomb underneath.

'Know what I'd like to do? Get Rix and CL in here and blow them to kingdom come,' he said.

'It's a dud,' I pointed out.

A small smile lifted the corner of Eddie's lips and he shook his head.

'What? How do you know?' I asked.

'I just do.'

'Well, if you're so sure, we've got to tell someone,' I said, irritated by his smug smile.

'No!'

'We've got to, Ed. Anyone could get killed. Some of the little kids from the street come into the Bomb Building when we're not here. They could just get blown to bits.'

Eddie frowned as he took in the truth of this. 'OK,' he said. 'We'll cover it. Put in a kind of floor. Make it safe.'

This wasn't what I'd been hoping for but it was a step in the right direction, and now that Eddie had got the idea, there was no stopping him. He even managed to get Manny and Bob involved in the project. While they went home to get nails and tools, Eddie and I collected planks and thicker bits of timber from the ruins. I pointed out that it would be safer to build the floor in two pieces outside the den, then carry it inside.

'No – three pieces,' Eddie said. 'Then we can always lift the middle bit up if we want to look at the bomb or anything.'

By the end of the morning we had fitted a raised floor that sat neatly over the bomb. Eddie was thrilled with it and he convinced Bob and Manny that it was safe to step inside the hut to admire the finished job.

'See, we can use it as our den again,' Eddie enthused. 'This afternoon we could make up a game and –'

'I'm g-g-going sw-sw-swimming this af-afternoon,' Bob said. 'Who w-w-wants to come?'

'OK, yeah,' I said, glad of the excuse not to come back here.

'I can't,' Manny said. 'My mum says I might catch infantile paralysis.'

That's what polio was called in those days and it was the scourge of our summers. Every year, dread rumours swept around about how you could catch it in swimming pools or cinemas or from drinking fountains. Every year, newspapers printed terrifying photos of the metal contraptions called iron lungs, in which, it was thought, many of the victims of infantile paralysis would have to spend the rest of their lives.

'What about you, Ed?' I asked.

'We can't leave Manny on his own,' Eddie said.

'I've got to stay in this afternoon anyway. My grandad and nan are coming,' Manny said.

'Ed?' I pressed

'Oh, OK then,' he said reluctantly.

We spent the afternoon at the swimming pool and the evening playing in the street, but we could tell that Eddie was longing to be back at the Bomb Building.

When we called for him the next morning he'd already left the house and we knew where we would find him.

'I'm not going in that flipping hut, I don't care what Eddie says,' Manny grumbled as we slowly cycled up the hill.

'Nor me,' Bob said. 'Gives m-me the cr-creeps.'

To our surprise, far from wanting us to go into the den, we found Eddie fitting a padlock to the door.

'Nicked this hinge and padlock from CL's toolbox.' He shot a glance at me and rattled the padlock to show how secure it was. 'No little kid's going to get in there. And this whole area round the hut is out of bounds. No one comes up this path except me.'

'Who says?' Manny challenged.

His father's work in the Seamen's Union had made Manny much more politically conscious than the rest of us and he was always quick to spot a violation of his rights.

'*I* say,' Eddie replied. 'That way, no one gets hurt.'

'You can't just decide,' Manny insisted. 'We ought to vote.'

'Stuff your vote,' Eddie said, and Manny's opposition collapsed.

We spent most of the day playing a kind of hide-and-seek game involving escaped prisoners of war and German guards, but not even Manny dared to defy Eddie and hide in the forbidden area near the den.

My mum was sitting at the kitchen table when I ran in for tea. She got up at once and went into the scullery. I followed her and caught her quickly wiping her eyes.

'You're late,' she said, turning to the sink.

'Why are you crying?'

'I'm not. My eyes are sore, that's all.'

I knew she was lying and I couldn't bear the idea that she was sad. I flung my arms round her waist and pressed my head against her shoulders to comfort her. She trembled and started to sob.

'Don't. Don't!' I said, my own eyes filling up. 'Mum, don't – please!'

Her whole body shook for a while, then she forced herself free of my grip. She lifted her apron and dabbed her eyes.

'It's nothing,' she said, turning round and smiling at me. 'Honest.'

'You don't cry for nothing.'

She sighed at my persistence.

'It's just silly little things,' she said, stroking my hair and smiling a heartbreakingly sad smile.

'What things?'

'Oh, you know ... I miss Kate and ... and I worry about Michael and —'

'What? Me?'

'No, of course not,' she laughed, and pulled me to her and hugged me.

'Dad?' I asked.

'No-oo!' she said, but I felt the slight stiffening in her body. 'Now go and eat your tea or you'll be late for choir.'

I went into the kitchen and sat down in front of my tea: a couple of pilchards and some lettuce.

'Did you have a nice afternoon?' my mum asked cheerfully as she came in carrying a plate of bread and marge.

I nodded, knowing that she was trying to change the mood. But she couldn't fool me; she was worried about my dad's gambling and his involvement in the black market. She put the plate on the table and I grabbed her hand and kissed it to let her know that I understood.

'Don't be soppy!' she said, pulling her hand away and grazing my cheek with the small diamond of her wedding ring.

'Ow!'

'Oh sorry, love.' She licked the end of her finger and rubbed the graze.

'Eat up, or you'll be late.'

It was a long choir practice that evening. There were two weddings booked for Saturday the thirteenth and Mr Daniel, the choirmaster and organist, made us rehearse all the hymns for those as well as the hymns and psalms for the coming Sunday services.

Mr Daniel was a brilliant musician and he demanded very high standards from us. We moaned about all the hard work, of course, but we were proud of the fact that we had the reputation of being the best choir in south-east London.

We were just starting the last run-through of Psalm 36 when the Rev. Maddox came in from the vestry and sat in the front pew watching the rehearsal. Having an audience spurred us on to sing our very best and as the last, long note of the psalm faded away the vicar stood up and gave Mr Daniel a mock military salute. 'Adrian, you are a miracle worker.'

Mr Daniel smiled nervously and crossed his arms, hiding his hands in his armpits, as if to protect the tools with which he worked the miracles.

'And, of course, thank you, choir!' the vicar added.

After the choir practice Bob and Eddie and I were kicking an old tennis ball around outside the church hall, when the Rev. Maddox came past.

'Beautiful singing tonight, lads,' he said. 'Tongues of angels!'

We snorted, modestly dismissing the praise.

'No, seriously. It merits a glass of squash at Parachute Pete's place; are you on?'

He laughed when he saw our embarrassment. 'Don't worry, I've been called worse things in my time. Parachute Pete – sounds pretty good to me. Come on, back to my place and I won't take no for an answer.'

We crossed Fleetly Road and followed him up Malham Hill towards the vicarage. He opened the door, led us across the huge entrance hall, and ushered us into a room which smelled of lavender-scented polish. The inside shutters were closed, although it was still light outside, and a green reading lamp was glowing on the desk.

'My HQ,' the vicar said jokingly. 'This is where we'll meet for confirmation classes in the autumn. I hope you're looking forward to that as much as I am.'

We nodded enthusiastically.

'Now then, refreshments,' he said, heading for the door. We waited, hardly daring to look at each other in case we got the giggles. A minute later he came back carrying a tray with a plate of biscuits and four glasses of weak-looking orange squash.

'Don't stand around like chumps! Make yourselves comfortable.'

We sat down on the small leather sofa in front of the desk. Bob and Eddie leaned back, leaving only enough space for me to perch at the front where there was no stuffing. The wooden strut of the sofa cut into my bottom.

The vicar handed a glass to each of us then sat on the

edge of the desk. He lifted his glass and drained the squash in one long draught.

'Well,' he said, putting his glass back on the tray. 'Well...'

He picked up the plate.

'Biscuit?'

We each took a Rich Tea biscuit and nibbled at it.

'Well now ...' he said, then paused. 'I spend a lot of time thinking about you three. Do you know why?'

We shook our heads.

'Because you're our tomorrow. You're the rocks that our church's future will be built on. So we need to make sure you're solid rocks, don't we?'

We nodded.

'Loving God and Jesus is such a simple thing and yet sometimes we all have moments of confusion and doubt. So, if there's anything that you're not sure about, any questions you want to ask, I'm always ready to –'

'All this stuff about forgiving people when they do bad things, that's wrong,' Eddie said. The vicar was astonished by such an instant response and he looked at the ceiling to give himself time to think, but Eddie went on, 'It just means they go on doing it and no one stops them.'

'No, well, obviously God requires repentance from the –'

'But what if they don't repent?' Eddie cut in, already ahead of the argument. 'S'posing they just go on ... hitting people or hurting people, and no one stops them. That's not right. I mean, look at the people who killed Jesus. Someone should have stopped them.'

'Ah, but what did He say on the Cross? "Father, forgive them for they know not what they do." It's the only way forward, Edward. Love has to triumph over hatred. You know that in your heart.'

Eddie paused, but Bob was ready to take the matter further.

'Wh–What ab–ab–about Hitler? W–We hate him and the G–Ger–mans.'

'We don't hate them, Bob –' Rev. Maddox started.

'I do. They k–k–killed my gran and b–bombed me and m–m–made me have a s–stutter.'

'Well yes, but –'

'That's right,' Eddie butted in. 'We didn't forgive the Germans, did we? We bombed them back. We had a war and we killed them until they gave up. You know, you were a commando.'

'A padre.'

'It's the same thing. You helped to fight Hitler.'

'Well, of course we have to stand up to evil.'

'There you are, then,' Eddie said, in triumph.

'Yes, but it's more complicated than that, Edward,' the vicar said, leaning forward and patting him on the head. 'Love and Forgiveness. That's the central part of Christ's teaching and we must never forget it.'

Eddie knew better than to go on. When adults patted you on the head it meant that the conversation was at an end. Anyway, the vicar looked at his watch.

'Good grief, is that the time? Better drink up your squash and get off home before your mothers start tearing their hair out.'

We gulped the rest of the insipid squash and followed the Rev. Maddox to the front door.

'God go with you. And don't forget, this door's always open when you need to talk things over.'

We went out and he closed the door behind us.

'Blimey!' I said when we got out on to the street. 'You didn't half go on. I was dead squashed in the middle. My bum's gone all numb.'

'Yeah, but he's wrong,' Eddie argued. 'He's a good vicar and everything but that stuff he said is stupid.'

'Yeah. I h–h–hate H–Hitler and the G–Ger–mans, don't you?'

We nodded.

'Not just them,' Eddie muttered, then spat on the pavement.

10

The next day Bob went with his family to watch his dad play cricket and Manny was out visiting his grandparents, so Eddie and I cycled up to the Bomb Building alone. It felt strange being up there now; not scary exactly, because I knew the bomb couldn't just explode on its own, but it was hard to forget about it, hidden under the floor of the den. Eddie disappeared into the hut for ten minutes and I wasn't sure if I was pleased or annoyed that it was out of bounds to me.

'It's a bit boring here,' I said when he came out again. 'Why don't we ask our mums if we can go down to Blackford?'

Blackford, our nearest big shopping centre, was over two miles away and outside our permitted territory.

'They'll only say no if we ask,' Eddie said with a glint in his eye.

I grinned and nodded at his silent suggestion.

'Great!' he said. 'Race you!'

He grabbed his bike and sped towards the exit and I chased after him. We shot out on to the road, turned right and swooped down the hill past the Rabbit Club.

Normally we stopped at the junction with Manstead Road but today we skidded recklessly on to the main road without slowing.

We raced past Maldain Road School, side by side. Eddie stuck two fingers up to the empty building and I laughed and did the same.

'Wooooohooooooo!' Eddie screamed, looking over his shoulder to check for traffic, then swerving across the road and back again. I copied the crazy manoeuvre, then followed him as he jumped his bike up on to the pavement. Two women walking towards us stepped aside as we shot by.

''Ere, get on the road, you!' one of them shouted angrily.

'Get lost!' Eddie yelled.

We bumped back down on to the road and stood up on our pedals and pumped hard as we came to the long slope that marked the usual limit of our territory. We reached the top, settled back on to our saddles and free-wheeled down the other side. Eddie and I smiled at each other; we were bowling along on our bikes, the sun was shining, we were breaking all the rules and we didn't care: we were wild and free.

As we approached Blackford, the traffic became heavier and we were forced to ride in single file. We passed Wolfe's College and grimaced at each other at the thought of the new school in September. Five minutes later we swept under the railway bridge and there, on the left-hand side, was Blackford Greyhound Stadium. I caught a glimpse of my dad's office window behind the trees and I wondered if he might be looking out.

We crossed the river bridge, turned left into the High Street, and stopped outside the Colosseum so that I could touch the stage door in my ritual homage to Stan Laurel and Oliver Hardy. They had performed at the theatre a couple of years before and even though I hadn't seen them I was always thrilled by the fact that they had been there. My film-star heroes had walked through this door, they had looked at my world: these grey streets and dowdy houses and boarded-up windows and bomb sites and queues outside shops with almost nothing to sell.

'Come on, let's go,' Eddie said impatiently as I stood there trying to catch some Hollywood glitter.

We put one foot on our pedals and were scooting along the pavement when a man and a woman stepped out of a shop doorway right in front of me. I swerved to avoid them and then jumped off the pedal when I saw who I'd nearly hit.

'Dad!' I said.

'Andy!' my dad said. He looked round. 'You on your own?'

'No, I'm with Ed,' I said, pointing to where he was wheeling his bike back towards us.

'Oh, right. Wotcha, Eddie!'

'Hello, Mr Adamson.'

'So what you two doing down here then?' my dad asked with a conspiratorial grin.

'Nothing,' I said.

'Nothing, eh? Does your mum know?'

I shook my head.

'Why aren't you at work?' I asked.

'Give us a ride on your bike,' my dad pleaded, turning to Eddie. Then he took up a boxer's stance and threw a couple of joke punches at him. Eddie laughed.

'No, I'm just doing a bit of shopping,' my dad said, turning back to me. 'It's your mum's birthday next week.'

'I know.'

'I thought I'd get her something nice so I asked someone to help me. Women always know what other women like.' He waved his hand to indicate his companion, then he put his arm round my shoulder and squeezed me. 'Susie, this is my son, Andrew. Looks a bit of a ruffian but he doesn't bite – much! Andy, this is Mrs Wallace; she works with me at the stadium.'

'Hello,' I said, holding out my hand.

'Pleased to meet you,' she said, shaking my hand. She smiled and I noticed a smear of lipstick on one of her very white teeth. 'I'm going to make your dad come and choose a present for my husband when it's his birthday.'

'Fair's fair,' my dad conceded.

A breeze blew past, almost lifting Mrs Wallace's straw hat from her head. She laughed and clamped it back on to her wavy black hair. She had the greenest eyes I'd ever seen and her earrings and necklace matched the colour exactly. She was quite pretty although her face was rather long and her nose and chin were a bit pointed and reminded me slightly of a witch.

My dad took a packet of Woodbines from his pocket. He slid a cigarette out, put it in his mouth, and then jokingly offered the packet to Eddie.

'Yeah, all right,' Eddie said, pretending to reach for one.

'Just you try!' my dad laughed, slapping Eddie's hand away. 'If I catch either of you two having a puff I'll knock you into the middle of next week.'

He lit his Woodbine, inhaled deeply, and blew one of his perfect smoke rings. It hung for a moment in the air then the breeze blew it apart.

'Oh well, on we go, in search of the ideal present,' my dad sighed, hanging his head in mock exhaustion. 'See you later!'

He turned away, then stopped.

'Here,' he said. 'Don't want to get you into trouble so I won't tell your mum I saw you. Besides, we don't want her to know about the present.'

'No,' I agreed.

'Zo, mum's ze vord, *mein führer*,' he said in a silly German accent. He winked at me, then walked away with Mrs Wallace.

'He's a right laugh, your dad,' Eddie said.

I shrugged casually, but my heart swelled with pride.

On the way home we took a detour up to the playground at Hilly Park and sat on the swings watching the young kids playing on the slide and the roundabout. They were doing the things that had excited us not so long ago but it all seemed so childish now.

'I wonder if my dad would be a laugh like yours?' Eddie said. 'I wonder what he'd be like. Now. When I'm growing up and everything.'

'Dunno. Nice.'

'Better than CL, anyway. I hate his guts.'

Our moods were usually short-lived affairs, so Eddie's continuing bitterness about Rix and CL puzzled me. He seemed like a different person.

'Cor, leave off, Eddie. CL's all right,' I said.

'He's a stinking pig. He flipping hit me, Andy!'

His voice cracked and I should have paid attention to it but, stupidly, I went on. 'You used to say he was like a dad. You used to say he wanted the best for you.'

'My real dad wouldn't hit me,' he said angrily.

'How do you know?'

Eddie glared at me and then, suddenly, broke down. His face creased, his eyes filled, and large tears began to course down his cheeks.

'He wouldn't! My real dad – would – never – hit me. Not after Rix had done that . . . He wouldn't!'

I sat looking at him helplessly as he hung his head, his whole body heaving with sobs. Then he jumped off the swing and grabbed his bike. He blundered away across the grass then, when he got to the path, he swung himself on to the saddle and rode over the brow of the hill and out of my sight.

I burned with shame at my stupidity.

It was overcast and rainy for the next couple of days but I was glad because it gave me the excuse to stay in. I didn't want to face Eddie. What would we say to each other?

I read and re-read my comics or listened to the radio, but I felt restless and bored and on top of that my dad let me down again on the Friday evening.

'What are we going to see at the flicks?' I said, running out of the front room when he came in from work.

'Sorry, I can't make it tonight.'

'You promised,' I said.

'Something's come up.'

'What?'

'Something. I can't even stop for tea. I'm just popping in to tell your mum, then I'm off again. Oh, come on, Andy, don't look like that. We'll go next Monday, I swear on my life.'

I went up to my bedroom, disappointed but worried, too. He was probably doing another black-market deal; perhaps tonight would be the night he would be caught by the police. A moment later I heard raised voices and I knew that my mum was as unhappy as I was about the last-minute change of plan.

On the Saturday afternoon Bob invited me across to his house to play with his Meccano set. We decided to build a bridge but we'd only bolted a couple of the pieces together when Bob picked them up and threw them back in the box.

'What?' I asked.

'It's j-j-just k-k-k-kids' s-stuff,' he said and I knew exactly what he meant. For years we'd loved building things together but suddenly it seemed tiresome and silly.

We sat on the window sill and looked at the rain pouring down on his back garden.

'Have you seen Eddie?' I asked.

'W-W-Went across yesterday and today b-b-but he's always out.'

I was dreading going to church because Eddie and I could hardly avoid seeing each other in the choir, but I needn't have worried: he was sitting on his wall when I came out of my front garden on Sunday morning. He jumped down and came towards me. He was smiling. It was going to be all right. We weren't going to talk about it. He punched me lightly on the shoulder and I punched him back. Everything was forgotten – we were best friends again.

Bob came running out of his house and joined us as we set off for church.

'Where you b-been, Ed? I k-k-kept c-calling for you but you were n-never in.'

'Been up at the den quite a bit.'

'Doing what?' I asked.

'Thinking.'

The next afternoon we went up to the Bomb Building and Bob made his second big discovery of the summer.

Eddie went down to the den as soon as we arrived and we sat on the flagstones of the Big House, waiting for him.

'What's he doing in there?' Manny asked.

'Trying to m-m-make us f-feel jealous so we'll want to g-go in there.'

'Fat chance! Who wants to be blown up by a flipping bomb?' Manny replied.

'It's a dud,' I said, and realized that I believed it. Of course it was a dud. We couldn't possibly have found a real, live bomb – that was the sort of thing that happened to other people. Our bomb was just a hunk of useless metal.

'Wh-What's that?' Bob said, getting up and peering at something on the ground next to a brick. He kicked the brick away and squatted down. He brushed his hand over the ground, then stood up sharply and scuttled away in alarm.

'What?' Manny asked, jumping to his feet and backing away.

'It's a-n-n-n-nother one,' Bob said.

'Don't muck around,' I said.

'I'm n-n-not. Look.'

I stood up and looked at where he was pointing.

A rusty bit of metal was poking out of the ground. I bent down and gingerly scraped some earth away.

'What you doing?' came Eddie's voice. He was panting from the climb up the Big Brown 'ill.

'Bob's found this thing,' I said.

Eddie squatted next to me and picked up a piece of slate. Together we scratched at the soil and uncovered a rusty iron ring sticking out from a square stone slab. Eddie got hold of the ring and tugged. He grunted and strained but it didn't move.

'We need a crowbar,' I suggested.

We found a metal pipe in the rubble and Eddie used it as a lever. He strained until the tendons in his neck stood out, but the slab wouldn't budge.

'It's dead heavy,' Eddie grunted. 'Take the other end of the pipe, Andy. One, two, three – Lift!'

We heaved in unison and the stone almost shot out of its frame; it wasn't heavy, it had simply been stuck. We laid the stone down and all knelt round the hole. A fetid smell of earth and coal and rot rose up out of the darkness.

'W-W-What a s-stink!' Bob said.

'It's the coal-hole,' Manny said, pointing to a chute that looked like a playground slide. 'That's where they slid the coal down into the cellar.'

'Blimey, the cellar of the Big House,' Eddie whispered. Then he stuck his head into the hole and shouted, 'Hello!'

We listened to the word echoing in the darkness and then heard a drip of water.

'Back up!' Eddie ordered, and rolled a pebble down the chute. There was a moment's silence, then a splash.

'I wonder how deep it is?' Eddie said.

'Can't be very,' I said. 'If we had welly boots . . .'

'You're not going down, are you?' Manny asked.

'Of course,' Eddie said.

We tore down the hill on our bikes and dashed indoors for our boots. Manny was waiting when I ran back outside.

'Eddie's round the bend,' he said, nervously ringing the bell on his bike as if the chime made him feel better. 'There's probably rats and diseases down there. We could catch all sorts.'

Bob was the last to come out and he was carrying a torch, 'F–F–F–For th–the d–d–d–dark,' he said, holding it up.

When we got back to the Bomb Building, Eddie eased himself into the hole and slid down the steep chute, using his heels to skid to a stop just before the end. He eased forward and put one of his legs over the edge.

'It's all right,' he shouted. 'It's not all that deep.'

I slid down to join him. Then the light dimmed as Manny heaved himself through the hole and inched his way down the chute. Bob followed and when he arrived at the bottom he stood so close to me that I could feel him trembling.

'What a pong!' Manny said, pinching his nose.

'Yeah, you've let one off,' I joked.

'No, really, it's like rotten bodies or something.'

He'd said what I had been trying to stop myself thinking. Nobody had ever discovered the bodies of the old ladies and their brother after the air raid. Perhaps, and

I suddenly grasped the cause of Bob's trembling, they had been trapped down here when the house had collapsed. Perhaps their skeletons were lying in this thick, oily water. And perhaps their ghosts still lingered down here.

'Scaredy-cat,' I sneered at Manny.

'Ssh!' Eddie said.

The shaft of light from above didn't illuminate anything beyond the bottom of the chute and he was swishing his boot through the viscous water, trying to work out the size of the space by the slap of the waves on the hidden walls.

'Give me your torch, Bob,' Eddie breathed.

There was a click and the beam of light shot across the water to a brick wall about six metres away. Eddie moved the beam to the right and lit up a heap of coal piled up against the wall. Then he shone the torch to the left until he came to two steps that led to a green-painted door.

He held the light fixed on the door and we waded through the black water towards it.

'I c-c-c-c-c-c-c-c–' Bob stuttered and we turned round. He hadn't moved and was a small shadow framed by the light from the chute behind him. 'C-C-C-C-C-C-C-C-Can't, Ed.'

Eddie sloshed his way back to Bob. He put his hands on Bob's shoulders, their grey silhouettes merging as their heads came together. The echoey acoustics brought Eddie's whispered words clearly to us across the jerking water: 'It's all right. I won't leave you. Come with us; it'll be OK, honest.'

Bob nodded. Eddie gave his shoulders a little encouraging squeeze, then they waded back to where Manny and I were waiting by the door. Eddie grasped the door knob and turned it. The door squeaked as it swung open and the torch lit up a corridor inside.

'Come on,' Eddie whispered and we climbed the two steps.

The corridor smelled of mildew and there was a chill in the air, but the floor was dry and covered with a thick plaster dust. The beam of the torch picked out a pile of rubble blocking the far end of the corridor – probably the remains of the staircase that had once led up into the body of the house.

On the right, just in front of the rubble, was an opening which led into a large room containing a rusty lawnmower, a watering can, some gardening tools and, leaning against one wall, some metal garden chairs and a metal table.

'Great!' Eddie said, turning to us. The light from the torch lit up the underside of his face, casting eerie shadows round his eyes and distorting his features. 'It can be our HQ. Look – proper table and chairs and everything. If we close the trapdoor nobody will even know we're here.'

'B-B-B-But h-h-how w-w-w-w-w-would we g-g-g-g-g-get out?'

'Just push, it's not heavy.'

'Yeah, but if it got blocked we could be stuck down here,' Manny objected. 'Anyway it's dark and there's probably germs and everything.'

But Eddie ignored him. He handed the torch to Bob and began unfolding the table and chairs.

'It's the tops – look,' Eddie pointed, when he'd set them out. 'It's like King Arthur and the Round Table.'

'It's square!' Manny mocked.

'Shut up, Solomon!' Eddie snapped, then looked round at the room, nodding in pleasure at everything he saw. 'It's great. You could sleep down here and nobody would know where you were.'

Manny opened his mouth in disbelief but he didn't say anything.

'Imagine,' Eddie went on, obviously thinking of his mum and CL. 'They'd be scared to death. And next morning you could walk in cool as a cucumber.'

'What about the gh-gh-gh-gh-gh-gho–?'

Bob stopped as something rattled in the rubble in the corridor. A shiver ran down my neck. As one, we turned and dashed towards the exit. Even Eddie.

We sloshed crazily through the water, sending waves slapping against the walls. Bob was the first to the chute and he raced up into the open air. Manny followed, slowly heaving his flabby form up the slope. He slipped and scrabbled for a foothold.

'Get out!' I screamed.

Finally Manny managed to pull himself out and I dug the toes of my rubber boots into the shiny metal surface and hurtled upwards. I fell on to the ground next to the others and we watched as Eddie followed us out into the open. The warmth of the air wrapped itself round us comfortingly and the bright light instantly calmed our fears. We looked at each other and burst out laughing at our panic.

'Tell you what,' Manny said when we calmed down. 'We could flog that coal down there and make a couple of quid, at least.'

Eddie shook his head. 'No, we can't. We've got to keep this place secret. It's a great place to hide and it can be our HQ. We don't want people to know about it. Do we?'

Bob, Manny and I glanced at each other – another secret to keep. We should have said we didn't care if people knew. We should have closed up the trapdoor and forgotten all about that dark cellar. We should have seen the danger. But we didn't.

'Do we?' Eddie repeated.

We shook our heads.

I was sure my dad would cancel our trip to the cinema again so I didn't bother to go downstairs when I heard him come home that evening. I finished washing the dirt of the cellar off my hands, then wandered into my bedroom telling myself that I didn't care because there weren't any films that I really, really wanted to see.

I sat on my bed and picked up the latest *Film Fun*, then I heard him coming upstairs. I kept looking at the page when he stopped in the doorway.

'Muggsy was lyin' on his prison bed readin' the *Sports News*,' he said in his Hollywood gangster voice. 'Deuce came in and spilled the beans – "Hold on to your cheap cigar, Muggsy. We're goin' over the wall at seven o'clock tonight and we ain't comin' back." Muggsy was so excited he threw his *Sports News* in the air!'

My dad grabbed my *Film Fun* and threw it across the room.

'Dad! That's my new one!' I cried, trying to sound angry.

'Ooh, ooh, it's my new one,' he said, bending over and tickling me until I was writhing on my bed, howling with laughter.

'So, what are we going to see?' he asked, letting me go and sitting down next to me.

'The flicks?'

'I promised, didn't I? What's on at the Rex?'

'*Johnny Belinda*,' I said.

'That's the one I want to see.'

'You don't like the Rex,' I protested. 'You call it the Bug Hutch and you say it smells.'

'Yes, but I want to see *Johnny Belinda*.'

'You don't even know what it's about.'

'Yes, I do. There's this bloke called Johnny and –'

'Wrong! It's about a woman who's deaf and dumb. And Jane Wyman's in it and she won the Oscar for Best Actress.'

'There you are, I told you it was good!'

'Oh, Dad!'

'It's that or nothing . . .'

'OK!'

We caught the tram to Croft Hill just before seven and we arrived at the Rex at ten past. The usherette showed us to the front row and we sat down just as the lights were going down for the first film.

I was reading the title – *Rory Calhoun in*

ADVENTURE ISLAND – when my dad whispered, 'I've got to nip out for a bit.'

'Where?'

'Just out. I'll be back later.'

'I'll come with you.'

'No!' he said firmly.

'I don't want to stay by myself,' I pleaded.

'Don't be a baby. I'll be back by the time the other one starts. Promise.'

He stood up and walked off, his footsteps drumming up the thin-carpeted aisle. I sat in the dark, damp cinema, feeling cold. I suddenly remembered that Bob had told me that a girl had been watching a film here when a huge rat had run over her foot. I immediately lifted my feet and put them on the edge of the seat and watched the film through my knees.

Adventure Island finished and *British Movietone News* started. I turned round and looked at the door. He should be back soon. The newsreel ended. The trailers ended. The lights went down for *Johnny Belinda*. The Warner Brothers logo came on to the screen. Then the title of the film.

Where was he?

Then the list of actors. I made myself read them carefully. Jane Wyman. Lew Ayres. Charles Bickford. Agnes Moorehead. I read them all.

He still wasn't there.

The credits were finished. The first scene was happening but I wasn't watching. He'd promised he'd be here. Perhaps he'd been caught with black-market stuff.

Or he was hurt. Perhaps he was dead. My heart was pounding so hard that my head was jerking with the pulse of my blood, making the screen jump. I tucked my knees under my chin to steady my head.

I'd have to go out and ask to see the cinema manager. Get him to phone the police to see if there'd been an accident.

I got up and blundered into someone coming down the row.

'Where you off to?' my dad asked.

I suppose I wanted to throw my arms round him and hold him tight. But we didn't do that sort of thing. Instead I just stood there clumsily, blocking his way. He smelled of beer and cigarettes.

'Sit down,' he said.

I held my ground, making him touch me, making him push me. I pushed back.

'Come on, Andy,' he whispered. 'People are looking at us.'

I allowed myself to be pushed down into my seat.

'Look, I'm sorry,' he said softly as I stared at the screen. 'I got held up. But I was only over the road in the pub.'

'I didn't know that, did I? I thought something had happened.'

'Look, I've said I'm sorry. I had to see this bloke.'

'Why? Is it black market?'

'No! I was ... Well, I wanted to see him because I was ... thinking of buying a car for us.'

'A car!'

'Only thinking.'

'Ssshhhh!' somebody hissed from behind us.

My dad nudged me and giggled. I didn't respond, so he nudged me again.

'Forgive me?' he whispered.

I nodded.

He squeezed my arm, then settled back and started watching the film.

The next morning Eddie couldn't wait to get back to the cellar. By the light of a couple of candles we cleaned out what he called the Control Room, piling the garden tools out in the corridor near the rubble, and arranging the table and chairs in the middle of the room. Then we sat round the table and listened while Eddie tried to convince us what a great HQ it was.

'We could even have a map on the wall like in a proper war bunker.'

To help win us over he invented a game where we pretended to be soldiers planning a battle. We took the game seriously for a long time but it all ended in laughter when Manny had to be a captured German spy and kept on doing '*Heil Hitler*' and '*Achtung, Achtung*' in a silly German accent.

As we were walking home for lunch Eddie announced that he was planning to build a sort of walkway across the flooded floor in the afternoon.

'Oh blimey, I d-don't want to k-k-keep going d-d-down there all the time,' Bob moaned.

'Oh, come on, it's great,' Eddie said, putting an encouraging arm round his shoulder.

Bob shook his head.

'Come on,' Eddie persisted.

'No!' Bob shouted and ran away down the road and into his house.

'Suit yourself!' Eddie called scornfully but, when he turned and shrugged at me and Manny, there was disappointment on his face.

'He hates it because it reminds him of –' I began.

'I know what it reminds him of!' Eddie snapped.

There was no sign of Bob after lunch but Eddie was determined to build the walkway, so we searched through the rubble for suitable bricks and planks and carried them down into the cellar. I was quite interested in the job, but Manny obviously hated working in the foul-smelling water and when he got a long splinter in his hand he rushed home in case it went septic. We knew he wouldn't come back.

'That's OK. We can do it just as fast, the two of us,' I said to Eddie, glad to have a chance to show him that I was his most loyal friend.

We worked side by side in harmony and when I suggested some modifications to his design, he immediately approved them. By the end of the afternoon we had constructed a broad and solid walkway from the bottom of the chute all the way across the water to the steps.

'It's super. We won't have to wear boots any more,' Eddie said, punching my arm. 'Thanks.'

I punched him back hard then scooted up the chute, laughing, as he chased me.

'Go and get your card. I'm going to give your mum her present,' my dad whispered when he got home from work.

I ran up to my room and pulled the card from under my bed, then went down and put it on the kitchen table.

'Happy Birthday to you,' my dad started singing, moving towards the scullery where my mum was preparing the tea.

'Happy Birthday to you,
Happy Birthday, dear Peggy,
Happy Birthday to you.'

My mum turned round from the sink with a coy smile on her face. She flicked a strand of hair away from her eyes with her wet hand and then laughed as a drop of water ran down her cheek.

'Da-daaaa!' my dad said, making a grand gesture. Then he put his arms round her and kissed her. And I laughed, happy to see them like that.

'Andy's got something for you in the other room,' my dad said, pushing her towards the kitchen.

'Oh, love, you shouldn't have,' my mum said, picking up the card I had drawn for her. 'Oh, it's lovely! Look at all those flowers. It must've taken ages. Look, Harry.' She put the card on the mantelpiece next to Kate's.

'And now your present,' my dad said, going to his briefcase and pulling out a bottle of gin. 'Booth's – your favourite!'

'Booth's – your favourite, you mean,' my mother said, laughing. 'Thanks.'

'And that's not all!' My dad dived into his briefcase again and I realized that the bottle of gin was just an extra. This was the real present. What would it be? Jewellery? He'd been coming out of a jeweller's shop in Blackford.

'Sorry, they're not wrapped,' he said, pulling out two tall thin books.

'Oh, Harry, they're lovely.'

I looked at them: *The Story of Australia in Pictures* and *The Story of Africa in Pictures*. There were some nice photos, but surely Mrs Wallace could have come up with something more interesting. My mum seemed pleased, but I was disappointed: two thin books, a bottle of gin that my dad would drink; she deserved better than that. I wanted to add to the excitement, tell her something to make her really happy.

'And . . .' I announced, 'Dad's going to buy a car.'

My mum looked at him in surprise. My dad's eyes flashed me a warning.

'Cor, you don't half exaggerate, Andy! I only said wouldn't it be nice if we could. Blimey, he thinks I'm made of money.' He raised his eyebrows at my mum and she smiled. 'Here, have we got any lemon? We could open the gin and have a drink to celebrate.'

'Honestly, Harry, any excuse.'

'What better excuse than my darling wife's birthday,' my dad said, giving her a cuddle.

★

At the end of Wednesday afternoon we climbed out of the cellar and put the stone slab back in place. We were just kicking dirt over the top to hide it when Eddie straightened up and hushed us. He stood, listening, with his head held very still like one of the foxes we sometimes saw in the bushes, frozen and scenting the air for danger.

Then we heard it, too. A car was stopping outside on the road. A door slammed, followed by another. The sound of voices. Coming into the Bomb Building.

'It's grown-ups,' Eddie said. 'Quick, this way.'

We half ran, half slid, to the bottom of the Big Brown 'ill and darted into the bushes.

We waited and waited, hearing distant voices borne on the wind. Then three men came to the brow of the hill and looked down towards us. We were well hidden by the foliage but we crouched lower and held our breath. The tallest of the men opened up a large sheet of paper and the other two gathered round. The tall man pointed to the sheet and then at the far end of the bomb site.

'It's the pigs who're gonna knock it down,' Eddie whispered.

'Pigs,' I muttered. 'Why do they need this place?'

'They're greedy capitalist bosses, that's why,' Manny said.

Eddie suddenly stood up, shouting, 'Get out of here! Get lost!'

The men looked down to locate this voice and Eddie ran out of the bushes to the bottom of the Big Brown 'ill.

He was stupid. He'd be caught. But we couldn't let him go on his own, so we ran after him.

'What are you lot doing here?' the tall man shouted.

'Drop dead, you!' Eddie yelled.

'Don't you dare talk to me like that! This is private property and you're trespassing.'

'Oh, get lost, you creep!' Eddie screamed.

'You're trespassing on our property. And if you don't leave at once we'll come down there and throw you out,' said the man. But his voice lacked conviction and Eddie pounced on the weakness.

'Come on, try it,' he sneered.

'You'll f-f-fall flat on your arse,' Bob said, catching Eddie's wild defiance. Then he ran a few paces up the hill and stopped there, inviting the chase.

The tall man put one foot on the slope and realized that Bob was right, it was too steep for him. He looked round for another route, but the gentler side slope was hidden by bushes.

'Right!' he shouted, stepping back. 'You're breaking the law and I'm calling the police!'

'Do what you damn well like,' Eddie bawled, then he picked up a stone.

'I'm warning you!' one of the other men said, pointing at Eddie.

'No, I'm warning you!' Eddie screamed. 'This is ours. You try and take it and you'll be sorry.'

Eddie hurled the stone and the men ducked as it sailed just over their heads, then they scurried back out of sight as he picked up another one. We whooped and howled at this victory. Eddie launched the second stone and it sailed up and over the lip of the hill to clatter loudly on some bricks.

'Right,' came the tall man's voice. 'We know who you are and we're reporting you to the police.'

'Up yours!' I yelled.

'Capitalist lackey!' Manny shouted.

'They can't see us,' Eddie whispered. 'Let's get out of here and let 'em stew.'

We slipped into the bushes and made our way silently along the paths towards the side exit. We clambered through the fence and pounded up the road. At the top Eddie stopped and peered round the corner.

'They're still looking for us,' he said in triumph at the success of his ruse. 'Come on.'

The men's car was parked outside the entrance to the Bomb Building and as we drew level with it Eddie pulled out his penknife. He opened the blade and drove it at the side wall of the front tyre. The knife bounced off the rubber.

'What the . . .?' I gasped.

'Ed!' Bob piped in shock.

Manny said nothing – he was running down the hill towards home.

Eddie stabbed at the tyre again, but the blade of the knife snapped shut, trapping his finger against the handle.

'Sugar!' he said, swiftly pulling the blade open. Dark blood welled out of the deep cut.

'God, Ed, you're nuts,' I breathed.

Ed looked at his finger then flicked it towards the car.

Spots of blood splashed dramatically against the side window. He watched his blood begin to slide down the glass, then he laughed and pointed to it.

'It's bloody war!' he said.

He stepped forward and kicked the front door. The violence of the moment thrilled me and I pushed him aside and let fly with another kick at the car. Then Bob did the same. We were all wearing plimsolls and we only made tiny dents and scuffs in the metal, but we fled away down the hill feeling that we had won a battle against the enemy.

The choir practice that evening was longer than usual as we went through the arrangements for the two weddings on the following Saturday. In particular, Mr Daniel had worked out some special settings of the hymns for the wedding in the afternoon. They relied on a complicated harmony from the trebles and we rehearsed them over and over until he was satisfied. Then, as we finally finished, he handed out sheets with the order of service for the weddings.

Eddie was reading the sheets as we walked down the church path and when we reached the gate he suddenly stopped still.

'Oh no!' he said.

'What?' I asked.

'Read that.'

He handed over one of the sheets and I noticed that blood was seeping through the bandage on his cut finger.

'St Thomas's Parish Church. Saturday the thirteenth of August 1949,' I read.

'Under that,' Eddie said.

'Marriage Service. Two thirty p.m. Sidney George Rix – Diane Yvonne Carver,' I said.

I was about to go on to the next line when I stopped.

'It's them,' Eddie said, confirming what I'd just realized. 'It's Rix and Carver.'

13

'I'm not going to sing for their damn wedding. I'm not, so there.'

That's what Eddie kept saying whenever the topic came up over the next couple of days. I knew how he felt; I didn't want to sing at Rix and Carver's wedding either, I really didn't. But I knew it could cause all kinds of problems if we didn't turn up, and I also realized that Saturday was the thirteenth – unlucky thirteen.

By the Friday morning, I was getting desperate to find a solution to the problem and I made a stupid suggestion. 'Supposing we just pretended to sing.'

'Look, if you're so keen to get your lousy sixpence ...' Eddie sneered, referring to the money we got for singing at weddings.

'I don't want lousy sixpence,' I cried indignantly. 'But we've done rehearsals and stuff. And Daniel's done that special harmony.'

'Who cares about his stupid harmony? If you want to sing for Rix and Carver and make them feel everything's OK, you can – but I'm not.'

'I wouldn't go,' Manny said.

'You can't anyway, you're a Jew,' I snapped, and he gave me a reproachful look.

'Well, I've d-d-decided – I'm not g-going,' Bob said firmly.

Eddie gave him a smile, then looked at me.

'Andy?' he asked.

There was no way out. 'Yeah, OK,' I said.

Then Eddie outlined his plan. We would go to the wedding on Saturday morning and sing as well as possible, but we wouldn't go back in the afternoon. Instead we'd meet after lunch and cycle down to Blackford so that our parents would think we were at the church.

'And then on Sunday,' Eddie went on, 'when Daniel goes to pay us for the weddings, I vote we tell him we don't want any money. Not even for the one in the morning.'

'Good idea,' I said, admiring Eddie's diplomacy. Perhaps this self-imposed fine would keep us out of trouble.

'All in favour?' Eddie asked.

Bob and I raised our hands.

Just then Greg, one of the young kids from up the road, came strolling towards us. He had a lollipop in his hand and he was dipping it into a bag of lemonade powder.

'Hey, wh–where d'you get that?' Bob asked.

'Miss Geale's,' Greg answered. 'She's just had a delivery.'

Sweets!

We rushed indoors and begged pennies off our mums,

then ran together to the sweet shop. Word had got around quickly and there was already a long, long queue outside. As kids came out clutching their bags, we asked what was available. At first there were rhubarb and custards, aniseed balls, bullseyes, Fry's Chocolate Creme bars, sherbet lemons and American Hard Gums. But, as we slowly shuffled forward, word came that the hard gums were finished. Then, shortly afterwards, the bullseyes and the Fry's Chocolate Creme Bars.

'Oh, I really f-f-f-fancied chocolate,' Bob moaned.

After twenty minutes we arrived at the door, but now we heard there were only aniseed balls and sherbet lemons. That was all right, I liked both of those. We shuffled into the shop getting tenser as we got closer to the counter: would there be any sweets left?

There was a groan from the front of the queue and we heard Miss Geale say, 'It's aniseed balls or nothing.'

There were five people in front of us and I prayed that there would be enough to go round. Finally, we were at the counter.

I held out my money and asked for some aniseed balls.

'Finished,' Miss Geale said curtly.

'That's a swizz. He got some,' I said, pointing to the man who was on his way out of the shop.

'That was the last. All I've got left is liquorice wood or locust.'

'They're not proper sweets.'

'Take it or leave it,' Miss Geale said.

It was a difficult choice. You could chew on the liquorice wood for ages, but the taste wasn't always very strong. Locust was definitely more like a sweet, although it was actually a kind of caramelized bean pod. It resembled a long date and had a very syrupy taste, but it had one terrible disadvantage. Not only did it look rather like dog poo, it smelled a bit like it, too. It was all right once it was past your nose and in your mouth, but a whiff of it could put you off completely.

'Come on, I haven't got all day,' Miss Geale grumbled.

'Locust, please' I said, handing her two pennies.

She popped three locusts into a bag and passed it to me. I quickly held it away from my nose. Eddie, Bob and Manny all bought liquorice wood, then we left the shop.

'Eeuurr, locust!' Bob said, when we got outside. 'Let's have a s–s–smell.'

I held the bag out and he sniffed.

'Bah! It's di–disgusting!' he laughed.

'Don't bring it near me!' Manny squealed.

'Let me,' Eddie said, leaning towards the bag, then jerking his head away. 'Ah blimey, it's just like it!'

I took a deep breath and pulled one of the locust pods out of the bag. Bob and Eddie made vomiting noises as I shoved it in my mouth and chewed.

'Mmm!' I said, enjoying the concentrated sugary taste now that it was safely past my nose.

As soon as the pod was well mashed I opened my mouth wide and the others backed away, shrieking and cackling.

'Ahh, blimey!' Eddie snorted. 'Aaaah! It looks just like it! Oh, don't!'

'Oh, it's dis– Aaaah, it's disgusting!' Bob hooted,

doubling up with laughter and grabbing hold of the lamp post for support.

'Look, I'm a dog having a poo,' I mumbled.

I closed my mouth, puffed up my cheeks, and forced some of the squidgy brown mush out through my pouted lips. Eddie and Bob reeled against each other in helpless hysterics. Then my nose suddenly caught a whiff of the stuff and my stomach almost rebelled at the horrible smell, but I swallowed hard and the mess of locust went down my throat.

'Oh blimey, it's vile!' I laughed, sending us all into another fit.

The wedding on Saturday morning must have seemed perfect to the young couple who were getting married. The sun was shining, the church was packed and the best choir in south-east London was singing beautifully. They had no idea that three of the trebles were going through hell because, just before the service, Mr Daniel had bustled over to ask us if we were happy about the harmonies for the afternoon wedding. We'd glanced at each other guiltily, then nodded.

'Excellent,' Mr Daniel smiled. 'Don't be nervous, simply relax and let those lovely voices of yours ring out. It'll be wonderful.'

This rare friendliness and praise made us feel terrible. Then, just as we were leaving the church after the first wedding, Parachute Pete added to our discomfort by calling, 'Bye, lads; see you this afternoon!'

After lunch we met up and cycled away as if we were

going to church, but at Fleetly Road we turned left instead of right, then left again into Manstead Road and headed towards Blackford. The air was hot and heavy and although we cycled slowly we were breathless and sweaty when we arrived. As we passed the town hall, the clock struck two thirty and we knew there was no going back. The wedding had started.

We dawdled along the High Street, not sure what to do or where to go; then, as we passed Woolworth's, I happened to glance back and see a policeman step out into the middle of the road and stop the traffic. I suddenly realized that there was no traffic coming towards us, either.

'Hey, something's happening,' I yelled to Bob and Eddie. 'Look – the road's empty. Let's go and see.'

We sped off towards Lady Cross and as we rounded the bend we saw four policemen on horses trotting down the middle of the road in front of a huge crowd of marching men. Moving parallel to them on the pavement was another mass of people who were shouting and gesticulating at the marchers.

One of the mounted policemen signalled to us to get out of the way, so we pulled our bikes up on to the pavement.

'What is it?' Eddie called to a man standing at the gate of his tiny front garden.

'It's that Oswald Mosley's lot, innit? Cheek they've got – marchin' round 'ere after their darlin' Hitler dropped all them bombs on us. I wouldn't stand there, if I was you. Better nip in 'ere, quick.'

He held the gate open and we wheeled our bikes inside as the tide of people swept towards us.

'I'll give 'em this if they think of comin' in 'ere,' the man said, holding up a garden spade. 'Look at 'em. Fascists in the road and Communists on the pavement. Scum, the lot of 'em! The police ought to get out of the way and let 'em bash the daylights out of each other.'

The members of Mosley's Union Movement marched along silently, letting their slogans do their talking for them: 'PUT BRITAIN FIRST', read the large banner at the front of the column. Behind that, other placards proclaimed: 'JEWISH COMMUNIST PLOT', 'STOP COMMONWEALTH IMMIGRATION', 'KEEP BRITAIN WHITE'.

In contrast to the silent marchers, the people surging along the pavement were screaming abuse and chanting, 'Out, out – Fascists out! Out, out – Fascists out!' Some of them were carrying placards, too, with slogans such as: 'STOP NAZI HATE', 'MOSLEY = HITLER', 'REMEMBER 6 MILLION DEAD'.

'Look, it's Mr Solomon,' Eddie said, pointing to the group just passing us.

I read the words: 'SEAMEN'S UNION SAYS NO TO FASCISTS' and there, holding one end of the banner, was Manny's dad. He was shouting at the marchers and I caught a few of his words, '. . . my people . . . murder . . .' before his voice was lost in the tumult.

The chanting and clapping grew louder and louder, and I found myself caught up with the thrill of the rising hysteria.

'Whose side are you on?' I yelled to Eddie and Bob.

'Don't know. You?' Eddie replied.

'The Commies,' I decided, feeling a kind of allegiance to them because of Manny's dad, and not liking the silence of the Union Movement marchers.

'Me too,' Bob said.

'All right, then,' Eddie agreed.

The people poured past for almost ten minutes, then the crowd thinned and we saw a line of policemen bringing up the rear of the march.

'Let's shoot round the back streets and see it again,' Eddie suggested.

'Don't go gettin' yerselves mixed up!' the man said as we opened the garden gate.

We jumped on our bikes and raced along the streets parallel to the main road. When we reached the market car park we left our bikes against the wall of the public toilets and ran down an alley to the main road just in time to see the mounted policemen going by.

The pavement was crowded with shoppers, so the protesters were being forced out on to the road, closer to the marchers. The shouts and chants rose to a new level and one of the mounted policemen came trotting back, trying to keep the two groups apart. His horse's eyes showed white and frightened at all the noise and he started to rear. The policeman steadied him for a moment but the horse skittered sideways, driving some protesters further in towards the march. One of them stumbled against one of the marchers, who grabbed the placard out of his hands and hit him with it. Suddenly the lines broke and there was a heaving melee of fighting people. The shoppers scattered as the kicking, punching group surged towards the pavement. There were screams and cries as people were crushed against each other. A bottle sailed through the air and shattered on the ground.

I felt a tug on my arm and Eddie pulled me back into the alley where Bob was already standing. A young man, with a cut over his eye, rolled and twisted his way out of the crowd and burst past us, chased by two older men holding sticks. They rained blows on to his head and shoulders as he dodged away through the market stalls.

There was another surge and more people crammed into the alley, flailing and kicking. Bob and Eddie and I ran ahead of the crush and out into the car park. We grabbed our bikes and scooted away, but as we passed the entrance to the public toilets Eddie jerked to a halt and I crashed into him.

'What?' I cried as Eddie dropped his bike and ran into the toilets.

Bob and I let go of our bikes and followed. The two older men had caught the young man in the entrance and he was curled up on the ground, trying to ward off their kicking and stamping feet. Eddie grabbed the elbow of one of the attackers and tried to pull him away.

'Leave him alone, leave him alone,' Eddie shouted.

The man turned round, seized Eddie's jaw and pushed him back against the wall.

'Scram, you little runt!' the man roared, then he flung Eddie towards us and went back to kicking the young man in the ribs. He delivered three blows, then lifted his foot and crunched it down on the man's arm. There was a howl of agony and suddenly the attack was over. The older men stood back, squared their shoulders, straightened their jackets and brushed past us out into the car park.

We backed away as the young man leaped to his feet, blood streaming from his cuts.

'Commies!' he shouted, his eyes wide with fervour. 'Commies!'

We scuttled out of the toilets as he staggered towards us. He paused for a second, looking round the car park for his attackers, then he stumbled after them in hopeless pursuit.

All round the car park men were running, dodging in and out of the cars, chasing and escaping, aiming blows, wielding sticks, scuffling. There was the sound of approaching sirens and a moment later three police cars skidded to a halt on the far side of the car park. Everything stopped for a second, as policemen jumped out of the cars, then people scattered in all directions.

Four policemen pounded past us in pursuit of the fleeing men, and we grabbed our bikes and pedalled away from the action. We stopped at Hilly Park and sat on the grass talking excitedly. We'd seen plenty of fights at school but we'd never seen crowds of men fighting like this. The violence had frightened and thrilled us at the same time. Just like a film, as Eddie said.

All the excitement had driven everything else from our minds and it was only when we were cycling down Dunlow Hill on our way home for tea that we saw the spire of St Thomas's in the distance and remembered. A cold gloom descended on us.

'What was the wedding like?' my mum asked as I ate my tea in the kitchen.

'All right,' I mumbled, staring at my paste sandwich and unable to meet her eyes.

'Did the bride look nice?'

'OK, I suppose.'

'What about all those harmonies you were telling me about – did you sing them all right?'

'OK, I suppose.'

'OK, I suppose,' she mimicked. 'Might as well talk to a brick wall.'

Of course I was bursting to tell her all about the amazing scenes in Blackford, but I couldn't and we finished our tea in silence. Then the next morning during breakfast I had to keep quiet again when my dad reported what various people had told him about the riot. Most of his account was wrong but I said nothing, besides I was beginning to worry about the thought of having to face Mr Daniel and the vicar.

When I arrived at the church Bob and Eddie were waiting for me. We nodded at each other in sombre greeting, then stood behind the church hall and waited until the last moment before dashing into the vestry. The other choir members were already getting into line and we pulled on our cassocks and surplices and joined them just as the Rev. Maddox came in. I studied his face for some sign, but he smiled and greeted everyone in his usual manner. We bowed our heads in prayer and then processed into the church.

Throughout the service I watched Mr Daniel, trying to assess his mood, but he was totally involved in the music. He only looked in our direction a couple of times to nod his approval at the choir's singing. Perhaps he wasn't as angry as we had feared. During the final moments of silent prayer at the end of the service, I prayed earnestly that God would make Mr Daniel and Rev. Maddox forgive us.

When we got back into the vestry we quickly took off our vestments, hung them on our pegs, and were heading for the door when Rev. Maddox called, 'Edward, Robert, Andrew. In here, please.'

We followed him into his vestry. Mr Daniel was already there, looking very ill at ease, and his eyes darted nervously away from us to stare at the wall above our heads.

'Do you know how privileged you are?' the vicar said to us, putting his hand on Mr Daniel's shoulder. 'To sing in a choir like this? With a top organist and choir-master? Do you? It's an honour. And how do you repay that honour? Hmm? You let me down, you let the choir down and, worst of all, you let Mr Daniel down. Have you any idea how much work he put into those arrangements for yesterday? Have you? Arrangements he'd written especially for your voices?'

We shuffled uncomfortably at the vicar's tone, restrained and reasonable. He paused for a long time.

'I can't begin to tell you how disappointed I am,' he went on. 'You know what store I set by you three – how

I want you to be the rocks of my church. And now, you let us down like this.'

I felt tears begin to swell in my eyes and I bit my lip to stop them.

'Why?' the vicar asked. 'Andrew? Come on, tell me.'

'Forgot,' I muttered lamely.

'Forgot?' he barked, my obvious lie unleashing his anger.

I shrivelled. And the vicar moved on to stand in front of Bob.

'Robert?'

Bob shook his head. And the vicar moved on to Eddie.

'Edward?'

Eddie lifted his head and told the truth, quietly but clearly. 'They're our teachers and we hate them.'

'I – I beg your pardon?' the vicar said, shocked by Ed's directness.

'Mr Rix and Miss Carver. They're our teachers – well, they were, only we've left now,' Eddie said, stumbling in his desire to get it right, to open up his heart and make someone understand. 'Anyway, Mr Rix gave me the cane for nothing. I didn't do anything! Ask anybody, honest. And that's wrong. That's not Christian, is it? And they don't even come to church, so it's not like they're even proper Christians or anything. So –'

'How dare you!' Rev. Maddox thundered, and Eddie jumped in shock. 'Who do you think you are? A little boy, coming in here and telling me who's Christian and who's not. I'll not have it! Do you hear me?'

The vicar walked away to the corner of the room to

calm himself and Mr Daniel stood alone, blinking and rolling his eyes.

Eddie tried again, desperate to undo the damage.

'We're sorry,' he said. 'We didn't want to mess up Mr Daniel's harmonies or anything. But we couldn't come because it was Rix and ... Well, anyway, we're really, really sorry and we don't want our sixpences for the weddings, not even the morning one.'

There was a long silence, then the vicar came back and stood next to Mr Daniel.

'We've decided to suspend you from the choir,' he said. 'You may sing Evensong tonight but then you are banned from all choir activities for two whole weeks.'

A look of panic crossed Eddie's face. It was the worst possible punishment. His mother would ask questions, demand explanations. He hadn't told her about Rix's caning at the time; he couldn't tell her now. His mother would be upset again. Perhaps there would be another beating from CL.

'No, please, don't,' Eddie begged. 'Please! We've said we're sorry.'

'I've made up my mind,' the vicar said, walking towards the door.

'Please! It's not fair!' Eddie cried. 'What about forgiving? We've said we're sorry. You should forgive us. You told us that. You said we should forgive people. Even the Germans.'

'Edward, I am not prepared to discuss this any further. You've done wrong, you're being punished – you must learn from this lesson.'

The vicar opened the door and we filed out of his room.

It was hot and humid that afternoon. We sat on Mr Barrington's wall in the shade of his lime tree going over and over the problem, but there was no way out.

'My mum'll go c-c-crazy,' Bob said, breaking a long silence.

'Mine, too,' I said.

'Yeah, but at least your dad won't belt you,' Eddie murmured. Then he pulled his feet up on to the wall and buried his face in his knees.

We thought briefly about making a stand by not turning up for Evensong but in the end, of course, we had to go. It meant that our mothers wouldn't find out for another week.

We sang as well as we could. We behaved with dignity, hoping that at the end of the service Mr Daniel or the vicar would tell us that they'd changed their minds.

They said nothing.

Eddie was in a frightening mood the next morning. He insisted on going up to the Bomb Building even though we pointed out that the developers might come back.

'What are you, windy?' he challenged us. 'Anyway, let 'em come. I'll really smash their car this time.'

We trailed round the Bomb Building after him while he talked about ways of stopping the developers from working on the site.

'We could dig booby traps and stick nails in the tyres of their lorries,' he said, unconsciously picking at the thick scab on his knife-cut. Blood began to well out and run down his finger.

'You'll make it go septic,' Manny warned.

'Who cares!' Eddie snarled.

'No, but . . . honest, you can die if it goes really bad.'

'Who bloody cares!' Eddie screamed.

Bob and Manny and I froze. Then a terrifying look came on to Eddie's face, wild and angry.

'We'll blow them up,' he said. 'We'll blow them up with the bomb.'

'Don't be crazy, Ed,' I laughed.

The fury faded and he looked at me in desperation, pleading with me to understand and take his side. I shrugged and tears welled up in his eyes. He turned and ran away up the path, leaving us stunned.

'He's loony,' Manny finally said. 'You can't just blow people up.'

'He didn't mean it, idiot! He's just fed up with ... Parachute Pete and ...' I trailed off.

'Nearly lunchtime,' Manny said, glancing at his watch. 'I'm starving.'

'You're always s-s-starving, F-Fat Gut.'

'You should eat more: you might grow a bit, Short Arse.'

I listened to the radio commentary of the Fourth Test all afternoon and it was so exciting that I forgot everything else. New Zealand had been bowled out for 345 and England were batting. Len Hutton and Bill Edrich were on top form and runs were coming fast. I lay on the sofa with the windows open and a breeze billowing the net curtains and I could visualize every ball bowled and every stroke made.

My dad came in just as the last over of the day finished.

'How we doing?' he asked, leaning over the sofa and ruffling my hair.

'Brilliant. England are 432 for four. Len Hutton got 206!'

'Eeh bah gum, double century for the Yorkshire lad,' he said in a silly northern accent.

'You two going to the flicks tonight?' my mum asked as she cleared up after tea.

'Not tonight,' my dad said, lighting his Woodbine.

'It's Monday,' my mum said.

'I know what day of the week it is. Have you been nagging your mum about the flicks?' he said, turning to me.

'No!'

'There's no need to bite people's heads off!' my mum complained, clattering the plates together.

'There's no need to break the plates, either!' my dad snapped as she disappeared out into the scullery.

There was a noise of plates being banged down on the draining board. My dad raised his eyebrows and took a huge drag on his cigarette. I got up and took the rest of the tea things out.

'Come on, don't let's row,' my dad called from the kitchen in a conciliatory tone. 'There's just something I can't get out of tonight.'

'Oh yes – and what's that?' my mother asked.

'We'll go tomorrow, Andy,' he went on, and my mother closed her eyes and shook her head at his evasion. I ran my finger down her arm and she opened her eyes and forced a wry little smile for me.

'What's on at the Splendid?' he called.

'Erm, *The Secret Life of Walter Mitty*. It's got Danny Kaye and Boris Karloff,' I replied, ready to give him the times of the programmes if he asked.

'The secret life of Harry Adamson, more like,' my mum said loudly.

'I heard that, Peggy Adamson.'

'You were meant to!'

My dad appeared in the doorway and leaned against the doorpost looking at my mum. He took a drag on his Woodbine then pinched it so that the lighted end fell into the empty coal scuttle. He put the cigarette stub behind his ear, ran his fingers through his hair, and sauntered towards her. He put his arms round her waist and she stiffened as he kissed her neck.

'Don't be mean, Peg.'

'I'm not mean. I just want to know where you're going, that's all,' she said, trying to shrug his arms off, then laughing as he nibbled her ear. 'Get off!'

'You'll be angry,' he said, nuzzling her neck again.

'I won't.'

'All right, then. I put some money on the gee-gees last week and I've got to see a bloke about it.'

'You owe money!' my mum said, swinging round and sloshing water on to the floor.

'There you are, you're angry.'

'Harry, you know I hate getting into debt.'

'Ah, but we're not. I put it all on Gordon Richards' horses at Bath last Wednesday. Five races. Five wins. Cleaned up. And it wasn't even my money, it was this bloke's. I've got to take him his winnings and pick up my commission. See!'

He pulled my mum close and kissed the tip of her nose.

'Have a bit of faith in your old Harry,' he murmured.

She smiled and he kissed her on the lips. I saw her relax and press close against him.

I laughed and wolf-whistled. 'Oooh, Hollywood!'

'Shut up, you little peeping Tom,' my dad joked, breaking the embrace and pretending to dart at me. I dashed, giggling, to the door and along to the front room just in time to catch the beginning of *Dick Barton*.

About twenty minutes later my dad popped his head through the front window, 'I'm off.'

'Can I come down the road with you?'

'Well, I'd be delighted with your company, you little leprechaun, sure enough I would,' he said, making a funny face.

I ran out and caught up with him as he opened the front gate. For some reason I wanted to put my hand in his like the old days when I was a kid, but I didn't.

'So, it's Walter Mitty tomorrow night,' he said as we strolled down the road.

'Yeah, it's supposed to be dead good.'

And then I risked it – I hooked my arm in his. He started to shake it off, then smiled and let it stay there.

'Tell you what, save me coming home tomorrow, we can meet at the stadium. About six, not before, because I can get some extra work done. We'll get a bite at Lyons and go straight to the flicks.'

'Can we afford it, Lyons?'

'I told you, I won on the nags!'

'Who's the bloke you put the money on for?'

'Oh . . . just a bloke I know.'

We reached the tram stop and I let go of his arm. No tram in sight and no queue, so one had probably just gone. It might be ten minutes. I had plenty of time.

'Dad . . .' I hesitated, then forced myself to say it, 'I got into trouble at church.' And now that I'd started, I had to go on. So I told him.

'What's wrong with this Rix bloke, then?' he asked when I finished.

'He's just . . . horrible,' I said. 'So we didn't want to sing for him.'

'Sounds fair enough.'

'Yes, but Mum'll do her nut. And Bob's and Eddie's mums, too.'

'So you want me to have a word?'

'Can you?'

'Consider it done, *sahib*. It will be an honour to serve the little prince of Nunjee-Poo.'

'Dad, it's serious!'

'I've told you, I'll do it. Don't worry, I'll save you from the wrath of the ladies, I promise,' he said wiggling my ear. 'Goodo! Here it comes.'

He put out his hand and the tram screeched and clanked to a stop. He tapped my cheek and winked at me.

'I'll be late tonight and leaving early in the morning so I'll see you at six at the stadium. Six. OK?' he said as he stepped off the pavement.

He jumped on to the tram and climbed the stairs. The tram jerked and started to move off. I saw him arrive on the top deck. He bent and waved at me through the window, then settled into the back seat. I watched him being carried away from me and my heart was filled with love for him. He was the best of all dads; he was funny and kind and understanding and now he was going to save me and my friends from getting into trouble.

The next morning I was leaning out of my bedroom window when Eddie came out into his backyard. I cleared my throat loudly but he deliberately bent down and pretended to tie his shoelace. I wanted to tell him that my dad was going to sort everything out, so I coughed again but he stood up and wandered indoors without even glancing up at me.

At eleven o'clock I started listening to the cricket on the radio. Despite Eddie's bad mood it was going to be a really good day: a thrilling cricket game to listen to and then a great evening out with my dad.

Almost at once, the promise of the day faded. The English batsmen made mistake after mistake and collapsed from 432 for 4 to 482 all out – a lead of only 137. It would need great bowling to get New Zealand out for less than that. By late afternoon it was obvious that England stood no chance of winning and the game crept towards an inevitable draw. I turned off the radio and checked the time. Four fifteen. Dad had said six but I could walk slowly and then hang around outside; it would be more interesting than staying here.

'I'm going,' I announced to my mum in the kitchen.

'Not like that, you're not,' she said, looking up from her knitting. 'Change your shirt, wash your face and comb your hair – you look as if you've been dragged through a hedge backwards.'

I ran upstairs and five minutes later I presented my new clean self.

'There, that's much better,' she said, studying my face intently. She brushed my hair to the side and smiled. 'Goodness, you look so grown-up.'

I grinned, pleased.

'Here,' she said, picking up her purse and scrabbling among the coins, 'for the tram.'

'I can walk.'

'Go on, take it. Have a nice evening, love.'

She kissed me, then laughed and wet her thumb to wipe off the lipstick she'd left on my cheek.

A tram came just as I got to the end of the road so I jumped straight on and arrived at the car park of Blackford Greyhound Stadium at quarter to five. My dad's office was a strange concrete box on stilts that had been built on to the side of the main building. As I walked past the iron staircase that led up to it, I saw that his door was closed. It was too early to disturb him so I went to the far side of the car park and sat down on the grass bank next to a big sycamore tree. There was a cooling breeze in the shade and I watched the traffic going over the bridge in the distance.

At just after five o'clock, a door opened and workers began leaving the stadium. They emerged from the dark interior, blinking at the fierce summer light, and strolled towards the main road, the men taking off their jackets and the girls pulling at their sticky blouses to let the cooler air flow past their skin. Within five minutes they had all gone, leaving the door open: a black gash in the grey concrete.

A movement caught my eye and someone emerged from the shadowy exit. I recognized her at once. It was Mrs Wallace. She closed the door and locked it with a big key. Like the others, she strolled in the direction of the stadium gates, but when she got to the stilts she swung round and began to climb the stairs to my dad's office. Perhaps she was going to give the key to him.

I sat waiting for her to leave, but half an hour later she was still inside the office. They must be working. I stood up and walked slowly round the car park, hoping that my dad would spot me. I got to the gates of the stadium and looked up at his window, but all I could see was the reflection of the sun and the sky.

And then a game started in my brain. I'd count to a hundred and if she still hadn't come out I'd go up and tell my dad I was there.

I got to a hundred but I didn't go. I started counting again, more slowly. I got to a hundred and still didn't go. Once more, very slowly, and this time I would really go. I got to a hundred then added an extra thirty. In the distance I heard the clock of the town hall chime a quarter to six. Near enough to the time he'd said.

I walked over to the stairs and started to climb. I looked down through the pattern of holes in the wrought-iron steps, seeing the ground get further away with each step I took.

I reached the top and knocked gently. There was no reply, but I twisted the door knob and slowly pulled the door open.

A moment later I was running down the metal stairs

and across the car park. I reached the sycamore tree and ducked behind it, my heart thudding wildly. I heard the office door bang open and I peeped out and saw my dad. He was putting his jacket on. He stood at the top of the stairs and looked all round the car park before leaning over the hand rail to check under the stilts. Then he went back into the office.

I waited behind the tree and found myself humming the tune of 'Cigarettes and Whisky and Wild, Wild Women'. I giggled nervously as I realized the relevance. Mrs Wallace must be a wild, wild woman and like the song said, 'They drive you crazy, they drive you insane.'

But I stopped giggling as I remembered what I'd seen: the papers scattered on the floor, my father and Mrs Wallace on the top of his desk, the green clip-on earring that slipped off Mrs Wallace's ear as she turned her head and caught the movement of the closing door. I tried to get the picture out of my mind by concentrating on the red lorry heading towards the centre of Blackford, passing over the river bridge and disappearing from view. Was my dad in love with Mrs Wallace? Would he leave me and my mum and go and live with her?

The town-hall clock struck six and I stepped out from behind the tree and sat down on the grass as if I'd just arrived. The song started up in my head again and I could hear how the singer sang it as 'Cigareets and Whusky and Warl, Warl Wimmin'.

My dad came out of his office, followed by Mrs Wallace. I waved and stood up and walked across the car park. We met at the bottom of the metal stairs.

'Hello, old lad,' my dad said. 'Been waiting long?'

I was ready for that and shook my head. 'Just got here.'

'You remember Mrs Wallace, Andy? She's been help-ing me with my work. All finished, thanks to her. Ooops! Forgot to lock the door.'

He ran back up the stairs, pulling a bunch of keys out of his pocket. Mrs Wallace looked at me and smiled. I smiled back.

'You're off to the cinema,' she said.

I nodded and suddenly thought of *Johnny Belinda*. He'd left me alone in the Rex that night in order to meet Mrs Wallace. And the other times when he'd been too busy to take me to the cinema and I'd worried about the black market, it was because he'd been seeing her. And last night he hadn't been giving the winnings to a man he knew, he'd been seeing her. It was all lies and lies. The whole thing was spreading out like a stain across my life and I wished with all my heart that I hadn't found out.

'Right,' my dad said, coming down the steps. 'We'll be perfect gentlemen and escort Susan to her tram, eh Andy?'

We got to the tram stop and stood awkwardly in the queue as the traffic roared past across the river bridge. The tram arrived and we shuffled forward until Mrs Wallace climbed on board.

'See you tomorrow. Thanks for your help,' my dad called.

She turned briefly to acknowledge his words, then squeezed her way into the middle of the other standing passengers on the lower deck. The tram rattled away.

'Okey-dokey, off to Lyons we go. You hungry?' He put on a deep growly voice, '"Hungry as a Lyon". Be a good advert, that. I might send it to them. They pay for stuff like that.'

We walked side by side over the bridge and he suddenly took hold of my hand. I held on until we reached the far side of the bridge, then let go.

'What's the matter?'

'It's too hot,' I said.

When we got to Lyons he asked for a table next to the window, but they were all taken so we had to sit in the middle of the room surrounded by chattering people. We examined the menu and he tried to persuade me to have liver and bacon like him, but the thought of it made me feel sick. I ordered poached egg on toast.

It was only the second time I'd ever been to a restaurant and I decided I didn't like it very much. It was too noisy and too smoky and I hated watching people shovelling food into their mouths and chewing and swallowing while they talked and laughed. It seemed a disgusting thing to do, something that ought to be done in private.

'Why didn't you come up to my office when you got there this evening?' my dad suddenly asked.

'Just didn't.'

There was a long, long silence.

'It was good that Susan came and helped me,' my dad said, stubbing out his cigarette.

I nodded and pretended to look round the room and be interested by what I was seeing.

Our food arrived and while my dad devoured his liver

and bacon I forced myself to eat some of the toast and the white of the egg. But when I sliced into the yolk and it dribbled across the toast, I couldn't eat any more and pushed my plate away.

'Whatta you wanta now, *signor*? Icer de creama?' my dad asked.

'No, thanks.'

'What's the matter with you?'

'Not hungry,' I mumbled.

He lit a Woodbine and sat back making a big show of enjoying himself while he drank his coffee. I picked at my fingernails. He smoked another cigarette and then finally looked at the clock.

'Oh well, time for the flicks.'

'Yeah,' I said, trying to sound enthusiastic. 'It's Danny Kaye.'

I stood outside on the pavement while he paid for the meal and when he came out I made a point of thanking him and telling him how good it was.

'Yeah, it was great apart from the food and drink,' he joked bitterly.

I laughed hard, then desperately tried to keep talking: pointing out things in shops we passed, commenting on cars, and telling him things about the film we were going to see. It was a relief to get to the cinema and sit quietly in the darkness.

'You going to have something?' my dad asked during the interval when the lady appeared with the tray of ice creams.

I shook my head and he sighed in irritation.

'Where you going?' I asked as he suddenly got up.

'To the lav. Do you mind?' he snapped.

I watched him walk up the aisle and I sat there counting the seconds, sure that he'd walked out of the cinema and left me there. Finally, after an eternity, the door opened and he came back in.

'I thought you weren't coming,' I whispered as he sat down.

'Oh, for God's sake,' he hissed.

The Secret Life of Walter Mitty started. I sat through it as if I'd been frozen and when, mercifully, the film finally ended, I stood up and nearly buckled at the knees. My dad hurried out of the cinema and away along the dark pavement, and I staggered after him feeling that my legs would give way at any moment.

'Oh, come on,' he called, striding ahead.

The air had grown cold while we'd been in the cinema and there were haloes of mist round the street lights as we hurried along the back streets.

'You aren't half going fast,' I panted as we climbed the hill up to Hilly Park.

The park gates were always locked at dusk but the low fence never kept anyone out and it was a favourite place for courting couples. My dad sped towards the fence and vaulted over. Usually, when we took this short cut together, he would give me a hand to jump over, but that night I had to haul myself across while I watched him disappearing away into the darkness. My trailing foot caught on the fence and I fell in a heap in the rose border on the other side.

I got up and saw him silhouetted against the yellow glow of London as he strode across the wide open space at the top of the hill. He disappeared below the sky-line and I raced after him, terrified of losing him in the dark streets on the far side of the park. When I got to the gates I slowed because I could see him waiting on the other side. I climbed the fence and stepped on to the pavement.

With no warning he grabbed my shirt front and backed me up against the gates.

'You saw us,' he stated in a low voice. 'You saw me and Susan. You got there early. You came up to my office and saw us . . . together. Then you ran away and sat under the tree and pretended that you'd just arrived.'

I couldn't deny it. A strange childish whine escaped from my throat as I nodded.

He let go of my shirt and stood next to me, his back against the park gate, so that we were both looking away down Dunlow Hill towards the dim outline of St Thomas's spire. He pulled out a cigarette and lit it.

'Are you going to leave us?' I asked.

'That depends on you, doesn't it?'

'No.'

'Your mum's not going to want me around if you tell her, is she?'

I thought about this terrible new power: the power to tell, the power to hurt, to end my parents' marriage. I didn't want it. I hated this power. I wanted to be a little boy who didn't know anything.

'Do you love her?' I asked.

'Who?'

'Mum!' I shouted, angry that he had to ask.

'Of course I do, you know I do.'

'Then why are you …?'

'Oh, Andy,' he said, shaking his head and turning to look at me. 'There are things that are … too hard to explain. One day when you're grown-up, you'll … maybe you'll understand … What can I say? I'm sorry, that's all I can say. I'm sorry.'

I looked down at St Thomas's and thought of Eddie begging Rev. Maddox: 'We're sorry and we'll never do it again. Please!'

A very faint drizzle began to fuzz the light from the street lamp. My dad looked at it and wiped his face.

'So are you going to tell her?' he asked.

I shook my head.

For a moment he looked as if he was going to cry, but he wiped his face again and threw his cigarette end away. Sparks burst on to the road as it hit.

'Better get home, then,' he said.

I thought that my mother might have gone to bed, but the light was still on in the front room as we walked up the path.

'Hello, love,' my dad said as he went into the room. I stood outside in the corridor and watched him kiss her cheek.

'Did you have a nice evening, dear?' she asked me, looking over his shoulder.

'Yeah.'

'Oh, good. Ni' night, then.'

'Night,' I said.

I went up the stairs and I knew I had entered a new world.

15

The next morning I woke up early and thought of my dad with Mrs Wallace. No matter how hard I tried to stop it, the memory kept coming back, making me feel hot and sweaty. I pulled the blanket off and lay there reading comics. I heard my parents get up but I stayed in my room. I didn't want to see him.

Finally at about eight o'clock I heard him shout, 'Bye, love, I'll see you this evening. I'll be late.'

'What time?' my mother called.

'It's Wednesday, there's a race meeting on, remember?'

'You said your boss was doing this one for a change.'

'He is. But I'll have to stay for a while.'

'What time?' my mum repeated.

The door slammed.

He was staying out late. He was seeing Mrs Wallace again. Last night he'd said he was sorry, so I thought he would stop. But he couldn't stop. Like the song said, she was driving him crazy, driving him insane. And when five o'clock came she would climb the stairs to his office . . .

I jumped out of bed and ran down to the kitchen. My

mum was in the scullery, washing up. She glanced over her shoulder and smiled.

'Hello, dear.'

I had to look away in case she saw the secret written on my face.

I spent most of the morning trailing after her, singing cheery songs, making silly jokes and helping with the household chores. Our happiness seemed so fragile and I wanted her to get her fill.

While we were doing the washing-up after lunch I looked at her standing at the sink and everything seemed wrong. I hated knowing about Mrs Wallace when she didn't. Her ignorance made her seem so pathetic. I went to put my arms round her, but my elbow knocked a saucepan which splashed into the water.

'Oh, for God's sake!' she cried. 'Look, my pinny's all wet now.'

'Sorry,' I said, trying to wipe her with the tea towel.

'Oh, get off!' she snarled, slapping my arm hard with her wet hand.

'Ow! That hurt.'

'Serves you right. You'd try the patience of a saint, you would – under my feet all morning.'

'There's no need to bloody hit me!' I shouted, throwing the tea towel on to the draining board.

I headed towards the kitchen, but she grabbed hold of me. There was a stinging slap on the back of my thigh just below the line of my shorts, and then another one.

'Don't you dare swear at me!' she shouted.

I wrestled my arm free and spun round. She hadn't hit me like that for years and I was shocked.

'You hurt me,' I whined, and I could hear how like a little boy I sounded, playing on my mother's soft heart. But her lips were set in a thin line and her eyes were dark and determined.

'Good! And I'll do it again if you ever swear at me like that.'

For an instant, I was tempted. For an instant I almost told her about Dad and Susan Wallace. The words were there, ready. Then in the next instant I saw the pain and chaos it would cause and I held back. But I was not a wheedling little boy any more; my knowledge made me older, gave me a kind of power. I glared at her.

'I'm warning you,' she said, raising her hand.

'You'd better not,' I challenged and held her gaze.

She lowered her hand and looked away.

I walked calmly through the kitchen and along the corridor, but I was trembling when I opened the front door. I went out and headed straight towards Eddie's house. I couldn't go on being on bad terms with him. I needed a friend.

I rang his bell and the door opened almost at once, as if he'd been waiting for me.

'Hiya, Andy,' he said, and the relief in his voice matched my feelings at seeing him.

'Wotcha,' I said.

'They're all out. Want to come in?'

He led the way up to his bedroom and I peered out of his open window to look at my house. There was a movement in the kitchen and I ducked back inside.

'What?' Eddie asked.

'My mum.'

'Did you tell her about choir just now? I heard her shouting at you.'

'No, it was something else. You told yours?'

'Not yet. She'll do her nut when I do.'

'It's OK, my dad's going to . . .' I stopped as I realized that I couldn't count on his help now.

'What?'

'My dad was going to say something, but he probably won't.'

'Why?'

'Cos he's a sod.'

'They're all sods!' Eddie said. He grinned, then lifted his head and screamed at the top of his voice, 'So-o-ds!'

'So-o-ds!' I howled, imitating his stance.

'So-o-ds!' he began again and then spluttered and broke into wild giggles.

A moment later I was caught up in his laughter and we whooped and howled and rolled on the floor, reunited by this moment of madness, reunited by our anger and hatred of the grown-up world.

'Let's go out,' he said when we stopped laughing. 'That pig CL'll be home from work soon.'

We cycled up to the Bomb Building, but I held back when Eddie started along the path towards the den.

'Come on,' he said.

'You said it was out of bounds.'

'Not for you.'

He winked. We were together again. Outlaws.

He unlocked the padlock and we went inside the hut. Somehow, the air seemed much cooler in there and I was struck by the stillness as we stood side by side, looking down at the floor.

'Do you want to see it?' Eddie whispered.

'Yeah,' I said, and my voice trembled.

He lifted the central section of the floor and propped it against the wall, revealing the bomb. He had scraped the earth away and there were two pieces of folded paper laid across the fins.

'What's that?'

'My school report,' Eddie said.

'Why?'

There was a pause before he said, 'There's signatures on it.'

I got it at once: Rix and Carver. You put the names of people you hated next to the bomb. For the first time I understood what the bomb meant to Eddie. Understood how you could hate someone enough to want to blow them up.

'What about the other one?' I asked.

'An envelope with someone's name on it.'

I knew it must be CL; I nodded.

'Can I put something? Next time?' I asked.

'If you want,' Eddie said, a shadow of a smile flitting across his lips. I felt as if I had passed a test.

We stared at our bomb for a few minutes, then lowered the floor back into place and locked up the hut again.

We sat around at the top of the Big Brown 'ill talking

and throwing stones down into the bushes until the darts-factory siren sounded. Five o'clock. As we cycled home my mind was flooded with thoughts of what was happening in my dad's office, so I was astonished when I rang the bell and he opened the door.

'Here he is!' he called. 'Where've you been, dirty stop-out?'

'Nowhere,' I said, hating him.

'Nowhere? Oh, it's lovely there. Did you have nice weather?'

'Get off,' I mumbled as he tried to put his arm round my shoulder.

'Ooh, ooh! Sulkypuss,' he mocked, but I brushed past him.

The tea was already laid out on the table. It was salad with three really thick chunks of corned beef on each of our plates instead of the one thin slice we usually got.

'A friend of a friend gave me a couple of tins,' my dad explained.

'Black market, you mean,' I said.

'If you don't want it ...' he teased, taking my plate away.

I loved corned beef and I was really hungry, but I forced myself not to grab the plate and eventually he put it back. All through the meal I kept my eyes down while he chattered and joked, but I allowed my mum a brief smile when she brushed her hand across my hair on her way out to the scullery. She seemed to have forgotten our lunchtime row and I felt protective of her again.

My dad sat back at the end of the meal and lit his Woodbine.

'Wooaaa, lovely grub, darling,' he called to my mum. 'Even worth having to wait for His Nibs, here.'

'I thought you were going to be late,' I said, scowling at him.

'Well I wasn't, was I?'

'I bet your assistant was surprised,' my mother said, coming into the kitchen.

A buzz of shock fizzed through my chest and my eyes snapped round to look at her. Did she know about Mrs Wallace? Did she?

'What do you mean?' my dad said after a moment.

'I bet your assistant was surprised you didn't work late tonight,' she repeated. 'What's her name? Sophie?'

'Susan.'

'That's right, Susan.'

'I don't know about surprised. She was dead pleased,' my dad said.

'She was, was she?' my mum said, starting to collect the plates. She turned to me. 'Hey, you'd better get off to choir.'

'Just going.'

My dad was staring at his cigarette smoke and I felt sure that he was thinking about Mrs Wallace. I deliberately banged my chair against the table.

'Hey, mind the furniture,' he said automatically.

I glared at him but he was already miles away again, lost in his thoughts.

I met up with Bob and Eddie and we cycled away as if

we were going to choir practice, but turned up Westdale Street instead and stopped at the Ritzy. They were showing a John Wayne film called *The Wake of the Red Witch* and we looked at the poster and tried to imagine the story. Then we cycled along Blythe Road and stood outside Banner's Fish and Chips, watching the queue until the smell of the cooking made us feel too hungry.

'Come on, let's do a mystery tour,' Eddie suggested. 'You've got to follow exactly where I go and do everything I do.'

He raced off and we sped after him, copying every gesture he made: hands off the handlebars, put them back on; head turn to the left; ring the bell; lift right foot off the pedal and hold it out to the side. We braked, laughing, at the junction with the main road and were waiting for a gap in the traffic when Bob suddenly lunged backwards. His pedal caught in my front wheel and we both staggered to remain upright.

'Bob?' I heard someone say and I turned to see Mr Newman walking towards us. He was carrying a cricket bag and was glowing and tanned from his day out. 'Where are you off to? I thought you had choir on Wednesdays.'

Bob nodded at his father.

'So, what are you doing here?'

'W-W-W-W-W-W-W-W-W-' Bob said, then flicked his head to try and free the words. But it was no good. 'W-W-W-W-W-W-W-W-W-W-W-'

Mr Newman's mouth tightened in irritation and I was just about to break the rule and speak on Bob's behalf when Eddie beat me to it.

'We've been banned from choir because we missed a wedding.'

'You what?' Mr Newman asked, looking at his son.

'Bob wanted to tell you but I stopped him. And he only missed the wedding because of me,' Eddie said.

It was a brave attempt to take responsibility, but Mr Newman wasn't interested.

'Is that right?' he asked Bob. 'You're banned from choir?'

Bob nodded.

'Oh, well, that's going to make your mother happy, isn't it? What on earth's the matter with you?' Mr Newman went on, glowering at Bob. 'Do you do it on purpose, let everyone down like this?'

Bob hung his head and this irritated his father even more.

'Oh, don't stand there like a little ninny. Get home, now. Go on!'

Bob scrambled his bike round and pedalled away at top speed. We watched him until he disappeared round the corner. Then Mr Newman turned and raised his finger at us.

'As for you two scoundrels,' he warned, but the anger had gone and there was an amused glint in his eye. 'You'd better watch your step at Wolfe's next term. Right?'

We nodded.

'Because I'm going to be checking that you don't even breathe out of turn.' He paused, then winked. 'By the way, I need big ugly gorillas like you for my rugby teams. Make sure you get your names down for after-school training sessions. Build up those muscles, and we'll have you in the under-thirteens in no time, eh?'

We both let out a silly laugh, then he marched away swinging his cricket bag.

'Flipping hell!' I breathed when he was out of earshot. 'I hate rugby.'

'Forget the rugby,' Eddie said. 'Bob's going to cop it from his mum and you can bet your bottom dollar she'll go straight round and tell ours, too.'

'Oh blimey, yeah!'

'Damn Rix. It's all his fault.'

When I got home I called, 'Night,' and went straight upstairs, hoping that no one would call me back. I had just got into bed when my dad came into my room. I turned away and stared at the wall. My bed bounced as he sat down on it.

'Andy,' he said, gently rocking my shoulder, but I refused to turn and look at him. There was a long silence, then he sighed and went on in a soft voice that made him sound hoarse. 'I've told your mum.'

Told her? My heart jerked with shock and my face began to burn. Why? Yesterday it had to be kept secret and now he had told her.

'What did she say?' I asked.

'Well, she wasn't exactly pleased, was she? All the lying and stuff. You can't blame her.'

His hand came down on my shoulder again. This was it, he was leaving. My mother had kicked him out. My eyes began to fill at the thought of him going down the stairs and out of the front door forever. He squeezed my shoulder and I felt a sob rise in my throat, but I clenched my jaw to stop it.

'Anyway, I told her there was no point getting all het up and in the end I won her round. You know me, gift of the gab. She's off telling Eddie and Bob's mums now.'

'Why?' I gasped, finally swinging round to face him. The sudden movement sent a tear spilling down my cheek.

'What's up? I thought you'd be pleased,' he said with a puzzled smile.

'What?' I asked in confusion. Pleased? Pleased that my mum was going to tell my friends' mums about him and Susan Wallace?

'I thought you didn't want Ed and Bob to get in trouble. No awkward questions about Mr Rix and all that.'

'Oh, choir,' I said, suddenly realizing. 'I thought you meant . . .'

'What?'

In an instant my father's amused expression turned to a hard stare. And I understood that this was how it was going to be. The secret was so deep that we wouldn't even admit that there was a secret. I couldn't even share it with him. It would lie between us, a cold silence. I understood and I hated him for making me feel so lonely. He held my gaze and I could hear the smoker's wheeze in his breathing.

'Meant what?' he repeated.

'Nothing.'

He grinned.

'Well, pal,' he said, lifting up his tie and wiggling it like Oliver Hardy. 'Another fine mess I've gotten you out of.'

I lay down again and turned to the wall. After a moment he sighed and got up.

'Thanks for your help, Dad,' he said bitterly, banging the door closed.

My mother didn't say anything at breakfast the next morning, but there was a frostiness in her manner so I ate quickly and got up to leave.

'Two things,' she said before I reached the door. 'I don't want to be lied to ever again, do you understand?'

I nodded.

'Your dad says you had a reason for what you did, but I don't care – you let the vicar down so you'll write to him and apologize.'

It turned out that Eddie's mum had said almost exactly the same thing to him.

'No questions, nothing. Just write a letter,' Eddie reported, bubbling with relief, as we sat under Mr Barrington's lime tree sheltering from the steady drizzle. 'Mind you, CL tried to stir it up. Told my mum I was a troublemaker. He's the damn troublemaker. Your dad's super, though. How'd he get your mum to do it?'

'He's got the gift of the gab,' I said, and Eddie glanced at me, picking up the bitterness I couldn't keep out of my voice.

My dad's gift of the gab and my mum's visit to the Newmans didn't save Bob, though. When we knocked on his door his mother answered.

'Is Bob coming out?' I asked.

'He's in his bedroom and he's staying there,' she said.

'Is he ill?' Eddie asked.

'He's in disgrace,' she replied and closed the door.

We knew that Manny wouldn't be allowed out in the drizzle, so we went up to the Bomb Building alone. Which is why, crucially, Bob and Manny weren't with us when we met Cap.

16

Eddie and I had been in the Control Room for about half an hour, sorting through the pile of stuff we'd collected for weapon-making, when there was a thumping noise. We froze. Someone was stamping on the stone slab of the entrance.

'Manny?' I whispered, looking at Eddie.

He shook his head.

The stamping stopped so we crept out of the Control Room and down the corridor. Silence. We waited a bit longer, then I led the way across the walkway and up the chute. I got to the top and pushed the slab.

'A jack-in-the-box,' a voice said, and a man's face peered over the lip of the stone.

I let go of the slab in shock and fell down on to Eddie. We slid to the bottom of the chute and almost toppled off the walkway into the black water. Then light poured in on us as the trapdoor was opened.

'Come out of there,' the voice commanded.

We scrambled up the chute and out of the hole.

'Sit down and put your hands on your head!' the man ordered and, unquestioningly, we obeyed.

The drizzle had stopped and the sun was shining brightly so I had to squint to look up at the man standing there, legs apart, hands on hips. It was impossible to make out his face against the glare, but I could see the sunlight glancing off his tightly-waved black hair. I was sure he was going to tell us off for trespassing, and when he tucked his thumbs behind his wide leather belt I even wondered if he might use it to hit us. At the same time I was puzzled by that belt and his workman's boots – they didn't really go with the suit and tie he was wearing. What level of authority were we dealing with?

Usually we could place people instantly: their dress, their behaviour, and their voices told us exactly what class of person they were and how we should react to them. Cap confounded the rules. One minute he would speak in a heavy south-east London accent, then he'd switch to a Welsh accent or a posh voice and it was impossible to know which one was real. He was unpredictable and exciting.

'You know how I found you?' he asked us as we blinked up at him. He pointed to our bikes lying on the ground next to the coal-hole.

'Careless, that is,' he said. 'Especially to someone with my training. See that?'

He waggled his tie but we couldn't make out the colour or design against the blazing light.

'Intelligence Corps,' he announced. 'A Special Operations man isn't likely to miss much, is he? Got to have your wits about you to stay alive in battle.'

We were already interested, but now he hooked

us completely with the first of his startling changes in direction, coupled with a change of accent from educated army officer to London labourer.

''Ere, I know you, dun' I?' he asked, and he obligingly moved round so that the sun was no longer behind him and we could see his features at last.

He had a long, thin face with a dark beard shadow that was almost blue against his pale skin. And it was true: he did seem familiar. But from where? Then I registered the greeny-yellow bruising round his eye and the scabs on his nose and forehead and it all came back.

'The march,' Eddie said, beating me to it. 'In the toilets, last Saturday. Those blokes were kicking and punching you. Three against one.'

'Damn Communists! What do you expect of scum like that?' the man said, reverting to his army-officer voice.

'Eddie tried to stop them,' I offered.

'Yes, you did,' the man agreed, holding out his hand. 'Decent of you. Good to have you on our side.'

Eddie stood up and shyly shook hands with him, and I followed suit.

'Captain Stanley Evans. But you can call me Cap. By the way, you know Evans, the wicketkeeper, plays for England? He's my cousin. Good old Geoffrey; doing the Evans clan proud at the moment.'

'You mean Godfrey,' I said, correcting him.

'Ah, that's his professional name. He prefers the family to use his real name: Geoffrey. What a tip-top chap. You'd love him. Biggest practical joker you've ever met. Heart of gold, though.'

Eddie and I glanced at each other, thrilled to be talking to the cousin of an England cricketer.

'Do you still see him?' I asked.

'Of course I do.'

'Could you get his autograph for us?'

'See what I can do. But we're both busy chaps, you know.'

'You still in the army?' Eddie asked.

'No, back on Civvy Street now, but ... er ...' he looked round and then leaned towards us conspiratorially, 'I still provide intelligence for the Ministry of Defence. The war may be over but there are plenty of threats to the nation's security. Look at last Saturday.'

'Is that why the Communists were beating you up?' I said.

'The beggars paid for it later, I can tell you. Now, what about this place? What you got here, a camp or something?'

Cap seemed genuinely excited by the Bomb Building and wanted to know everything: the history of the place, what games we played, what animals we'd seen, who else came there. It wasn't like talking to an adult at all; he seemed to catch our enthusiasm for the place and to share it. Indeed, when we told him about riding our bikes down the Big Brown 'ill he asked for a demonstration, then borrowed my bike and had a go himself. He put his foot on the concrete block in honour of our ritual, then he launched himself over the edge. He slewed from side to side and almost fell, but he reached the bottom and turned round with a big grin on his face.

'Come and show me round down 'ere,' he called, adopting his cockney accent. 'I wanna see this shelter where them five people was killed.'

We led him along the path to the ruins and he peered into the dim interior where the family had died. Then he bowed his head as if he were praying.

'You never play here,' he said at last in a new, husky voice with a strong Welsh accent.

'Never,' Eddie confirmed.

'You've done right,' Cap said, closing his eyes and nodding to himself. 'They come back. Their spirits come back here from time to time.'

'How do you know?' I asked and a shiver ran through me.

'I can feel their presence.'

'Are ghosts real, then?' Eddie asked.

Cap opened his eyes and looked at us both intently. 'Oh, yes. They're real, all right.'

'Have you seen one?' Eddie asked.

'You don't see them. You ... feel them,' Cap replied.

I took a step backwards and almost fell as I stumbled on a brick.

'Don't be afraid,' Cap said.

'I'm not,' I lied.

'They don't harm those who have never harmed them.'

We stood looking at the ruins for a bit longer, then we led Cap down to the tall billboards at Manstead Road and back along various paths. We tried to hurry past the track that led to the hut, but Cap stopped and peered through the bushes.

'What's that?'

'Just a stupid den we made,' I said quickly.

'We don't use it any more,' Eddie added, 'cos we've got this great cellar. Do you want to see it?'

'Love to.'

He whistled in admiration when he slid down to join us at the bottom of the chute. He picked up a stick and dipped it into the water to see how deep it was; then he knelt and looked under the walkway to check the construction.

'You built this? Well done, it's a top job,' he said, and we glowed with pleasure as we followed him across to the Control Room.

We lit a candle and Cap shook his head as he looked round.

'I can't believe my eyes. This is just like the cellar I found in Dunkirk in 1940. The Germans were advancing and the British Army was trapped. So I set up an operations room in the cellar and deployed a battalion of my men round the town. We held the Germans off for a day or so to allow our lads time to get to the beaches and away on the boats. Had a few hairy moments in that place, I can tell you.'

'Like what?' Eddie asked.

'Oh, nothing to make a fuss about,' he said modestly and changed the subject. 'I tell you what would be dashed good fun. We could make a kind of army assault course outside. What do you think?'

We were thrilled as he described the climbing walls and obstacle course he would help us make. Best of all, he said he would get a block and tackle and some cable to construct what he called a 'death slide' from the top of the Big Brown 'ill down to the elm tree.

'That would be a pretty decent ride, wouldn't it – whizzing over the tops of the bushes on a pulley?' he said. 'Like being Tarzan.'

We were speechless at the thought of someone doing something so wonderful for us.

'Don't gawp at me like that. I'm not talking about a miracle,' Cap said, tapping the side of his head. 'Just takes a brain with a bit of know-how. Should've seen some of the engineering we had to improvise during the war. When you're in a tight corner you find a solution or you die, don't you?'

We nodded earnestly.

'I know what this place needs,' he announced as he looked round the cellar again. 'A map on the wall.'

'That's what I said,' Eddie agreed.

'I'll fish out one of my Special Ops maps of Europe for you.'

'Cor, really?'

'Only on loan, of course, and you'll be responsible for making sure it doesn't go AWOL – they're top secret. Now, what else?' he continued, pacing the room, inspecting the ceiling and walls. 'It's a bit dark down here with candles. You need a couple of Tilly lamps like we had in Dunkirk. The paraffin gives a good light and a bit of warmth at the same time. You can pick 'em up cheap down Blackford market.'

We sat round the table chatting and Cap asked some

questions about us, but we soon worked the conversation back to the war and quizzed him about his exploits. He was reticent about giving full details, often shrugging or just smiling when we tried to prise something out of him, but it was apparent that he'd seen action in North Africa, Italy, France, Germany and had even done what he called 'clandestine work for the Yanks' in the Pacific islands.

By the time we scrambled up the chute and out into the early evening sunshine, we were totally captivated by him and could hardly believe our luck when he said he'd like to meet us the next day.

'Aren't you working?' Eddie asked.

'Damned Reds cracked a couple of ribs,' he said, wincing slightly as he pressed his side. 'Got time off.'

'What do you do?' I asked.

'I'm in construction at the moment. It's just my cover, of course. There are a lot of Communist agitators in the building trade so I've been asked to keep an eye on them from the inside. But that's between you and me, right?'

We crossed our hearts and spat to show our agreement.

'Excellent, I knew I could trust you. You're good types. See you here tomorrow, at ten hundred hours.'

He shook our hands and we dashed home quickly, realizing that we were late. My father opened the front door but I ignored him and ran down the corridor. My mum was sitting at the kitchen table and, as my dad came into the room, I made a big show of putting my arms round her neck and kissing her cheek. She laughed and pushed me away but I sat down and I shifted my chair closer to her. I could sense my dad watching all this but I never allowed our eyes to meet.

When I collected the plates at the end of the meal, he jokingly grabbed my arm and pulled me so that the cutlery fell on the floor.

'Honestly, Harry!' my mum said. 'You're a bigger kid than he is.'

I helped her do the washing-up and then told her I was going out again.

'So, what's good at the flicks for tomorrow?' my dad asked as I passed through the kitchen.

'Nothing,' I said.

'Don't you want to go, then?' he called plaintively.

'No,' I shouted, slamming the front door behind me. Eddie and Manny were already outside, playing cigarette cards.

'Wotcha!' Eddie said, expertly flicking a card so that it landed on one that Manny had just thrown. He picked up the two cards and put them in his pack. 'I've just been telling Manny about Cap. He's wizard, isn't he?'

At first Manny was interested in what we had to say about our new hero, but when we went on about Cap's exploits during the war he got irritated.

'Blimey, anyone'd think he was flipping General Montgomery, listening to you.'

'No, but he's really smashing,' Eddie protested. 'Honest, you can meet him tomorrow and I bet you like him.'

'I'm not here tomorrow. My nan and grandad are taking me on a cruise down to Southend. I'm going on the dodgems and everything.'

The idea of steaming down the Thames to the sea distracted us for a while, but we soon went back to talking about Cap again and Manny said we were boring and went indoors.

'He's just jealous,' I said.

We got our bikes and rode up to the Bomb Building, both secretly hoping to find Cap there, but the place was deserted.

'I suppose he's a bit like a spy, really,' Eddie speculated. 'That's why he does all those voices.'

'Do you think we should tell him about the bomb?' I asked.

'No,' Eddie said immediately.

'He was in the army and everything.'

'I know, but ... it's our ... it's our only ...' Eddie cast around for the right word and couldn't find it.

But I nodded anyway, knowing what he meant: the bomb was our strength. Our secret weapon. In case.

17

We called for Bob at nine the next morning, but Mrs Newman said he was still in disgrace so we went up to the Bomb Building without him. We carefully hid our bikes in the bushes, and sat waiting for Cap. At exactly ten o'clock we were startled by a loud clap from just behind us.

'Too busy jabbering. You'd both have been dead,' Cap said, waving a dagger at us. He pointed to a small swastika badge at the end of the handle. 'See that? An SS officer presented this to me when I captured him. It's only ceremonial – not really sharp enough to kill anyone.'

He slid the dagger into a silver scabbard which had another swastika on it.

'Want to hold it? Just think, perhaps it was touched by Hitler.'

We each held the dagger for a few seconds, then Cap took it back. He passed one hand over the other and the dagger disappeared. We opened our mouths in surprise. He slid his hands together again and the dagger reappeared.

'Sheeee! How d'you do that?' Eddie gasped.

'Trade secret,' Cap said.

'Do it again,' I urged and, unwisely, Cap obliged.

This time we were watching closely so we saw the simple trick as he slipped the dagger up his sleeve. It was disappointing because we'd wanted to be amazed and dazzled by his skill, but Cap wasn't at all disconcerted. 'I let you see it on purpose. I'm not going to show you the real trick, am I? I'd be breaking the rules of the Magic Circle.'

'Are you really in the Magic Circle?' Eddie asked.

'Of course I am. And some of the tricks came in dashed handy during the war, I can tell you. Especially when I was captured.'

'You were in a prisoner-of-war camp?' I said.

'Yes: Colditz. But not for long. I made damn certain of that.'

He had us hooked again and we spent the rest of the morning down in the Control Room listening to his stories of battles and escape. Just before we went for lunch, Eddie reminded him about the Special Ops map.

'Oh dash, yes, I forgot.'

'Can you bring it this afternoon?' Eddie asked.

'Can't get home, I'm afraid. Got a meeting with someone,' Cap said, then put his finger to his lips. 'Don't ask who.'

I was keen to get back up to the Bomb Building so I gulped my lunch, but my mum made me stay to do the washing-up and feed the animals. Even so, I was out before Eddie, whose mother had kept him in until he had written his letter of apology to the vicar.

'I'll have to do mine tonight,' I said. 'What did you put?'

'Oh, just blah-blah, sorry, sorry. Load of lies!'

We were disappointed that Cap wasn't at the Bomb Building when we got there. Half an hour passed and we began to worry that he wouldn't come. Then I realized that we hadn't hidden our bikes. As if he had just been waiting for us to do things properly, he appeared the moment we'd wheeled the bikes into the bushes.

It was a brilliantly sunny afternoon and Eddie and I suggested starting work on the assault course, but Cap insisted on going down into the cellar. We sat round the metal table and I could smell the beer on Cap's breath, so I told him that I knew he'd been in a pub.

'Well spotted! We'll make an intelligence officer of you yet.'

We asked him to tell us more stories about the war, but Cap said he was tired of the subject.

'Messy business, best forgotten,' he said. 'Get your fathers to tell you about it. What did they do for king and country?'

My dad had been unfit for military service because of deafness in one ear, but I'd always been proud of his work in the fire service. Compared to Cap's adventures, though, his efforts seemed puny and I gave a very brief and dismissive account of his war career.

'Well, we needed firefighters, you know,' Cap said generously. 'What about your old man, Eddie?'

Eddie explained that his father had been killed in the docks just as the war started.

'That's a coincidence. I lost my dear old pater when

I was two, like you. He was killed in a riding accident. So you and I are a bit like twins,' Cap said, putting his arm round Eddie's shoulder. I felt a surge of jealousy at their closeness.

'My brother Michael's in Malaya, fighting in the jungle,' I said, trying to get Cap's attention, but he didn't seem interested so I blundered on. 'Sometimes I think I might see him on the newsreels at the cinema.'

Cap's reaction was startling. He let go of Eddie, sang the opening of the signature tune, then lifted his head up, flapped his arms and crowed like the cockerel at the beginning of *Pathé News*.

'I prefer *British Movietone News*, myself,' he said as we laughed.

He began talking about films and we discovered that he loved them as much as we did. We discussed films we'd seen, and started drawing up a list of our all-time favourite films and stars.

'Tell you who I love: Gregory Peck. People say I look a bit like him,' Cap said, standing up and striking a gun-fighter's pose. Then, in a perfect imitation of the actor's voice, he added, 'The best-looking cowboy in the whole Wild West, boys.'

Most people, like my dad, did corny impressions of easy voices like Humphrey Bogart or John Wayne, but Cap had a real talent for mimicry. He started with Peck and went on to do brilliant impersonations of every star we named. He even improvised scenes between Laurel and Hardy, doing each of the voices and sending us into fits of laughter.

'Cor, you're dead good. You ought to be on the stage or the wireless,' Eddie said.

'I might give it a go one day. Try one of them talent shows.'

Then, once again, he switched directions entirely and picked up my earlier reference to Michael in Malaya. He wanted to know where he'd been and what he'd done, but my skimpy knowledge disappointed him.

'You ought to follow what he's doing. He's a king and country man, like me, your brother – helping to protect the Empire and stop the Commies. They're everywhere. Look at the places they've overrun: China, Poland, Hungary. It'll be here next. They're infiltrating everything: trade unions … newspapers … the BBC. Half this Labour government are double agents just waiting to cuddle up to Comrade Joe Stalin. Why do you think we've got all this rationing? All those Lefties want to turn this place into another Russia. Nationalize this, ration that.'

'My dad says they'll ration the air next,' I said.

'He's got his head screwed on, your dad. The Germans had the right idea, they knew what the Reds were up to.'

'But you were fighting the Germans,' Eddie pointed out.

'That's because they got too big for their boots and we had to put them in their place. But the Commies are the real enemy.'

Usually we weren't at all interested in politics, but Cap made it exciting. Down in that dingy cellar, the communist threat felt real and imminent and it was reassuring to hear him explain how Sir Oswald Mosley was leading the fight against it. As we cycled home later I was ashamed to recall how I had stupidly taken the side of the Commies when we'd watched the march.

CL was just coming out of Eddie's house as we arrived.

'You're late again,' he snapped. 'You know tea's at five when I'm on nights. How is it that everyone else fits in except you? And you can write that letter to the vicar again – there are six spelling mistakes.'

'You shouldn't have read it! It's private,' Eddie fumed.

'Do it again and do it properly,' CL ordered.

'God, I hate him,' Eddie muttered as we watched CL hurrying towards the main road. 'Why didn't my mum meet someone like Cap?'

I didn't mention Cap to my parents because I sensed they would try to stop me seeing him, but he was an unseen presence in my house all evening. I kept looking at my dad while we ate tea and thinking how Cap was so much more alive and colourful and interesting and energetic. He could do proper imitations of actors. He could tell real war stories, not just talk about stupid things like dog racing. He was doing important things for the government, not being a black-market spiv. And, like Eddie, I wished that my mother had chosen a better husband. Cap would never betray her by getting mixed up with another woman.

'Sure you don't fancy the flicks tonight?' my dad said, lighting his Woodbine after tea.

'There's nothing on,' I mumbled.

'There must be something,' my mum said. 'Still, it'll make a nice change to have you both here on a Friday.'

She smiled and I forced myself to smile back.

'I was looking at that bike of yours,' my dad said. 'You can't go to your new school on that old rattler. I was thinking of getting you another one.'

'I like mine,' I said.

'No, it's clapped out. What do you like best, Phillips or Raleighs?'

'I don't want a new one.'

'Of course you do. It'll be great. Just think, the school's not far from the stadium. You'll be able to ride round and see me. You could bring your friends and I could show them round the place. They'd love that. Be dead impressed.'

'Yeah, they could see your office,' I said.

A terrible silence chilled the air between us. My father looked away.

My mother didn't seem to notice. 'The butcher says they're talking about cutting the ration on bacon and ham again,' she complained.

'It's the Labour government,' I said. 'The Lefties are just waiting to cuddle up with Comrade Joe Stalin.'

'Of course they aren't,' she said. 'Anyway, Russia was our ally during the war. We'd never have beaten Hitler without them.'

'Yeah, but the Commies are the real threat.'

'That's my boy,' my dad said, relieved that the subject had changed. 'You tell her, she won't listen to me.'

'Yeah, but you don't support Sir Oswald Mosley, do

you?' I snarled to show him that I wasn't on his side.

'No, I damn well don't.'

'Well, he's the only one who sees the truth. That's why they're trying to gag him.'

'Gag him? I'd string him up. Anyway, what do you know about Mosley?'

'Plenty.'

'Well you can just un-know it. I'm not having you spouting Fascist rubbish in this house.'

I glared at him and went up to my room. I spent the evening reading my comics, then remembered the letter of apology for the vicar. I scribbled it quickly and ran down to show my mother.

'Yes, that's fine,' she said.

'Let's have a butcher's,' my dad said, putting out his hand.

'I did it for Mum, not you,' I said, snatching it out of his reach. 'You don't even go to church.'

His jaw tightened with the effort of staying calm.

'Night,' I said, giving my mum a kiss.

'Ni' night, darling,' she said.

'And me,' my dad said, grabbing me and planting a bristly kiss on my cheek before I could get away.

I deliberately rubbed my cheek as he looked at me.

I went to bed and as I said my nightly prayers I left my dad out of my list and asked God to bless Cap instead.

Cap was in a brooding, restless mood the next morning, his mouth set in a sullen expression which my mother always called a 'pet lip' when I did it. He said he was fed up with the Control Room and, instead of going down there, he spent the morning mooching around the bomb site, throwing stones and kicking things in a desultory fashion. He broke off a branch from a hazel bush, stripped it of leaves, and used it to swipe at flowers and the bees and butterflies flying round them.

Eddie suggested planning the assault course but this plunged Cap into even deeper gloom, so we tried to cheer him up by chatting and telling jokes. Nothing worked, though, and when the darts-factory siren sounded at twelve thirty I was glad to have an excuse to leave.

'It's lunchtime. Better go.'

'Yeah, see you, Cap,' Eddie said.

Cap gave a barely perceptible bob of his head and headed for the side exit of the bomb site. We watched him clamber through the broken fence and out on to the road, then we ran in the opposite direction, along the path and up the Big Brown 'ill towards the other exit.

Neither of us resented the boring and aimless morning we'd endured. On the contrary, our main concern was for Cap.

'Hope he'll feel better this afternoon,' Eddie said when we got home.

'Hope he'll be there,' I added, and Eddie pulled a worried face.

We raced back after lunch and were relieved to see Cap waiting for us near the coal-hole. And his whole mood was different.

'Sorry, Eddie, forgot that damn map again,' he said,

getting up and pulling the slab off the trapdoor. 'I'll try and remember tomorrow.'

All his energy and enthusiasm had returned and he was his chatty self again. He switched from role to role during the course of the afternoon and we were entranced. We laughed at his witty comments, his sharp turn of phrase and his brilliant mimicry, but there was something more than that. He made us feel what no other adult had ever done: that our opinion really counted. He wanted us to believe what he believed and it flattered and dazzled us that he cared.

For a couple of hours at the end of the afternoon, we sat in the Control Room and listened while he told us more about the dangers posed by the growth of communism. He used what both Eddie and I believed was his real voice – the clipped tones of an army officer – whenever he spoke about politics.

'I'll tell you chaps one thing, I wouldn't leave my dear old mother living if the Reds invaded England,' he announced dramatically. 'She'd be better off dead than at the mercy of those beasts. I've seen them at work. They're sub-human.'

'But I don't get it,' I said, remembering my mother's words. 'They were our allies. They helped us to beat Hitler.'

'More's the pity. Look what's happened since Hitler: they've taken over half of Europe, and they won't rest until the whole damn world's gone Commie. You mark my words, it's only a matter of time before the Russians get the A-bomb, then you'll see what's what.

'Winston Churchill knows,' Cap went on. 'The Iron Curtain, he called it. But Sir Oswald Mosley is the only one who can see the whole picture. That's why it's so important that youngsters like you understand what's going on – you're our hope for the future of this country. The Union Movement needs you.'

At this point he pulled out the Nazi dagger and asked us if we wanted to swear to fight the communist threat. Eddie and I placed our hands on the dagger and swore.

That night, as I lay in bed, I couldn't think of anything else but Cap. I went over and over the things he'd said about Communists and I felt proud that I had sworn to help stop them taking over Britain and the Empire. And I hoped that Cap would keep his promise to speak to Sir Oswald Mosley about setting up a junior branch of the Union Movement with Eddie and me as founder members.

As I slipped into sleep, I dreamed that Eddie and I were swimming in a deep pool of rainwater that had formed among the piles of bricks at the Bomb Building. Cap was watching us. There was green scum on the water and Cap scooped it away so that he could see us better. And I was happy that he liked us so much. But suddenly I was frightened. Something was wrong. Far away I heard myself whimper.

18

'It's not fair! The vicar said we couldn't go to church.'

'He meant to the choir and you know it,' my mother said, peering at the mirror on her dressing table and plucking a grey hair from the side of her head.

'It'll be horrible; everyone'll look at me cos I'm not with the choir.'

'You're coming and you'll give that letter to the vicar and that's that.'

I stamped down the stairs in anger.

'Hey,' my dad whispered, poking his head round the door of the front room. 'I'll tell your mum I need you to stay and help me, if you like.'

'I want to go,' I said.

'Suit yourself,' he snapped and went back into the room.

I wanted to sit in the back pew at church where no one would see me, but my mother made me walk all the way down to the front with her. Bob and his mother were sitting in one of the middle pews with Mrs Lang, but Eddie wasn't with them. The congregation stood up as the choir filed in and a couple of the younger choristers looked at me as they went past, but I stared ahead and pretended that I didn't care.

At the end of the service we were near the back of the queue, shuffling out of the church. The vicar stood at the door greeting people and my pulse throbbed in my throat as I handed the letter to him. Then, in an extra effort to please my mother, I said, 'I'm really sorry, Vicar.'

He inclined his head gravely in acknowledgement.

'I should think so,' my mother said, giving my shoulder a shake.

I hesitated, hoping that the letter and apology might change his mind about the ban, but he turned away and beamed at the old lady behind us.

'Dead jammy, getting out of church!' I said to Eddie when we met up that afternoon.

'Oh yeah? How'd you like it if your mum said you were too wicked to go? Anyway, CL made me do all the washing-up and polish everyone's shoes. The pig. Come on, I've got to take my letter to the vicar.'

We cycled round to the vicarage and I held Eddie's bike while he dashed up the path, shoved the letter through the letter box, and raced out again. We sped away through the quiet streets and up to the Bomb Building. Sunday afternoons were empty times back then – nothing was open and most people stayed at home – so we were surprised and delighted to find Cap waiting for us in the Control Room.

'Mother always takes a nap after lunch on Sunday so I thought I'd drop by to see how my lads were doing,' he said. 'What've you been up to?'

We told him about the letters for the vicar and gradually, prompted by his questions, the whole story about Mr Rix and Miss Carver started to come out.

'Seven?' Cap winced after Eddie had recounted the caning, blow by painful blow. 'That's a bit much. But you survived. Like me with those Commies the other day. We've been through the fire, and we're like steel. And one day we'll get our own back.'

He made a fist and playfully punched us both on the arm.

'Seven?' Cap repeated. 'That's a hell of a licking. I bet you've still got the stripes on your bottom, haven't you?'

'It's still a bit bruised.'

'Show us,' Cap said.

Eddie stood up and prepared to slip his shorts down, then suddenly stopped.

'Get off it,' he said, affronted.

Cap pointed at him and began to laugh.

'He thought I meant it!' Cap snorted. 'Daft as a brush, you are. Come on, Andy – true confessions. Eddie's told us his. What about your dark, dirty secrets?'

I almost said it. I almost told him about my father and Mrs Wallace. I ached to share my worries and fears with him. Perhaps he would say some simple, obvious thing that would make the whole problem go away. But I just couldn't force myself to speak. I grinned, embarrassed, and shook my head.

'Oh well, time I was getting back,' Cap said, looking at his watch.

We followed him across the walkway, up the chute,

and out into the late-afternoon sunshine. Clouds of midges were swirling in the thick, warm air.

'You coming here this evening?' I asked.

'Might do,' Cap said.

'Oh, go on. Please, Cap,' I insisted. If he arrived before Eddie, perhaps I would get up the nerve to say what I hadn't dared to say earlier.

'Time alone will tell,' Cap said and then strode away, swinging his arms to clear a path through the midges.

Halfway through tea my mother burst into tears and left the table. I sat, mortified, because I had caused it all by refusing to go to Evensong.

'You'll do as you're told or I'll smack you!' she'd shouted.

'That's enough!' my father had said, banging his hand on the table. 'If he doesn't want to go, he doesn't have to.'

My mother had looked at him, shocked, then she'd run out of the room and up the stairs.

'OK?' my dad asked when she'd gone.

I was completely torn: I hated making my mother unhappy and I hated accepting my father's help, but I didn't want to go to church and miss the chance of talking to Cap in private.

'She'll be right as rain in a minute,' my dad said, seeing my hesitation. 'Go on, off you go.'

Instead of waiting for Eddie, I cycled straight up to the Bomb Building, but Cap wasn't there. I went down into the cellar and crossed the walkway. The darkness in the corridor scared me but I forced myself to keep going. I fumbled into the Control Room and groped for the table, trying to find the matches and candles, but suddenly panic overwhelmed me. I ran back to the chute and scrambled out into the friendly open air.

Ten minutes later Eddie and Manny arrived on their bikes; now there was no chance of talking to Cap alone. I had upset my mother for nothing. We went down to the Control Room and Manny was just describing his trip to Southend when we heard the secret three-note whistle that Cap had taught us. Eddie whistled back. We all looked expectantly at the door as footsteps sounded in the corridor.

'Thought I might –' Cap stopped as he caught sight of Manny. 'Who's that?'

'He's a mate of ours,' Eddie explained. 'He wanted to meet you so –'

'Did I say he could come?'

'No, but . . .' Eddie trailed off as Cap's disapproval filled the room.

'What's your name?' Cap demanded, staring at Manny.

'Emmanuel Solomon.'

'I thought as much, with a nose like that. You're a Jew, aren't you?'

Manny nodded.

'Yeah, but he's OK. He's our friend,' Eddie said.

'I thought you two were Christians. You said you went to church.'

'We do,' I said.

'You know the Jews killed Jesus Christ, don't you?'

I can still recall the turmoil inside me as he said this. In some sort of garbled way I believed he was right, but I felt that it was hurtful of Cap to mention it in front of Manny.

'It's true,' I said to Manny, trying to break it gently. 'It's in the Bible. But we have to turn the other cheek and forgive you. That's what Jesus said.'

I looked at Cap, hoping that he would be nice to Manny and turn the other cheek. Instead, he began talking to Eddie and me as if our friend didn't exist. He chatted about films and cricket and he asked questions and told jokes and laughed. The only time he acknowledged Manny's presence was when he repeated that he was going to talk to Sir Oswald Mosley about setting up a youth group. 'Just for you two, of course,' he added.

Throughout all of this, Manny sat in silence, eyes down, in his own private little ghetto. I willed him to get up and leave, so that I wouldn't feel so embarrassed and awkward on his behalf, but he sat there, cowed, enduring Cap's ostracism.

Even when we got home at the end of the evening there was no reaction from him.

'You coming back up there tomorrow?' I asked, sure he would say no.

Manny thought for a moment, then nodded and started to wheel his bike away down the path towards his back door.

'You don't have to,' Eddie offered.

'I want to,' Manny called.

Eddie and I sat on my front wall and looked up and down the empty street. The street lamps were on and a bat was hawking the insects round the nearest one. We watched it flitting in and out of the light.

'Manny must like him,' I said, unconvinced.

Bob was subdued when he was finally allowed out again on the Monday. His stutter was worse than usual and he seemed unwilling to talk about his punishment, though Eddie and I eventually prised out the news that his mother had slapped him when she'd heard about the choir.

'It d–didn't hurt m–much cos I d–d–dodged and she hit my shoul–shoulder. She was g–g–going to give me an–another one but my dad said I w–w–w–wasn't w–w–worth the eff–effort.'

'Did you have to write a letter to the vicar?' I asked.

'No.'

'We did. Our mums made us, didn't they, Ed?'

'I w–w–w–wouldn't even if they tried to m–make me. Bl–Bl–Bloody vicar. It's all his fau–fault. Him and my d–d–dad.'

'No, it's Rix's fault. He started it,' Eddie said.

'They're all s–s–s–stink–bums!' Bob said, then stuck his bottom out and let off a rippling fart that sent us into gales of laughter.

'Where's Manny? He's late,' Eddie complained.

'Oh, let's leave him,' I said. 'Cap'll be there by now.'

'Who?' Bob asked.

'Ca–' Eddie started. 'Gor blimey, that's right! You weren't here.'

I was as surprised as Eddie to realize that when we'd last

talked to Bob we still hadn't met Cap. Only four whole days. And in that time he had become the very centre of our lives: the best, the most important man we knew.

So we started telling Bob about Cap and, just as it had with Manny, our enthusiasm provoked a negative reaction.

'The b-b-bloke in that b-b-bog di-didn't l-l-look much like a w-w-war hero to me,' Bob commented drily as I went on about Cap's bravery in battle.

'Honest, Bob, he's wiz. You'll see,' Eddie promised.

Then, after all that, Cap didn't turn up. We spent the whole morning idly mooching round the Bomb Building waiting for him before we gave up and cycled home for lunch. Manny was outside, sitting on his wall.

'Where were you?' Eddie asked.

'Talking to my mum.'

'Cap wasn't there anyway,' I said.

'Is he going to be there this afternoon?' Manny asked.

'Hope so. Why?'

'Just want to tell him something,' Manny said, then sauntered away down his path, leaving me uneasy.

I went in for my lunch and decided to make it up with my mum after our row the previous evening, but she wasn't in a conciliatory mood.

'Oh, stop doing that,' she said when I tried to give her a hug as she stood at the sink. 'You're not a baby any more, you know.'

I ate my meal quickly and was back out on the street in half an hour. I sat on the front garden wall waiting for the others and wondering if Cap would turn up. And if he did, I realized, I didn't want Manny and Bob to be there. I didn't want to share him.

Eddie must have had exactly the same thought because the minute he stepped out of his front gate he took a quick look round and said, 'Let's go on our own.'

We cycled away fast, casting guilty glances over our shoulders until we arrived at the Bomb Building. We hid our bikes, slid down the chute, and were lighting a candle in the Control Room when we heard Cap's whistle. I saw Eddie's face break into a smile of relief and happiness that I knew was mirrored on mine.

'Hello, lads,' Cap said as he came through the doorway. He sprang to attention and gave us a salute, followed by a wink, and we knew that he was as pleased as we were.

'What happened this morning?' Eddie asked.

'Sick parade. Bit of a bore. Anyway the medic cast his expert eye over me and said he'd never seen a man with such powers of recovery. Captain Stanley Evans is in the pink and raring for action.' He looked round. 'On our own today?'

We nodded.

'Just the elite corps!' he said, rubbing his hands in pleasure. And we all grinned, delighted to be together. Cap reached out and stroked our cheeks, then gripped our chins and raised our heads. 'You're my boys,' he said, gazing at us. We giggled shyly and ducked out of his grip, delighted and embarrassed by his words. He gently punched our chests and we threw a couple of mock punches at his arms.

Then he was off. For the next hour and a half he dazzled and impressed us for the last time. Prompted by our questions, he skipped from subject to subject, mixing his imitations of film and radio stars with anecdotes about the war and cricketing stories that he'd heard from Godfrey Evans – he no longer called him Geoffrey I noticed. My face ached from the almost permanent grin on it and my chest was filled with all the affection I felt for Cap.

Then he switched mood and began talking about Mosley and the Union Movement. He told us that it was our duty to see that Britain continued to be great and to make sure that the British race was kept pure. When he said he was counting on us to stand shoulder to shoulder with him in the struggle to defeat the communist threat, my eyes watered with pride and gratitude.

We were just in the process of swearing a solemn oath on the Nazi dagger, when there was a grating sound, followed by a call from outside.

'Eddie? Andy?'

It was Bob.

Cap put his finger to his lips and we froze. There was the sound of someone sliding down the chute and Cap put his dagger in his pocket and ghosted away into the darkness of the corner as Bob and Manny appeared in the doorway. They looked at the dark figure in the shadows and then back at us.

'We've been searching all over,' Manny said.

'Hilly P-P-Park. Everywhere,' Bob confirmed.

'You knew we were coming here,' I said coldly.

'We couldn't see your bikes or anything and the slab was closed so we thought you'd gone somewhere else,' Manny said.

They both looked over at Cap and there was a long, awkward silence. He seemed ill at ease and hostile and I was annoyed that their intrusion had changed his mood so quickly – they were spoiling everything. Finally, Bob walked over and held out his hand. There was an agonizing pause as Cap stared at him.

'It's Bob – he's our pal,' Eddie said.

'P-P-P-Pleased to m-m-meet you.'

Reluctantly Cap shook Bob's hand and I was amazed to see him struggling to think of something to say. How could he be so relaxed and confident with us and so tense with other people?

'How old are you?' he asked. The sort of automatic question that any adult might ask.

'Same age as us,' Eddie replied, saving Bob from a stuttered reply.

'Bit of a shrimp, aren't you? When you going to start growing?'

Bob shuffled uncomfortably.

There was another long, long pause, then I tried to give Cap the chance to show how fascinating he could be.

'Why don't you tell them what you told us, Cap? You know, about all the things that are threatening us and stuff.'

He thought about it for a moment then nodded and sat down at the table. Eddie and Manny sat opposite him and Bob and I shared the last chair.

Cap cleared his throat and started talking about the Union Movement and its objectives. I saw Manny bristle a couple of times when Jews were mentioned, but I was less worried about what Cap was saying than how he was saying it. When he'd explained it to Eddie and me he'd made it seem so exciting and heroic, but now it just sounded dull, as if he was reciting a lesson he had learned. After about five minutes, Bob shifted his weight on our shared seat and I knew he was getting bored. I wished I'd asked Cap to tell an exciting story about the war, or do one of his brilliant impersonations instead.

After ten minutes Bob started to fidget and look round the room, but Manny was obviously listening very closely and when Cap paused for a moment he seized his opportunity.

'My dad says Mosley's a Fascist. He says he's an old-guard aristocrat trying to keep the workers down.'

I held my breath as Cap slowly lifted his eyes and gave Manny a look of contempt.

'Oh yes? And what the hell's he, your dad? A Communist?'

Manny shook his head. 'He's a Marxist.'

'Same thing,' Cap snorted. 'They're all Russian sympathizers.'

'Karl Marx was German,' Manny said. 'He died years before the Russian Revolution. Anyway my dad says that what they've done in Russia isn't proper Marxism. He says that when the workers understand about real Marxism they'll unite all over the world and bring the capitalist bosses to their knees.'

Bob stopped fidgeting and the cellar filled with a terrible tension as Cap slowly got to his feet.

'Unite?' Cap sneered, bending towards Manny. 'And what's the first thing your precious workers do when they unite? They go on strike. Look at the dockers. Look at the miners. It's poor old Britain that'll be brought to its knees by all these strikes. And then the Reds will come marching in, killing and looting.'

'Of course they won't,' Manny said, standing up.

'I know what you Jews are after,' Cap went on. 'You want to see this country crushed by your Communist friends.'

'That's stupid, why would I want to do that? I'm British, too.'

'Don't you call me stupid,' Cap warned, his face twisted with anger. 'You're not British and you never will be. You're a Jew.'

Bob got up and took a small sideways step so that he was standing right next to Manny. His eyes flicked from me to Eddie and back again. The battle lines were being drawn. Whose side were we on?

'Anyway, it was wrong what you said yesterday,' Manny said. 'Jesus was a Jew. And it was the Romans who killed him, not us.'

'Don't be stupid. Jesus was a Christian,' I fired back, knowing I was out of my depth, but hoping I could stop the confrontation.

'He was a Jew, Andy,' Manny explained patiently. 'It's in the Bible. My mum told me. He was from Galilee and he was descended from Abraham and King David.

194

That's why they called him the King of the Jews.'

I had some vague notion that Jesus was the Son of God, but I didn't really understand it so I kept my mouth shut.

'And my mum says the reason people try to blame Jews for things is because we are God's chosen people.'

This seemed like an outrageous boast and I wasn't surprised when Cap immediately took it up.

'See what they're like, the Yids?' he asked, appealing to me and Eddie. 'They think they're better than everyone. Better than you, better than me.'

'I didn't say that, I ...' Manny started.

'Typical Commie Jewboy,' Cap raced on. 'You can always tell a Jew: big fat gobs going jabber, jabber, jabber. Hitler knew how to shut you up, though, didn't he?'

There was a jolt inside me. Eddie and I stood up, shocked. Yes, Manny ought to stop boasting about Jews, but Cap's response was terrible. Parachute Pete's descriptions of Belsen had made a huge impression on us. Surely Cap didn't mean that Manny should be taken to somewhere like Belsen? I couldn't believe it. Nor could Bob.

'Hitler w-w-w-w-was ...' he began. But the words wouldn't come and he started again, 'Hitler w-w-w-w-w-w-w-w-w-was ...'

'Hitler w-w-w-was r-r-r-r-right!' Cap said. Then he grinned at me and Eddie, inviting us to admire his wit.

'Don't, Cap,' Eddie begged in a whisper that was barely audible. But Cap heard him.

'Someone's got to say it, Eddie. That's how they get away with it. They sneak their way into power. Lawyers with their jabber, jabber. Moneylenders robbing us blind and taking their pound of flesh. Nobody dares to say anything and before you know it they've taken over.'

'Yes, but Hitler did terrible things, Cap,' I said, looking for a way for him to take it back.

'Hitler said what everybody knows, Andy. The Jews are scum.'

There was a brief pause, then Manny spat at Cap. He was probably aiming for his face but the ball of spit was heavy and it fell on Cap's Intelligence Corps tie instead. Cap looked at it in disgust, then grabbed Manny.

'Wipe it off!' he screamed. 'You filthy little Jewboy. Look at my tie! Wipe it off.'

He shook Manny until his thick glasses slipped down his nose.

'Leave me alone!' Manny cried.

'Wipe – it – off!'

Manny scrabbled in the pocket of his shorts and pulled out a handkerchief.

'All right, all right,' he wailed and Cap stopped shaking him.

Manny righted his glasses and we could see his magnified eyes welling with huge tears as he leaned forward and wiped the spit from Cap's tie.

'God, you're filth,' Cap said when he looked down at the damp patch on his tie. 'Gassing's too good for you.'

The tears spilled from Manny's eyes and rolled out past his glasses and down his cheeks so slowly that they moved like oil. He opened his mouth but no words came and, finally, the tears finished their journey and dripped off his chin.

I was horrified. I knew that what Cap was doing and saying was wrong, but I didn't want to know it. I didn't want to think anything bad about him; didn't want to lose the excitement and adventure and heroism he had brought to my life. But my admiration and affection was draining away and I couldn't bear it – it would leave me with no one. I wanted Bob and Manny to go now. Now, before it was too late. Before I would be forced to take their side.

'Come on,' Bob said, pulling Manny's arm. But Manny was fixed there, defeated and weeping, paralysed by Cap's hatred. Bob looked at him and then, almost in tears himself, he shouted at Cap, 'You're a p-p-p-p-pig!'

'You're a p-p-p-p-pig!' Cap mocked, like some ten-year-old kid in the playground.

This attack on Bob roused Manny from his submissive torpor. He sucked his saliva together and spat again. This time, at the ground in front of Cap's feet. The action – ancient and ritualistic – was a gesture of such total contempt that even Cap was taken aback by its power and he merely stared as Manny turned and walked slowly out of the room, followed by Bob. We heard them cross the walkway and haul themselves up the chute and out of the cellar.

My heart was pounding wildly and I glanced helplessly at Eddie. He was staring at his feet.

'You shouldn't have brought him here,' Cap said. 'He spat at me! You shouldn't have brought him here.'

Shame and guilt swept aside all my other emotions.

'Cap!' I called as he headed for the door. 'Please!' My voice broke in supplication.

Cap's footsteps scrunched down the corridor and thudded across the walkway. When the thump of the closing slab was followed by the sound of him sliding back down the chute, Eddie turned to me with wide eyes and whispered, 'He's coming back.'

My first thought was of punishment. I'd seen the dark and dangerous anger in his eyes when he'd glared at Manny. All that fury was going to burst on us for having brought our friends here. I shivered.

'That's better,' he said, coming back into the room. He smiled. 'Just us again. You want to watch who you mix with. I don't want my boys hanging around with the wrong types. It only takes one bad apple to rot the whole barrel. We don't want that, do we?'

We weren't going to be punished. Cap still liked us, still wanted us, still valued us. I was so relieved that I forgot all my doubts about him and nodded earnestly. He ruffled my hair.

'Eh, Eddie?' Cap asked, turning to him.

'Yeah,' Eddie mumbled, still looking down.

'Come and shake on it then.'

Eddie shrugged and came forward slowly. As soon as their hands gripped, Cap pulled Eddie towards him. He flipped him round and held him in a neck lock, laughing.

'Gotcha!'

'Stop it! Don't!' Eddie giggled as Cap began to tickle him.

'You all right, then?'

'Yeah! Don't!' Eddie squealed, trying to squirm out of the lock.

'Right, then,' Cap said, letting him go.

We all stood laughing and the bad feelings retreated, but our chatter was forced and clumsy during the next half-hour and Eddie and I were happy when we realized it was time for tea.

'Back this evening?' Cap asked.

'Yeah, of course!' we said enthusiastically, but it was a great relief to climb out of the cellar with its dark tensions. We freewheeled our bikes down the hill, enjoying the rush of the wind and the golden light of the open air.

Our friends weren't in the street when we got home. I was certain that Bob wouldn't say anything to his parents, but Manny might tell his. I could just imagine their reaction when they heard what had happened to their beloved son. If only Manny and Bob hadn't come. If only Cap had been nice to them. But it couldn't be changed.

'Manny can't help being a Jew,' I said as we got off our bikes.

'Cap shouldn't take the mickey out of Bob,' Eddie said.

'No, it's not fair.'

We were testing the water, seeing how far we would let ourselves criticize Cap. Away from his presence, the cruelty of his behaviour was a lump of nastiness that we couldn't just wish away.

'We going up there this evening?' Eddie asked.

The real test.

It took only a second to decide, 'Ye-es!'

'Yeah,' Eddie agreed, his face intense as he imagined the pain of breaking contact with our hero. We couldn't let go of him; we needed him too much.

Despite that, I hesitated when, after tea, my dad asked, 'Fancy the flicks tonight?'

He asked it casually, without looking up from his *Daily Express*, but I knew he was desperate for me to say yes and part of me ached for the simple pleasures we used to share before . . .

My slight hesitation must have given him hope because he lowered the paper. But my pain and resentment came flooding back: he'd probably leave me alone in the cinema again; he'd use me so he could go and see Mrs Wallace. No, I'd had enough of his lies and his cheating.

I shook my head.

'Suit yourself,' he said, raising his paper and hiding his face.

Cap was waiting for us when we went back to the Bomb Building that evening. He was sitting on the top of the Big Brown 'ill and we knew he'd been to the pub because he smelled of beer.

'Come on, lads. Sit next to me – one on either side. That's it.'

He had a two-pint bottle of Whitbread Pale Ale in his lap and he ripped the paper seal from the top and unscrewed the stopper. Beer fizzed out and slid down the brown glass on to his hand, then he raised the bottle and took a long swig.

'To us,' he said, holding it out to Eddie.

Eddie took it, wiped the top, and took a gulp.

'Urgggh!' he said after he'd swallowed. He shook his head from side to side trying to rid himself of the taste. 'Urggh, it's like earwax!'

Cap laughed. 'Come on, Andy, show us what you're made of.'

I was determined to drink more than Eddie so I took a long glug and then another, swallowing before the taste hit me. Fizz bubbled up my nose and I coughed and spluttered but raised the bottle again.

''ere, steady on,' Cap said, taking the beer away. 'Don't want you gettin' blotto.'

He leaned back and drained half the bottle with a series of deep gulps, then set the bottle down between his legs and gave an enormous belch.

''Scuse I,' he said as we laughed. 'Come on, let's go down the HQ, the bloomin' midges are beginning to bite.'

Eddie and I had already crossed the walkway and climbed the steps to the corridor when we heard a splashing sound.

'Just 'aving a quick slash,' Cap called as we looked round.

We'd often peed from the walkway into the water but there was something wrong about Cap doing it and we hurried along the corridor to the Control Room to get away from the heavy splattering noise.

'Phew, I needed that,' he said, coming in and sitting down at the table just as we lit the candle. He belched again and lifted the bottle to his mouth. He gulped steadily, tipping the bottle until the last bit of foam slipped down his throat. Then he sent the bottle rolling across the floor into a dark corner.

From the moment we'd met him that evening he had been speaking in his coarsest South London accent and, despite our laughter, we hadn't liked the crude, brutish character that he'd been playing. But as the bottle chinked against the hidden wall, he switched to his army officer persona. His whole bearing changed as he gazed at us.

'You know what the trouble is with this country? We haven't got enough youngsters like you: upright, loyal types who'll always do their best. It was quality chaps like you who made this little island the centre of the best empire the world has ever seen. And look what this socialist lot are doing – breaking it up and handing it back to the natives. It could make you weep.'

He lifted his head and stared at the ceiling as he con-templated the break-up of the Empire. The light from the candle caught the tip of his chin and nose while the rest of his face was sunk in shadow.

'Still,' he said, sitting up straight and clapping his hands to dismiss his unhappy thoughts. 'Nil desperandum. While we've got lads like you, there's hope for the future. We can still make Britain a place fit for heroes. Att-ennnn-tion!'

He sprang to his feet and we followed suit, standing up straight, feet together, shoulders back, arms held stiffly to our sides. He moved towards us in mock inspection, even slipping an imaginary stick under one arm.

'Look at you. Strong, healthy boys. Firm young bodies. Good-looking.' He stroked my midriff. 'Tummy in, Andy.'

I tensed my stomach muscles.

'Better! Keep those shoulders up, Eddie. That's the way. Stand aaaaat – wait for it! Stand aaaat – ease.'

We did our best imitation of soldiers, stamping our feet apart and putting our hands behind our backs.

'Excellent. That's the way. Tough and ready for anything. Not like those other two. What a degenerate shower! That Jewboy with his thick glasses and his big ugly nose. And that little squirt with the stutter. What kind of a future would Britain have with them? Not exactly empire builders, those two, are they?'

He laughed dismissively and Eddie and I let out small snorts of uneasy agreement.

'You two, though,' he said, gripping us each by the shoulder. 'You're my boys. We're comrades. Brothers in arms. We'd go to the ends of the earth with each other. Do anything for each other. Anything – am I right?'

We nodded earnestly. This was what we wanted to hear. School had let us down, parents had let us down, the church had let us down, but the world didn't have to be a horrible, disappointing place filled with injustice and betrayal and lies. There could be decency and honour and loyalty and pride.

'Good. That's how I feel, too,' Cap went on. 'Because I trust you. You know that, don't you? I'd trust you with my life.'

A shiver of pride and excitement fizzed through me,

making tears well up in my eyes. I clamped my teeth together to stop such a cissy show of emotion.

He let go of our shoulders and walked into the darkness at the edge of the room. We could just make him out, facing the wall, head down, as if he was wrestling with some insoluble problem. There was a long, long silence that seemed to last for minutes. But there was no question of Eddie or me moving. We were on parade. Our leader was sunk in deep meditation and until he spoke we would wait.

'I won't be here tomorrow,' he said finally in a quiet voice. 'I've got to go back to work. This is the last time it's going to be like this.'

Eddie let out a little gasp and I felt my heart begin to melt with dismay. Still we stood unmoving, watching his dark shape in the shadows. Then he raised his shoulders as if he had made a decision and he turned and walked towards us.

'You're going to have to trust me,' he said, stopping in front of us. 'I told you I trust you. You're going to have to trust me. Whatever happens . . .'

He paused as if unable to go on and his distress brought those unwelcome tears swelling in my eyes again.

'Aren't we going to see you, Cap?' Eddie asked, his voice thick with unhappiness and fear.

'Of course you are,' Cap said, a quick smile breaking on his face. Reassurance flooded through me, but I saw his eyes de-focus and stare away at some invisible point beyond our heads.

'When?' I asked, almost choking with hope.

'Oh ... soon.'

'And we'll build the death slide and make the assault course?' Eddie urged, desperate to make the future with Cap solid and real, a future in which we would work side by side and turn our playground into the most wonderful place of adventure and heroism and comradeship.

'Don't worry,' Cap said, still staring off into the distance, 'we'll turn this place into a ...'

He shook his head and closed his eyes as if overcome by the vision of what he was planning.

'I've got to go,' he said, turning away.

'No!' I burst out, the tears finally brimming over.

I stepped forward and grabbed his arm, pressing my face against the dusty sleeve of his suit, dimly aware that Eddie was doing the same on the other arm.

'Don't! Don't,' I cried.

He lifted his arms and pulled us round and crushed us to his chest. I could hear his heart pounding. He kissed the tops of our heads, then pushed us both away.

'Did I tell you to dismiss?' he barked in mock military outrage. 'Right, I want you to stand at ease and face that wall and you don't turn round or move until I go.'

We did as we were told. We listened as he went, getting further and further away from us. Out into the corridor. Across the walkway. Up the chute. Leaving us behind. And all that time we stood at ease, facing the wall.

And longer. Our hearts aching in the silence.

Then Eddie broke rank and blew out the candle and, without a word, we made our way out into the twilight.

Thick dark clouds had covered the sky, trapping the day's heat so that the air was close and sticky. Faintly, far away over the centre of London, thunder was rolling.

19

The next day Bob and I came to blows at the top of the Big Brown 'ill.

Eddie and I spent most of the morning wandering aimlessly around the bomb site, missing Cap. And, although we didn't say it, missing Bob and Manny, too. So we were surprised and pleased when we heard them calling us from the top of the hill. We ran to meet them, but the hostility of Manny's first question warned us that there wasn't going to be an easy reconciliation.

'Is that pig here?'

They were pleased to hear that Cap had gone but they called us traitors for having taken his side. I pleaded that we hadn't taken anybody's side but I knew it wasn't true. Our silence had been a betrayal of our friends, one of those Sins of Omission Rev. Maddox had spoken about.

Then Bob began to test our loyalties, criticizing Cap, calling him a Little Hitler and launching into a list of specific and damning complaints.

'He's just a big bu-bully, p-picking on people. And, anyway, he's f-f-full of w-wind. What h-happened to that st-stupid army training thing he was going to b–build and that m–map he was go–going to bring?'

We had no answer to the charges and Bob rushed on, casting doubt on everything Cap had told us. He finished up by saying that he didn't believe that he had taken part in so many battles.

'Of course he did. He was in Special Ops,' I blustered.

'Special f–f–flipping Ops. What does that m–mean? How could he have been at D–Dunkirk and Africa and Italy and Gr–Greece?'

'Loads of people were,' I argued.

'And J–J–J–Japan and be a p–prisoner of w–war? You b–believe anything he s–s–says! I reckon he wasn't even in the f–f–flipping war.'

'Don't be stupid,' I shouted. 'He captured an SS officer and he's got a Nazi dagger to prove it – so there!'

'Nazi flipping d–dagger. You can buy those down B–Blackford Market. I bet that's where he g–got it. Off a f–flipping stall. He's just a l–l–liar.'

This was too much. I pushed Bob and he flew at me, fists flailing. We each landed a couple of punches, then Eddie and Manny pulled us apart.

'Look, cut it out, both of you. It's stupid. Stupid!' Eddie yelled, puncturing our fury with his disapproval.

We stopped struggling and, tentatively, Eddie and Manny let us go. We shook ourselves and glared at each other.

'It's all your fault,' Manny said, taking up the attack. 'Letting that Fascist pig come up here.'

'We didn't let him, he just came,' Eddie said. 'And if

you don't like him, then don't come when he's here.'

'We've got as much right as you have,' Manny said, his sense of justice outraged. 'You don't own the place. It's a free country; you can't tell us what to do.'

Eddie sighed, defeated, so I took over, 'Yeah, well you can't come down in the Control Room. That's ours.'

'No, it's n-n-n-not. I f-f-f-f-found it!'

'You don't even like it, cos it's dark and scary,' I sneered.

'Bob found it,' Manny insisted. 'You two can go and sit on that flipping bomb of yours. The cellar's ours.'

'Oh, come off it!' Eddie cried, alarmed to see this rift hardening into an actual demarcation.

But it was too late. Bob and Manny were already opening the trapdoor. We watched them go down the chute, then felt we had no choice but to go to 'our' den. We sat in there for a while with nothing to do, then we went outside and felt there was nothing to do there, either.

'It's just nuts,' Eddie said in dismay, as we heard Manny and Bob close up the trapdoor and leave to go home for lunch.

'They don't even like the cellar,' I tried to reassure him. 'They'll soon get fed up and we'll be able to go back.'

'That's not the point. It's . . . being split up. It's nuts.'

The split only lasted a day. The next afternoon there was a familiar car parked outside the Bomb Building when Eddie and I got there after lunch, and Bob and Manny were waiting for us, all differences forgotten.

'It's the b–b–b–builders again.'

'Two of them,' Manny added. 'The tall bloke with the map and a new one. They were just going in when we got here.'

We cycled round the corner and down the hill to the side entrance. Eddie opened the loose boards and started to climb through, then he stepped back smartly and put his finger to his lips. We heard faint voices and, when we peeped through the cracks in the fence, saw the two men strolling along the base of the Big Brown 'ill. They stopped and consulted a plan, then started climbing the side path up towards the top exit.

'What were they saying?' I asked.

'Dunno,' Eddie said. 'One of them said "difficult" but that's all I heard.'

'M–M–Maybe it's too hard to b–b–build and they w–w–won't do it.'

'They'll do it all right. They'll find a way. Fascists,' Manny commented.

We cycled back up to the top entrance just in time to see the car drawing away. We pedalled after it, calling out abuse, but the car accelerated smoothly down the hill leaving us far behind.

'I h–h–h–hate them,' Bob said, flicking a forlorn V–sign at the departing car. 'They c–c–come here and j–just … And we c–can't d–d–do anything.'

'Yes, we can,' Eddie said firmly.

'Oh, yeah – what?' Manny demanded.

Eddie grinned.

'We blow them up!'

Only ten days before, when Eddie had first suggested it, we had dismissed it as a crazy, impossible idea. He had been alone with his anger at the world, alone with his pain and his thirst for revenge. But things had changed. Since then, we'd all been hurt or humiliated and someone was going to pay for it.

A kind of wild excitement seized us and we hurried down to the hut. Eddie's hands trembled as he unlocked the padlock. Manny and Bob giggled as they stood at the door and watched as Eddie and I lifted the middle section of the floor and handed it out to them. They laid it down on the ground.

To show my fearlessness I sat down, cross-legged, in front of the bomb. Life was totally awake in me. My whole body zinged with silver energy. I stared at the rusty-red fins and the swell of the metal that led to the body of the bomb hidden in the clay. Eddie let out a tremor of laughter and sat down next to me.

Infected by our madness, Manny and Bob sat down opposite us. Eddie grasped my hand. His flesh felt icy against the burning of mine. I reached across and took Bob's hand: small and bony. Bob took Manny's plump hand. Manny turned his head towards Eddie. A ray of sun beaming through a crack in the wall lit up the thick lenses of Manny's glasses so that the tears standing in his eyes and wetting the dark red eyelashes could be seen in magnified detail. Were they tears of fear or was his political soul moved by this gesture of unity? Manny reached over and took Eddie's hand. The circle was complete and we all gazed at the bomb.

It felt like the solemn moment when the vicar turned from the altar and the whole congregation gazed up at the chalice of communion wine he was holding. Half in imitation of that intensity and half in a fit of bravado that wanted to take me to the very heart of the danger, I let go of Eddie and Bob's hands, rocked myself forward on to my fists and leaned down to kiss the bomb. As my face hovered over the metal, I imagined the blast, imagined the ripping of my flesh, the disintegration of my skull, the extinction of my life.

My lips touched the metal and tingled.

When I rocked back on to my haunches, Eddie leaned forward and copied my kiss. Then Bob. Then Manny.

'If they come here to smash everything up, they're going to get a nasty surprise,' Eddie said.

'B-B-Boom!' Bob said, his stutter giving a percussive, slow-motion quality to the imagined explosion.

A brief croak of laughter escaped our lips as we thought of it.

'What are those pieces of paper?' Manny asked, pointing to the envelope and school report that Eddie had stuffed next to the bomb.

'People I'd like to blow up,' Eddie replied matter-of-factly.

There was a pause as Bob and Manny absorbed this information. Then they both nodded and smiled as they caught on.

Bob tittered. 'Who'd you b-b-blow up, Andy?'

I got a flash of my father, looming over me as he pushed me back against the iron gates of Hilly Park, his breath puffing on my face as he said, 'You saw us. You saw me and Susan.' Him. I would blow him up. Then my brain shrank away from the idea.

'Dunno,' I said.

'CL,' Eddie said. The air tightened. Then he made a silly face to show it was a joke.

'P-P-Parachute Pete,' Bob suggested.

'Rix and Carver,' I said, to please Eddie.

'All t-t-t-teachers.' Bob added.

'What about your dad?' Manny pointed out.

'Him, too!' Bob said, then made it comic by adding, 'B-B-Boom!'

'All dads!' I said, using the plural as a jokey cover.

A smile crept on to Manny's face at the outrageousness of what we were saying. Then he made his choice, 'Cap. Fascist pig. That'd teach him. B-B-Booooom!'

He opened his arms wide to mime the explosion. My eyes met Eddie's and we told ourselves, *No, not Cap.*

Late that evening I was lying in bed with my hands behind my head, unable to sleep, my mind whirling with thoughts about the bomb. It was just a game when we'd thought about parents and teachers being killed, but were we serious about leaving the bomb for the builders? That was just a joke, too, wasn't it? We couldn't really let someone be blown up.

At just after eleven thirty my father came in from work. There were clinking sounds from the kitchen as he poured himself a drink. I heard him go into the living room and a moment later there were raised voices. The row lasted less than a minute, then my mother came up the stairs and went into her bedroom. I strained my ears and heard her crying. A wave of anger swept through me and I wanted to hurt my father, punish him. No joke, no game – I wanted to get him in the hut and show him the bomb. Make him sweat and beg and then: B–B–Booom!

I was still awake half an hour later when I heard him come up the stairs. I shut my eyes as my door opened. He stumbled across the room in the dark and I smelled the whisky on his breath as he bent down and kissed my forehead. He brushed my hair with his hand, but I didn't move and a few moments later he tiptoed clumsily out of the room.

I slept late the following morning, then hung around the house and helped my mum with some housework, trying to show her I cared. I kept looking for signs of sadness but she actually seemed more cheerful than usual and I decided that she and my dad must have made it up, so I went out on to the street to see if my friends were there.

The weather was warm and close and the leaves were hanging limply on the trees. There was a line of large flying ants crawling groggily across the pavement and I quickly traced them back to a small hole at the base of our front wall. They often swarmed in sultry weather like this and seeing them pouring out in such a steady stream from this nest, I felt sure that the air would be thick with them by the afternoon.

'Andy!'

It was Manny. He was riding his bike down the hill

faster than I'd ever seen him. He squeezed the brakes and skidded to a stop near me.

'We've been waiting for you! Eddie and Bob are up there,' he nodded back up the hill. His voice was high with excitement and there was a smirk on his lips as he went on, 'You'll never guess what's happened.'

'You've messed your pants.'

'Ha ha. Funn-ee! You're the one who's going to mess himself,' he sneered. He waited for a second, then hit me with the news. 'They've started work at the Bomb Building. They knocked down the fence at the front and there's a bulldozer ripping everything up.'

He paused to let the information sink in then, with a vindictiveness that was totally unlike him, he moved in for the kill. 'And guess who's driving it. Your precious stinking Cap, that's who!'

20

Crouching low, I made my way up the side path of the Big Brown 'ill. I peered over the bushes and saw the bulldozer heading away from me, pushing a tumbling mass of rubble towards a huge mound of bricks and wood that stood at the side of the site. The driver was wearing an army helmet so I couldn't see his hair. He was shirt-less, and his scrawny arms and bony shoulders protruded from a grubby vest. I almost giggled with relief. It was all a mistake. That couldn't be Cap.

The driver wrenched the big gear stick and the bulldozer backed up and swung round. I saw the face. It was him. Looking so skinny and small and insignificant, but undeniably him.

We went down to the billboards at the far end of the Bomb Building, where the grinding, clattering noise of the machine was less overwhelming.

'We've g-g-got to d-do something,' Bob said, glaring up towards where Cap was working.

'Do what?' Eddie said flatly. 'We can't stop them. Doesn't matter what we do. It's finished.'

The bleak finality. I looked at the dense vegetation and

felt heartsick at the thought of our childhood wilderness being ripped to pieces, leaving scarred, bare earth to be tamed by rows of houses and neat gardens.

But worse than the pain of that loss, was the pain of Cap's betrayal. Why had he deceived us? Had he been laughing at us all this time? I squirmed at the memory of the secrets we'd told him, the things we'd believed about him. I felt ashamed and embarrassed as if I was standing naked under the gaze of mocking eyes.

'Why'd he do it?' I asked, looking at Eddie. He shook his head and I knew that he was numb with the same bitter disillusionment.

'We told you, didn't we?' Manny gloated. 'You wouldn't listen. You thought he was great. Cap this, Cap that. Well, now you –'

'Just . . . shut up, Manny,' Eddie warned.

'I only –'

'Shut your gob!' Eddie said fiercely.

He picked up a stone and hurled it into the air. It arced towards the ruins of the air-raid shelter and he watched it fall. He gazed at the spot and I knew what he was thinking. The ruins, too, would be swept aside by the bulldozer. We had respected the shelter and honoured the memory of the dead family, but now it would be desecrated. The ghosts would be dispersed. The ghosts whose presence Cap had said he could feel. The ghosts he'd told us were real. Was that another lie? Another part of his joke?

Eddie turned back to us, his face hard with anger. 'We don't tell him about the bomb. And we let him get it.'

'Yeah,' Bob said. 'He'll drive that b-b-b-bulldozer r-r-right through the hut and into the b-b-bomb.'

'We can't! That's murder,' I said.

'Of course it's not. We didn't put the bomb there. The Germans did,' Manny said. 'If anyone gets hurt, it's Hitler's fault.'

'That's right,' Bob said.

'I don't know ...' I began but Eddie cut me short.

'Who votes for not telling?' he urged.

The three of them held up their hands. I kept my hand by my side – they had a majority. I could get away without voting. My conscience could remain clear. But that wasn't good enough for Eddie, it had to be unanimous.

'Andy?'

I hesitated, torn.

'He doesn't care about us, Andy,' Eddie said, his mouth twisted with disappointment and hurt. 'Why should we care about him?'

I felt my bitterness rising. But still I hesitated.

'Come on, Andy,' Eddie insisted. 'Let's pay them back.'

And I knew. It wasn't just Cap. It was everything. The whole summer. Cap would have to pay for all of it.

I raised my hand.

After lunch we cycled up to Hilly Park and played in the playground, but we felt out of place among the younger kids. We had races along the paths on our bikes until we were told off by a park-keeper, then we sat on the grass, looking out over London. We tried to talk about other things but we kept coming back to the one topic on our minds.

'It's probably a dud,' Manny said, and I thought I heard a note of hope in his voice.

Yes, that would be the ideal outcome. Cap would get a fright when his bulldozer suddenly dug up a bomb, a fright so terrible that he would be sorry for everything he'd done – but the bomb would fail to explode.

'I w-wonder when he'll get down to the d-den?' Bob asked anxiously.

'Not today,' Eddie said. 'Tomorrow? The day after? I dunno.'

Not today. Perhaps two days. Something might happen. The bomb might go off on its own. Someone else might find it. We might change our minds.

As I'd anticipated, the flying ants were swarming when we got back home. Dense black clouds of them were swooping from one side of Fleetly Road to the other. Shop fronts were closed, traffic was nearly at a standstill and pedestrians were covering their heads and running to get away from the buzzing swarm. We stood on the edge of the chaos, watching the panic and confusion.

When the ants suddenly swept away along Lowther Road, Ed, Bob and Manny raced after them, but I called out that I was going home. I cycled quickly up Goldsmith Road to the Bomb Building. I wanted to see Cap without the others but I had no clear idea why. To warn him?

A Clayton Builders Ltd lorry was parked in the road outside the Bomb Building. I heard voices and darted into the garden of the house opposite and peeped from behind the privet hedge. A man came out of the Bomb Building, followed by Cap, who was putting on his blue checked shirt.

'If you ain't ready on time tomorrow you can walk 'ome,' said the other man.

'It's the duty of – ah – every British worker to – ah – strain every sinew to make Britain great again in this – ah – time of peace,' Cap said in a remarkable imitation of Winston Churchill. 'We should – ah – work . . .'

'Just shut it, Evans,' the other man snarled, grabbing his arm and twisting it behind his back.

'Ow, leave off!' Cap whined. 'That 'urts!'

'Then don't get on my wick,' the man said, jerking his arm.

'Ow! OK, OK,' Cap gibbered, bending almost in two to escape the pain.

The man yanked his arm again then let go and climbed up into the driver's seat of the lorry. Cap rubbed his shoulder gingerly before hauling himself up into the cab and slumping in the passenger seat. As the driver started the engine, I stepped out from behind the hedge. Cap saw me at once and his face broke into a smile. A moment later, he realized. The smile faded and he shrugged and made an expression of hopeless resignation.

The lorry pulled away and disappeared round the corner towards the Rabbit Club, leaving a trail of stinking, black fumes.

My bedroom was stifling when I went to bed that night. My mother had closed my window against the flying ants, but even when I opened it wide the air outside was close and sticky. I lay with all the covers off but felt sweat begin to form on my back and on the nape of my neck. Sleep was impossible and the worries started to swirl round my brain.

I got up and leaned out of the window.

'Ed!' I called softly. 'Ed!'

I heard him scramble from his bed, then his head popped out from his window.

'Hot, isn't it?' he said.

'Yeah, can't sleep. Keep thinking about . . . you know.'

'Me, too.'

'I went up the Bomb Building,' I said. Eddie didn't react, so I went on. 'I saw Cap. He was getting in the lorry. He looked dead sad when he saw me. Maybe he doesn't want to work there, but he's got to.'

I glanced at Eddie and he seemed thoughtful, so I dared to say what had been haunting me.

'Maybe we ought to tell him.'

'Maybe.'

I waited a long time while we both looked out at the thick grey clouds turning deep blue with the onset of night.

'Shall we tell him, then?'

'OK. Tomorrow,' Eddie said, then ducked back into his room.

I got back on the bed feeling light and calm. It was cooler now, too. I pulled the sheet over myself and fell asleep.

★

'We'll have to let the others know we're going to tell him,' Eddie said as soon as we met up after breakfast.

We knocked at Bob's house first and were surprised when his mum said that he'd left at seven thirty, and that he'd told her he was meeting us.

'Yeah, that's right,' Eddie said quickly, covering up for Bob. 'We're late.'

We couldn't understand where he was and why he'd lied to his mum, so we set out to look for him. We cycled all round our territory almost as far as Blackford before coming back via Hilly Park and down Malham Hill. We turned on to Fleetly Road near St Thomas's Church and saw Rev. Maddox coming out of the gate.

'Hello, lads!' he called cheerfully as we swept by.

'Hello, Vicar!' we responded automatically. Then we remembered.

'Stinking swine,' Eddie hissed under his breath.

We turned right up Westdale Street and explored all the roads near the Ritzy before heading home. Manny was sitting on his garden wall when we got back and he hadn't seen Bob either.

'Listen, we've decided to tell Cap about the bomb,' Eddie said.

'Why?' Manny asked, outraged.

'Come on, Manny, s'posing he got killed,' I said.

'Good job!'

'He hasn't done anything,' I argued.

'Only called me a Jew! Only said I should be gassed! Do you know what they did, people like him, in Germany? They took our skins and used them to make lampshades.'

'Oh, come on,' I protested, 'Cap wouldn't do that.'

'And he lied to you,' Manny went on. 'And now he's knocking down everything: the den, everything.'

'Yeah, but we can't let him get killed, Manny, we just can't,' Eddie said firmly.

As we cycled away Manny hurled his greatest insult at us: 'Fascist scabs!'

The whole of the top part of the Bomb Building had already been cleared and all the debris was piled at the side. We could hear the bulldozer but we couldn't see it, so we dropped our bikes and ran to the top of the Big Brown 'ill, scared in case Cap was demolishing the hut. But he was on the opposite side, clearing the area near the fence. We watched him for over a minute before he looked up and saw us. He immediately waved and switched off the bulldozer.

'Wotcha,' he grinned as he scrambled up to the top of the slope, but he stopped as soon as he saw our angry faces. 'You've got the 'ump wiv me, 'aven't you?'

'Why didn't you tell us?' Eddie asked.

'I said I was in construction.'

'You didn't tell us about – about this,' I said, gesturing at the desolation.

'I didn't know, Andy. I never know where I'm gonna be sent.'

'You did!' Eddie challenged. 'You knew! But you lied to us. You lied all the time: you said we'd build a death slide and an assault course. You said we had to trust you.'

'You *'ave* got to trust me,' Cap said.

'You said we were brothers in arms,' Eddie went on, painfully recalling every word of our last meeting. 'And look what you've done: you've ruined our place. The only place we've got.'

Cap shook his head sorrowfully.

'I thought you chaps knew me. Understood me,' he said. He had switched to his officer voice and, yet again, the rapid change disarmed us. When he walked away and stood looking forlornly down the Big Brown 'ill, Eddie and I glanced guiltily at each other and went to stand near him.

'I explained to you about working for the Ministry of Defence, didn't I?' Cap said after a long silence.

'Yes,' we mumbled.

'Well, put yourselves in my shoes. If they send me somewhere to collect intelligence for the nation's security, what do I do? Tell them I can't go because I've got some friends who play there? Eh? This place matters as much to me as it does to you, but there are things that are ... bigger than us.' Cap faltered, his voice overcome by emotion. 'Things – like duty. And sacrifice.'

My eyes began to water and I made a fist, trapping my thumb so that I could squeeze and hurt myself to stop the tears.

'It's time to grow up,' Cap commanded. 'You're not kids any more, you know. You're big enough to play your part. Has Britain ever let you down?'

We shook our heads.

'No. So you mustn't let Britain down. You told me you want to help set up the junior branch of the

Union Movement. I hope you were serious about that.'

We nodded.

'Good, because I'll tell you what I'm planning.'

He sat down and we sat beside him while he spoke quietly but urgently about the letters he'd sent to Sir Oswald Mosley about us, and the important projects we would be involved with.

His words worked their magic and once again we fell under his spell. Everyone else had let us down but Cap always filled us with new hope. He made us feel like brave young warriors. He excited us with visions of a noble society. He made us hungry for a better world than the one we lived in.

We were all of us, including Cap, wrapped up in this dream when we were startled by a shout.

'Have you found him?'

It was Manny. He was standing on top of the long pile of debris.

As usual, the intrusion of someone else immediately deflated Cap. The life and energy drained from his face and he became tense and clumsy.

'Oh yeah, have you seen Bob, Cap?' Eddie asked. 'We've been looking for him all morning.'

'Well, 'e's not 'ere, is 'e?' Cap growled. Then he yelled at Manny who was making his way unsteadily along the top of the rubble. 'Oi! Get off there, you! Get off!'

But Manny was looking down at something. He spun round, almost losing his balance as some bricks shifted under him.

'It's his bike,' he called. 'It's Bob's bike.'

The skin tightened on my face and I shot to my feet, followed by Eddie. We ran across to the rubble and scrambled up to the top next to Manny. There, halfway down the other side, lay Bob's bike next to a blue checked shirt that I recognized as Cap's.

Eddie stepped sideways down to the bike, picked it up and raised it up to me. As I bent down and took it from him I was aware of how much lighter and smaller it was than mine – a kid's bike. I dragged it up to the top and then bumped it down to the ground, followed by Eddie and Manny. We walked towards Cap, then stopped a significant distance away from him.

'Where's Bob, Cap?' Eddie asked.

''Ow should I know?'

'He's been here. This is his bike,' Manny said.

'Well, I ain't seen 'im and I ain't seen that bike.'

'You must've seen it,' I said. 'Your shirt was right next to it.'

Cap closed his eyes wearily.

'Oh all right then, 'ave it your way.'

'Where is he?' Eddie demanded.

'I'm punishing him, Eddie,' Cap said, adopting his officer voice. 'Teaching him a bit of discipline.'

He smiled apologetically – an appeal to his troops to understand the difficulty of leadership – but we couldn't be deflected now.

'Punishing him?'

Cap's smile faded in the blast of Eddie's angry disbelief.

'You don't know what he did, the filthy little beast.'

Cap's voice was querulous with indignation. 'I turned up here this morning and found him pissing in the tank of my bulldozer, didn't I? I 'ad to spend nearly 'alf an hour, draining the diesel and filling it up again.'

What had Bob been trying to do: stop the bulldozer in order to save Cap or was it just a piece of crazy defiance?

'Where is he?' I asked, stepping forward.

Cap's eyes flicked over to a large metal barrel that was standing near the flagstones of the Big House. I ran to it and looked in but it was empty apart from a couple of large chunks of concrete. Then, with a terrible lurch in my stomach, I realized what it was standing on: the trapdoor to the cellar.

I wrenched at the barrel, trying to drag it clear, but was too heavy and my arms were weak with panic. Then Eddie and Manny were by my side, tipping it and helping to roll it away.

Eddie dragged the trapdoor aside and the familiar stink of coal and stagnant water rose up from the darkness. He crouched and slid down the chute and I followed. We peered into the gloom.

Bob was lying about halfway across the walkway. He was on his side, curled into a tight ball, his knees tucked up to his chest and his arms over his face, his hands gripping the back of his head. Next to him, two pools of congealed wax and a litter of burnt-out matches showed how he had tried to drive the darkness away.

I thought of the panic I'd felt when I'd been down here on my own only a week ago. The way the unknown terrors had sent me racing blindly up the chute and out into the light. I imagined Bob alone, driven half mad by his terrible memories. Trapped down here, standing on that slippery chute, frantically pushing and sliding, pushing and sliding, as he tried to lift the trapdoor. With the ghosts from the Big House seeming to breathe on him out of the stinking black water.

'Bob,' Eddie said softly, kneeling next to him. 'Bob, it's us. Me and Andy. Come on, we'll go outside. It's nice and light out there. Come on, mate.'

He didn't move and Eddie looked up at me with anguished eyes. I squatted down and gently shook Bob's shoulder then took one of his hands and tried to pull it away from his head, but he whimpered and trembled so I let go.

'We can't carry you, Bob. Come on, please get up,' Eddie pleaded. 'Let's get out of here.'

He started to stroke Bob's back, then put his arms round him and cradled him against his chest, rocking him like a baby. Gradually Bob's body relaxed. His legs straightened slightly and he started to unroll. He took his arms away from his face. There was filth on his cheeks where he had rubbed his tears. He had stopped crying but his long eyelashes were still matted and wet.

'That's it,' Eddie encouraged him.

We stood up and hauled Bob to his feet. He crumpled when he took his first step but we held on to him and supported him across the walkway to the chute.

'Give us a hand, Manny,' Eddie called.

Manny lay on the ground and reached down for Bob. Eddie and I pushed from behind and he started to stagger up the chute. He grasped Manny's hands and was pulled from the terrible prison out into the open air. When Eddie and I clambered up he was sitting numbly on the ground. A few, fat raindrops were falling out of the low grey sky on to the bulldozer-scarred flagstones.

'That'll teach him not to mess with me,' Cap muttered as Manny and I got the bikes.

Eddie pointed a finger at Cap, 'You're dead.'

There was a chilling intensity in his voice and Cap sensed this was more than an idle threat. His eyes flicked anxiously from me to Eddie.

'Don't you threaten me, boyo,' Cap said, slipping into his Welsh accent. 'Don't try and curse me – I can do it better, see.'

But we weren't listening. It was over. We had clung to the hope that he could be our friend, our hero, but he was like all the others who had let us down. The final illusion of our summer had been shattered. Up to this minute our plans for revenge had been just a game to help us through the bad times, but not any more. Our minds were made up: we would not tell him about the bomb. We wished him dead. There was no way back.

We turned away from him and led Bob towards the exit.

'Hey!' Cap called.

He was standing, legs astride, and now that he had our attention he slowly raised his hands. He folded the two central fingers of each hand into the fist and pointed his index and little fingers at us, like some ancient Celtic sorcerer.

'Anything happens to me and I'll come for you, one – by one – by one.'

He jabbed his outstretched fingers at each of us in turn.

For a moment I was shaken by this curse, but then Manny raised his own hands, gave Cap two V-signs, and punctured the mood with a silly playground insult: 'And back to you with brass knobs on!'

We skirted the pile of rubble and made our way on to the street.

21

Bob's silence frightened us. He stared ahead and let Eddie lead him down Goldsmith Road. All three of us tried talking to him but we got no response until I pointed out that it was nearly lunchtime and he would have to go home to eat. Suddenly he started to shake his head in agitation.

'You've got to,' Manny said. 'You've got to tell your mum what's happened. They can call the police. It's against the law what he did. It's kidnapping.'

'N–N–N–N–N–N–N–N–N–N–N–N–N–' Bob stuttered, his chest heaving as if he was sobbing with the effort to get the word out. But the message was clear.

'It's all right. It's all right,' Eddie said soothingly and Bob stopped trying to get that little word 'no' past his jittering tongue. 'You can come to my place – my mum and the twins are out shopping. I'll tell your mum you're having lunch with me.'

After my own lunch I rushed round to Eddie's house. Bob was in the kitchen, sitting in an armchair with his knees tucked up under his chin, staring at nothing. Eddie and I sat near him and kept talking about anything we could think of in the hope that he would join in. He followed us with his eyes, but he stayed silent. Finally, at just after two thirty, Eddie spoke directly to him.

'My mum and the twins'll be coming back soon. Do you fancy going out for a walk?'

Bob considered this for a moment then nodded.

We walked slowly along Fleetly Road and Eddie talked about the swarming of the flying ants, describing the incidents that I'd missed after I'd left.

'You should've seen the people hiding in the shops. It was a right laugh, wasn't it, Bob?'

Bob nodded and there was a glimmer of pleasure in his eye at the memory but he stayed silent as we climbed Dunlow Hill and went into Hilly Park. The low grey clouds had blown away on the breeze and a veiled sun was shining over London. We sat down on the grass and Eddie pulled out an old tennis ball from his pocket and we began idly rolling it to each other. Under cover of the activity, Eddie broached the situation.

'Not going to tell your parents then?'

A shake of the head.

'Do you want us to?'

A violent shake of the head.

'Cos of your dad?'

A reluctant nod.

A break now, during which the game got frantic and involved throwing the ball hard in order to hit the others rather than let them catch it. Bob laughed out loud as Eddie clowned pain when he was hit. Then the game calmed down again.

'Can you talk?' Eddie asked.

A shake of the head and a slight watering of the eyes.

'Just try,' Eddie went on. 'Come on, it's only us. We don't care.'

Bob tried. He opened his mouth and puffs of air came up from his chest but his voice box and his tongue were frozen. Tears spilled from his eyes.

'Fancy a kick around?' Eddie said quickly, and he and I got up and ran around passing the ball to each other.

Out of the corner of our eyes we saw Bob roughly brush the tears away and stand up to play. For over an hour we took turns as goalie, attacker and defender, then Eddie kicked the ball a long way away down the slope towards the allotments.

'First to the ball, wins,' he challenged.

We raced each other to the ball and then sat down, panting. It was the remotest part of the park where few people ever came, and a moment later I realized that Eddie had chosen the spot deliberately. Eddie, wonderful Eddie, had found the solution.

'I bet you can sing,' he said, casually.

Bob looked up, hope in his face.

'Come on – no one can hear us down here,' Eddie urged. 'Let's sing something. "Buttons and Bows".'

Eddie started to sing and I joined in. A look of anticipation came on to Bob's face as he realized that he could, that he would, sing. He swallowed a couple of times. Then lost his nerve. And we lost faith in 'Button and Bows'.

'"Slow Boat to China",' Eddie said quickly. 'That's easy. One, two, three.'

Eddie and I started the chorus and by the time we had got to the end of the first line, Bob had joined in. His voice came out strongly and ours wobbled with excitement as it did. Eddie laughed in triumph and we had to start again.

For the next quarter of an hour we sang all the hits of the year, one after the other, giving Bob no chance to lose his nerve again: 'You Made Me Love You', 'Cruising Down the River', 'I'm Looking Over a Four Leaf Clover'. And, finally, Bob's favourite, 'Ghost Riders in the Sky'.

We were still singing it at the tops of our voices as we walked back up the hill and out of the park gates.

'"Ghost Riders in the Sky" – *say* it now,' Eddie demanded when we got to the end of the song for the third time. 'Come on, if you can sing, you can speak.'

'Gh-Gh-Gh-Gh-Gh-Gh–'

My throat tightened as Bob's stutter seemed to go on and on and on. But at last, with a jerk of his head, he slipped past it.

'"Gh-Ghost Riders in the Sky".'

'Yes!' Eddie shouted. 'Again.'

'"Ghost R–Riders in the Sky".'

By the time we got back to Goldsmith Road, Bob was joining in the conversation. His stutter was worse than usual but at least he could talk and people who didn't know the truth would simply think that he was having a bad day.

'You going to tell your mum and dad?' I asked.

'You're k-k-k-kidding.'

'Never?'

'N-N-Never.'

And he never did.

I was exhausted when I got home and in no mood for a confrontation with my father.

'It's Friday,' he said, during tea.

'Mmm?' I mumbled, playing for time.

'Friday – the day before Saturday,' he said jokily. 'Friday – the day you and me always go to the flicks, remember?'

My mother was watching me. He was taking a huge gamble because her curiosity would certainly be roused if I refused again. Then he upped the stakes dizzyingly.

'Anyone would think you'd gone off your old dad,' he said. 'What have I done?'

He had lit the fuse and handed the dynamite to me. I had the chance to blow everything to pieces. But he had gambled correctly. I couldn't do it.

'Nothing,' I said, giving my voice an unconvincing giggle.

'So? Are we going?'

I nodded.

'Goodo. What's on?'

I'd been so caught up with other things that I hadn't memorized the week's cinema details yet but I had noticed what was on at the Ritzy when Eddie and I had cycled past that morning.

'There's that musical with Doris Day, *It's Magic.*'

'Well, if it's magic, we'll have to go, eh? I fancy a musical.'

Musicals were his least favourite films.

The cinema was quite full when we arrived halfway through the second feature but we got our favourite places in the middle of the front row. My dad nudged me and smiled as we settled down.

'Have a choc ice,' he insisted when the lady with the tray came round during the newsreel. He squeezed my hand as he thrust the money in it and he waved to me as I joined the queue. He asked for a lick of the ice when I got back and I let him have one although I always felt a bit sick when someone did that.

'Thanks, pal,' he said, nudging me again.

He was making such an effort and I needed the warmth of our old relationship, so my resistance broke.

'They changed it,' I whispered when the title, *It's Magic*, came up on the screen. I knew he liked it when I gave him obscure bits of information about films. 'In America it's called *Romance On The High Seas*.'

'Cor, you know everything,' he beamed, ruffling my hair.

We walked along Blythe Road to Banner's Fish and Chip shop when we came out of the cinema, and he bought me some chips.

'Give us some then, meanie,' he joked. I held the packet out and we shared them as we walked home down Brock Road.

'Have you said anything to your mum?' he suddenly asked.

'What about?'

The long silence told me. And the barrier came between us again.

'She's been a bit off with me,' he finally said. 'I thought you might've let something drop.'

'Well, I haven't,' I snapped, and deliberately walked closer to the kerb to put a distance between us.

I kissed my mum when we got home and pressed myself close to her to make sure she gave me a hug as I said goodnight. Over her shoulder I stared at him coldly and hugged her tightly.

On Saturday morning I went to the cinema again, this time with Eddie and Bob. While we were waiting in the queue, I couldn't stop myself from asking the question that was on all our minds, 'Do you think Cap works on Saturdays?'

'Dunno,' Eddie said. 'He'd finish at twelve, anyway. Wouldn't have time to do much.'

'It's pr-pr-pr-prob-probably –' Bob glanced at the people round us before whispering, '– a dud.'

Reassured, we shuffled forward into the foyer and bought our tickets.

We sang the ABC Minors' song; we chuckled at a cartoon and an *Our Gang* short; we sat rapt and silent during Episode Five of the *Flash Gordon* serial, *Spaceship to the Unknown*; we fidgeted and talked through a particularly feeble cowboy main feature. Then we poured out of the cinema with all the other kids.

It was dull and close out on the street. The air was so thick that distant buildings appeared grainy in the warm, grey haze. As Bob and Eddie and I passed the MacFisheries shop we heard the urgent sound of a bell. Ignoring the traffic lights, a police car and an ambulance swept round the corner and went tearing away up the hill. We looked at each other and a terrible foreboding began to gnaw at us.

As we walked under the railway bridge we heard a train coming. Our lives were filled with superstitions and one of them was making sure we were never under this wide bridge when a train went over it. We started to run but it was too late – the train rattled and boomed above us before we could get clear. It was a bad sign. A bad, bad sign.

We took the short cut along Dog Alley, named by us because of the number of dogs who barked from behind the high fences at any passers-by. That day, there was not a single bark. The lack of noise from the dogs drew our attention to the more general quiet that lay over the area: no children playing, no people chattering behind the fences. It was eerie.

We came out on to the main road and saw that there was no traffic coming towards us. The feeling of dread deepened and we quickened our steps. The doors of The Bird in Hand were wide open and the pub was silent and empty. When we turned left on to Fleetly Road there were groups of people standing in front of the shops talking to each other. Beyond them, a crowd was block-ing the entrance to Goldsmith Road. A rope barrier had been strung across the road and a line of policemen stood behind it.

The pounding of my heart filled my chest as we pushed our way through the crowd.

'What's happened?' I heard Eddie ask.

'A bomb's gone off,' someone said.

'Hey, you can't come through here,' a policeman shouted as Eddie and Bob and I got to the front of the crowd and lifted the rope.

'We live here,' I said.

The panic in my voice must have made the man think that I was worried about my family.

'How far up?' he asked.

'There,' Eddie said, pointing.

'Don't worry, the bomb was up the other end, on the old bomb site.'

'C-C-C-Can we g-g-go home?'

'Yeah, I should think so. Alf, show these lads home, can you?'

Another policeman came over and we slipped under the rope and began walking up the road with him.

'Was anyone hurt?' Eddie asked him as we stopped in the middle of the road close to our houses.

''Fraid so. Some poor chap working up there. Killed outright I heard.'

Our eyes met then darted away, as if the policeman might see our guilt in the appalled look we gave each other. It had happened – we had killed Cap. We regretted it at once, would have done anything to take it back, but there was no escape. For the rest of our lives the weight of his death would be with us.

I ran to my house and as I opened the front door my mother came bursting out of the kitchen and along the corridor.

'Oh, thank God!' she said, sweeping me into her arms. 'Thank God!'

Wrapped in her embrace, I began to cry. Huge sobs of grief and guilt wracked me.

'Sssh! Sssh!' my mother said, holding me tight and smoothing the back of my head. 'It's all right. Everything's all right.'

22

All afternoon and evening I longed to pour the whole story out to my mother but I couldn't bring myself to do it. At the same time I was watching every word I said, every gesture I made, to make sure that she didn't suspect that anything was wrong. Three times I had to listen to her tell me how the explosion had rattled the windows and how she had rushed out into the backyard and called to Eddie's mum. I had to endure her questions: had we ever seen any sign of a bomb? Where did I think the bomb might have been?

'Just think,' she said, 'you could have walked on it and it might have gone off. I should never have let you play up there, I knew it was dangerous.'

Then there were the thoughts that flashed through my brain no matter how hard I tried to stop them. Cap on the bulldozer, slamming into our pathetic little hut. Had he heard a clink of metal an instant before the explosion? Had the force of the blast blown him to pieces? Was there blood everywhere?

Whenever I found myself alone, my head sank as

though unable to bear the weight of the agony in my mind. And under my breath I asked the same question over and over: what have I done? What have I done?

Mercifully, when I got into bed the strain of the day had worn me out and I slumped almost instantly into a deep sleep, untroubled even by dreams.

I felt myself surfacing, rising back out of oblivion, and the memory hit me like a blow to my stomach. I opened my eyes. My bedside clock said eight o'clock. It was Sunday morning and Cap was dead and I had helped to kill him. It wouldn't go away. And it was no good telling myself that he'd been killed by a bomb dropped by the Germans. I had wished him dead. I had stayed silent and let him die. And I knew, with devastating clarity, the truth of the doctrine of Sins of Omission.

'Andy?' my dad called as I stumbled out of bed and along the corridor.

I pushed open the door to my parents' bedroom and a sour smell hit me as I went in. My dad was still in bed and the curtains were closed.

'I missed a right to-do here yesterday, then,' he said, sitting up and pulling his pillows up behind his back for support. He leaned over and took a Woodbine from the packet on the bedside table.

'Yeah.'

'It could've been you who'd stepped on that bomb. What would I have done without my Andy, eh? Doesn't bear thinking about.'

He shook his head mournfully at the thought, then lit his cigarette and put the ashtray on the eiderdown. He pointed to the bed and I sat down. He rubbed his hand across my shoulders.

'Remember when you used to sneak into bed with me and your mum to cadge some cuddles on a Sunday morning, cheeky little devil. Too big for that now, eh?'

I nodded and he continued to rub my back. It was rare for him to touch me now and I longed to lie down and cadge one of those old-time cuddles. But I knew how good he was at deception, so I held back. I wasn't going to be tricked by him or anyone, ever again.

He coughed as he took a deep drag on his Woodbine, then he leaned towards me and lowered his voice, 'Want me to get you out of church this morning? Your mum's bound to nag you.'

Wreaths of smoke curled round me. So that was it. He was just trying to turn me against my mum. I got up and headed for the door.

'Andy? Oh, stay here,' he called plaintively. But I kept going.

I wanted to go to church. Perhaps I would find forgiveness there. And I wanted to see Bob and Eddie.

Mrs Newman and Mrs Lang were talking outside the church when my mother and I arrived. I saw at once that my friends weren't there, and when I asked Bob's mum where he was, she gave her reply to my mother, as if I wasn't there either.

'I don't know what's got into him,' Mrs Newman said. 'Won't eat. Won't talk. I wonder if he's sickening for something.'

'Same with Eddie,' Mrs Lang reported. 'It's a worry,

what with all this infantile paralysis around.'

'Oh, they'll be all right,' my mother said, passing her hand rapidly across my forehead in what could have been a tidy-up of my hair but which was, I knew, a quick check on my temperature. 'It's probably all this choir business. And this terrible bomb. And school coming up soon. They're just unsettled.'

I paid hardly any attention to the service. The hymns were dreary and Rev. Maddox's sermon was a dull history of the writing of the Gospels rather than the message of forgiveness and mercy I'd hoped for. Then, in the final prayers, came the surprise. The vicar asked us to pray for the king and his government, and to remember a number of old parishioners who were sick in hospital.

'And lastly, I would ask you to pray for the young man who was so tragically injured by a bomb in our parish yesterday.'

My body buzzed with prickling heat. Injured? Cap was injured, not dead?

'Hello, Andrew. Don't forget choir on Wednesday,' the vicar said, tapping my head as we passed him on the church steps. He lowered his voice in pretend conspiracy. 'Can't wait to have you back – the choir doesn't sound half as good without you three.'

'I thought he was dead – that man with the bomb,' I said.

'No, thank the Lord. Seriously injured, but alive.'

Seriously injured, but alive. There was hope. Perhaps he would get better. We wouldn't be murderers.

★

The afternoon crawled by. My dad slept on the sofa and my mum knitted in her armchair. I wanted to meet up with Bob and Eddie but each time I checked out of the window there was no one on the street and I was reluctant to go and call for them. Perhaps they were ill or their parents had made them confess.

Just after tea there was a knock on the door and I rushed to open it. It was Manny. I pressed my hand to his lips to stop him saying anything.

'Can I go out?' I called.

'All right,' my dad replied.

'What about Evensong?' my mum asked, but I pulled the door shut and ran down the steps, followed by Manny.

'Tell us what happened. I've been at my nan and grandad's,' Manny said when we got out on to the street.

'The bomb went off.'

Manny clenched his fist in triumph.

'Blimey, Manny,' I protested, shaken by his cold-bloodedness. 'Anyway, Cap's not dead – he's injured.'

His eyes blazed with a sudden idea, 'Let's go up and see.'

'You're crackers.'

'Why not? Come on.'

'What about Eddie and Bob?' I stalled.

'I'll go and get them,' he said.

There was no stopping him in this mood and a couple of minutes later he had called for the others and we were on our way up the hill.

'Cap's not dead,' I said in a low voice, even though there was no one to overhear us.

'Yeah, my mum told me,' said Eddie. And Bob nodded.

'Well, that's good, isn't it?' I asked.

They looked at me blankly.

The whole of the top entrance to the Bomb Building had been strung with barbed wire so we ran down to check the lower entrance near the Rabbit Club. It was untouched. We pushed the loose boards aside and dodged through the fence.

We climbed to the top of the Big Brown 'ill and looked down at the damage. There was a large crater where our hut had stood and the explosion had flattened the bushes all around. The bulldozer was lying upside down at the edge of the crater, its blade grotesquely twisted out of shape. The blast must have been enormous and I imagined Cap being tossed up into the air with the huge machine.

'Maybe the bulldozer protected him – from the blast and everything. Maybe he was just injured when he fell off,' I whispered, willing it to be true.

Eddie stayed silent, staring at the wreckage and lost in his thoughts.

'M-My m-m-m-mum sa-says he's in a b-b-bad way,' Bob said, half turning but unable to drag his eyes away from the destruction below.

'The vicar said it was serious,' I confirmed. 'But that doesn't mean he can't get better.'

'There's no point talking about it,' Eddie said quietly, almost flatly. 'Won't change anything. We'll just wait and see.'

He turned away decisively and we followed him, down

the Big Brown 'ill and out of the Bomb Building for the very last time.

Eddie had set our policy. We would wait and see and, in the meantime, we wouldn't talk about it.

We were very subdued for the next few days. We stayed down at our end of the street and occasionally raised enough energy to play bike hockey or cricket, but the weather was very warm and steamy so most of the time we sat around doing nothing. We didn't talk much and nobody mentioned Cap or the bomb.

Work on the Bomb Building began again on the Wednesday morning and that gave me a bit of comfort. Things hadn't stopped. Barely four days had passed and yet life was going on, new workmen were working there. Cap had been replaced and soon, I tried to convince myself, he would recover from his injuries and the whole incident would be forgotten.

That evening Bob and Eddie and I went back to choir. We were nervous as we approached the church but there was no need. As soon as we opened the vestry door Mr Daniel welcomed us with a huge smile.

'Thank Heavens,' he said, his black eyes rolling momentarily right up in their sockets. 'Balance again. Lord, how we've missed the balance.'

The next hour and a half of practice was a wonderful relief. How calming and reassuring to be back in the choir stalls singing with passion and precision. How familiar and solid everything seemed: the organ with its high ecstatic trills and deep throbbing notes that quivered in our chests;

the stained-glass windows that we'd gazed at throughout our childhood, their colours intensifying as the rich rays of the evening sun glowed through them.

Towards the end of the rehearsal, Rev. Maddox slipped in to listen, as usual, and sat in the front pew with a contented smile on his face.

'Bravo,' he applauded as we finished. 'That's more like it, eh, Adrian?'

'I should say so,' Mr Daniel said.

'Good to have you back in the fold again, lads,' the vicar said as we walked past him.

And that was what it felt like: we had been lost sheep but now we were safely back in the flock, with the door barred against the wolfish world outside.

As we turned the corner into Goldsmith Road after choir practice, the whole street expanded, then shrank in a dazzling flash. A second later a deafening thunderclap shook the houses. We jumped in shock then scattered for our houses as cold rain cascaded down in sheets. By the time I got to my front door, I was soaking. Another brilliant burst of lightning was followed by another ear-stunning crack of thunder and I dived indoors.

The long hot days were over and the first day of September brought cooler, showery weather. It felt as if the holidays were over. School was looming and for the next few days I was out with my mother buying my new school uniform.

After tea on Friday evening my dad made me put on the complete outfit: cap, mac, satchel and all.

'Out of the way, Peg. Let's get a proper butcher's at

him,' he said as my mum fussed around on her knees adjusting the turn-ups on my first pair of long trousers.

'You just wait a second ... There!' she said, standing up.

'Blimey O'Reilly,' he said softly. 'A real Wolfe's boy.'

My mum put her arm round his waist and he put his arm round her shoulders.

'That's our son, that is,' he said, giving her a little squeeze. 'Makes you proud, doesn't it?' His eyes were glistening and I was touched by the love on his face. Then after a moment he grinned. 'Here, you can wear it to the flicks tonight.'

'Oh, no! Dad!' I protested.

'Don't be ridiculous, Harry. I want it smart for Tuesday and ... Oooh, you teaser!' she laughed as he broke away from her, pointing his finger and cackling.

'Honestly, you two – fall for it every time!'

He pulled her to him and gave her a hug. She resisted for a moment, then relaxed in his arms as he kissed her cheek. It was obvious that she wasn't 'off him' any more; perhaps, I hoped, it was over with Mrs Wallace and everything would be like it was before.

There was a big queue outside the Gaumont and, as we joined it, my dad checked his watch. He jerked his thumb to a phone box across the road.

'Just got to make a call.'

'Who to?'

'Mind your own!' he said, flicking the end of my nose with his finger.

He dashed across the road and into the phone box. He dialled a number and started talking. It was a long call and the queue had started moving by the time he ran back to join me.

'Who was it?' I asked.

'No one.'

'It was her, wasn't it?'

He scowled at me and the anger and pain came flooding back. When we got inside the cinema I crunched myself into the corner of my seat, as far away from him as possible. The main film was a comedy and my father tried to join in the general laughter, but I could hear the forced note in his laugh and I hated him for it.

Then, to make things worse, part of the film involved someone being blown up by a bomb. It was meant to be funny but I could hardly look at the screen.

'I want to go,' I whispered as the bomb exploded.

'Why? It's good.'

I stood up and shuffled towards the aisle, not caring if he followed me or not. As I walked down the outside steps to the pavement he caught up with me and held my arm.

'What is it?'

'I want to go home.'

We waited at the tram stop for ages and I could feel him aching to speak.

'It wasn't what you think,' he said, at last. 'I was setting up a little deal. I didn't say anything because it's black-market stuff and I know it upsets you.'

I stared ahead, willing a tram to rattle round the corner.

'OK?' he asked. Long pause. 'It's the truth. Believe me?'

Tight-lipped and expecting him to slap me, I shook my head. He didn't slap me. His shoulders sagged and he stepped away. I knew he was staring at me but I refused to take my eyes off the tram tracks disappearing round the corner. We stood in tense silence until a tram finally arrived.

On the day before our new school term started we all went to the playground in Hilly Park. We knew it was the last time – we would never come here again once we were at secondary school. So we swung higher, took risks on the slide, rocked the rocking-horse until it clunked and jolted on its base, hooked our feet through the handles of the roundabout and spun upside down, our heads and shoulders dangerously overlapping the edge as the world whirled by in a blur.

On the Monday evening, we ached for the pleasures we were about to lose. We stayed out until the last possible moment, drinking in the evening – the glow of lights from the houses, the flit of the bats, the rich, dark blue of the sky – talking in subdued voices, avoiding the topic that was on all our minds: school. Only as we finally, reluctantly, responded to our mothers' calls to go indoors, did Eddie make oblique reference to it.

'Quarter to eight tomorrow morning. We all meet up. Here. OK?'

So we went in to face the fears that kept us turning restlessly in our beds, searching for sleep, then jolted us awake in the grey light of dawn. Were the rumours true? Did the older boys at Wolfe's College really shove 'new bugs' headfirst down the toilet? Did they whack you with hockey sticks?

And what extra agonies must Bob have gone through as he faced his life among the tough boys at Croxley Sec without us? He certainly looked pale and hollow-eyed when we met up at the planned hour. And he stood out in his maroon uniform next to the three of us in our dark blue. We waited awkwardly, with not much to say, until the distant darts-factory siren sounded eight o'clock.

'Better push off,' Eddie said.

He held out his fist and we all held out ours so that they touched. We'd never done it before but Eddie had a fine sense of ceremony and we knew what it meant. We were the four musketeers; all for one and one for all.

'If anyone's beastly to you,' Eddie said to Bob, 'get his name. I mean it, Bob. Get his name and we'll do him; right?'

Eddie looked at me and Manny for confirmation and we nodded.

'See?' Eddie said.

Bob smiled shyly and our promise of loyalty and protection gave him the courage to go. He pedalled away to the end of the road, paused while a tram went by, then sped out on Fleetly Road, waving quickly to us before he disappeared.

'Flipping hell,' Eddie breathed, his face buckling for a moment as if grief and tenderness for Bob were about to overwhelm him.

Then he grabbed his bike and slung his satchel across his back. We did the same. And we cycled away in single file towards our new school and our new lives.

23

Somehow we got through that first frightening, confusing week. The rumours about Wolfe's were true – there were duckings in the toilets and whackings from hockey sticks, but with over a hundred new boys in the First Year only a few unlucky people suffered. Manny was sneered at a couple of times as 'Jewboy', but he had his own defence mechanism: walking on until it was safe to mutter that satisfying insult, 'Fascist scum'.

At the end of the first day Bob said that everything had gone well for him, too, but on the second day he arrived home with the breast pocket of his blazer ripped.

'Who did it?' Eddie demanded.

'It's OK. I k-k-kicked him where it hurts. He w-won't d-do it again.'

His mother re-sewed the pocket, but the following day he came home with ink stains all over the back of his blazer and on his neck.

'It w-w-was someone else so I k-ki-kicked him, too,' Bob said defiantly. And his policy worked, because on the Friday he got back from school, smiling, with the news that nobody had picked on him.

So we survived. And there were so many new experiences that, most of the time, I managed to forget about Cap. But then, out of nowhere, the memory would suddenly come swooping back, leaving me sick with guilt and dread.

In late September I had my twelfth birthday. I got home to find cards from various aunts and uncles and one from Kate.

'Lots of love to my BIG brother,' it read. 'All grown-up – Boo Hoo!'

There was a card from my parents, too, but no sign of a present and I wondered if the expense of kitting me out for school meant they couldn't afford one. I was at the table doing some homework when I heard the front door open.

'Come out, come out, wherever you are,' my dad sang down the corridor.

My mum and I hurried out to find him standing on the top step. With a flourish of his arm, he indicated the new bike standing against the fence.

'Happy Birthday!'

I felt a brief burst of joy, then an explosion of doubts strangled my pleasure: it was too expensive; I couldn't thank him; it was a bribe; I didn't want it; where had I got it from?

'It's a Dawes,' my dad was saying. 'The bloke told me they're the best. I didn't know what colour but I chose blue, to go with your uniform.'

'Is it black market?' I said.

'Andy!' my mother cried.

'Is it?'

My father's mouth opened but he found no words, then he whirled round and down the steps. He grabbed the bike and wheeled it across the little patch of grass and out of the gate. He gave one thunderous look at me then stalked away, taking my present with him.

'You ... naughty ... ungrateful little boy,' my mum said, her voice tight with anger. 'Go to your room!'

I fled upstairs and got into bed with the covers over my head, trembling with shame and fear. As time passed and no one came to punish me, I calmed down and began to justify myself. All right, I'd hurt my mum but she didn't know what my dad was like. He was only trying to bribe me so I wouldn't tell her the truth. And anyway, the bike was black market or stolen or one of his dodgy deals.

Hungry, miserable, and torn between regret and defiance, I finally fell asleep.

When I left the house the next morning, the Dawes was standing in the side entrance, but I reached past it and took my rusty old bike. I did the same the following morning, too. But that evening, when Eddie and I arrived home late after rugby training, my father was waiting. He stood blocking our gate until Eddie had gone indoors.

'Get off that bike,' he said.

I got off and he grabbed the handlebars.

'Leave off!' I said, wrestling him for control of the bike.

'Andy!' he said sharply as he twisted the handlebars into an iron grip that I couldn't shift. 'If you knew the things we've gone without, how we've scrimped and saved for that bike, you would be ashamed of yourself. Now let go.'

'No.'

He leaned closer. 'I don't want to hit you – out here where everyone can see,' he whispered. 'But I will if I have to. Now please, please let go.'

I looked in his eyes and I knew he would do it. I let go and he wheeled my old bike away down the street. The next day I was forced to take the Dawes to school. Eddie and Manny were impressed and I had to pretend that I was thrilled with my birthday present.

The atmosphere at home stayed cold and awkward until a week later when Kate came back from Nottingham and rescued us from the gloom. My mother was delighted to have her home again and the place was filled with their happy chatter and laughter.

I was determined to find the right moment to tell Kate about Dad and Susan Wallace. I rehearsed the words I would use and I imagined how my big sister would sort things out, as she had done in the past, and I would be able to go back to the innocent, happy world that I had lost.

Then, only a week after she arrived, she announced that she'd found a job at a nursing home fifty miles away on the south coast and had to start at once. So Kate's chirpy presence went out of our lives again before I could share my troubles. A stiff, uneasy atmosphere settled back on our house. My dad and I no longer chatted or joked together and, using the excuse that I had too much homework at

Wolfe's, I stopped our traditional Friday expeditions to the cinema.

There was a burst of very late Indian summer at the end of October, so our half-term holidays were warm and sunny. The four musketeers were together again and it was great. We spent most of the time on our bikes, cruising the streets on long sorties out of our childhood territory and into areas of London that we didn't know. The bustle of the sprawling city was starting to call to us.

For over two and a half months none of us had talked about the Bomb Building. We'd seen the area being stripped of bushes and undergrowth; we'd seen the big elm tree felled and cut and burned; we'd seen the levelling of the Big Brown 'ill and the razing of the bomb shelter where the family had died. We'd seen our beloved playground become an unrecognizable desolation of churned-up clay, ready for building work to begin. We'd seen it all out of the corners of our eyes as we'd sped by on our bikes, but we'd never commented on it.

As for Cap, we never mentioned him and we each found our own way of coping with our fears and regrets. My way was to convince myself that Cap would get well, that perhaps he was already better and out of hospital. I even fantasized that he would forgive us and we would become friends again. I prayed every night for his recovery.

Although the unwritten rule was that we didn't talk about it, I brought it up with each of my friends separately during the half-term holiday. Manny was the least repentant. When I really pushed him, he admitted that he sometimes felt a bit sorry for Cap but he still believed he deserved it.

'Blimey, Andy, he thinks Hitler's OK. He thinks concentration camps and killing Jews is OK. So, it's funny – well, not funny, but sort of serves him right – that he got blown up by a German bomb. It's kind of like ... justice.'

Bob's reaction, when I asked him what he felt, was brief but eloquent. He shook his head in sorrow and stuttered painfully.

'Ju-Ju-Ju-Ju-Just p-p-p-p-p-p-p-poor bl-bl-bl-bl-bl-bloke, really.'

'Were you trying to stop him when you peed in the bulldozer?' I went on.

'Su-Su-p-pose so.'

As for Eddie, what we had done had offended his code of honour.

'It was wrong. We were cowards. We should have had a proper fight with him, not just ... And, anyway, it wasn't fair. We picked on him instead of all the other people like Rix. OK, he's a liar and he put Bob in the cellar and all that ... but what we did was wrong. Wrong. And I feel like ... I dunno ... like ... I've lost some-thing.'

I had longed to talk to Eddie, hoping for reassurance. Instead, his misgivings unleashed all the emotions I'd been managing to keep in control. He was right. I'd lost some-thing, too. I didn't know what it was, but it was gone and I didn't know where to find it again.

Cap began to dominate my thoughts. I had long, complicated dreams about him; dreams which jerked me out of sleep in the middle of the night and then floated near the surface of my dozing mind until the morning, clouding the rest of my day. I even found myself deliberately thinking about Cap or the bomb while I was talking to people, as if daring myself to bring it out into the open.

Then, on 18 November, my emotions finally boiled over. I can place it exactly because memorizing the date of the local paper was always the first part of my routine of learning the cinema programmes when I got home from school on Fridays.

On that afternoon, I glanced at the front page and then opened the paper, searching for the entertainment page. As I flicked past page five my eyes caught the word BOMB as part of a headline and I stopped to read the full sentence: BOMB VICTIM'S MOTHER IN HOSPITAL VIGIL. I knew, with a lurch in my stomach, that it was about Cap.

The article started with a retelling of the explosion and it confirmed what I'd guessed at the time: that Cap had been protected from the blast by the bulldozer. It then went on to describe how, having saved him from the bomb, the bulldozer had reared up from the force of the explosion and tipped over on top of him. My eyes tried to skip over the details, but I took them all in: the machine had crushed his chest, severed his right leg at the knee and ripped off his right arm at the shoulder.

Having read the terrible details once, I was compelled to re-read them again and again.

Then I looked at the two slightly faded photos next to the article and realized that they were of Cap. One was taken when he was about three or four, standing in a courtyard, wearing a floppy sun hat and clutching a woollen toy dog in his hands. The other showed him as a teenager, his face still chubby with puppy fat. He was squinting in the bright sunlight with a puzzled look on his face, as if someone had just asked him a question he hadn't heard properly. I stared and stared at the photos, trying to know Cap better.

Finally I moved on to the account of his mother who was staying at the hospital twenty-four hours a day to be with 'her only child'. It talked about her prayers in the hospital chapel and her praise for the doctors and nurses who were 'working night and day to save my boy'. He was in a coma and had to have help with his breathing but, she said, 'I'm sure he knows when I'm there.'

Those words of blind hope suddenly filled me with a sense of the fragility of human life and I rushed into the scullery to wrap my arms round my mum.

'What? What is it?' she chuckled as I clung to her. 'Andy?'

She tried to push me away but I wouldn't let go and we both stumbled against the sink.

'What is it?' she asked again, but I shook my head and held on tight. How could I begin to tell her my frantic fear that she and my dad might die or leave me? What words could I use to describe my desire to make everything whole and right? How could I explain that I didn't feel like me any more. She ran her hand across my hair. 'You are a funny boy sometimes.'

When my dad got home I held back, pushed and pulled by an inner struggle, but at the end of our meal I glanced at him and he winked. My resentment was overwhelmed by a rushing need for his love.

'Shall we go to the flicks tonight?' I asked.

The look of surprise and delight on his face almost broke me there and then, but I managed to suppress the fevered emotions swirling inside me.

'What's on?' he said, covering his own swirl of emotions by fussing with his Woodbine packet. He took out a cigarette and used it to hide his smile by running it across his lips, before popping it into his mouth and lighting it.

'There's *Key Largo* at the Astoria. Humphrey Bogart, Edward G. Robinson and Lauren Bacall,' I said.

'Mmm, Bogey and Bacall. That sounds like the one. *Key Largo* here we come. Peg?'

'What?' my mum called from the scullery.

'Andy and I are going to the flicks.'

'Oh, that's nice.'

We stood at the tram stop and he babbled non-stop, desperate not to let that silence fall between us again. I wanted to help him out, laugh at his corny puns or take up the thread of what he was saying, but I felt too choked to do anything but nod and keep my face fixed in a smile.

An old lady came and stood behind us. She had short grey hair and sad, dark eyes that made me think of Cap's mother. I imagined Mrs Evans crouched over her son's bed, clasping his hand and willing him to get well. Tears began to well up in my eyes and I looked away from the old lady to my dad, who had stopped talking. He had exhausted his chatter but, unable to bear an awkward silence, he began to whistle.

'Name that tune,' he said, repeating the melody.

It was 'Dance, Ballerina, Dance', one of the big hits of the year. I knew it at once but I couldn't open my mouth in case a long howl of pity and misery broke from me.

'Come on, it's dead easy. I'll buy you a choc ice if you guess it.'

He whistled the tune again, his eyes wide as if wanting me to read the correct answer in them. There was a rattle from down the road and the tram appeared. He turned his head to look at it, whistling all the time.

My tears brimmed over and slid down my cheeks. I wiped them away quickly but more followed, flooding my eyes. My dad turned round and saw me. He stopped the whistling and a look of anguish flashed on his face.

'Andy?' he said hesitantly.

I walked away as the tram screeched to a stop. Home. I had to get home. He caught up with me as I passed Miss Geale's sweet shop.

'Andy, what is it? What did I do?'

A strangled sob came out of my throat as I looked into his anxious eyes. My knees buckled and he caught me but my weight knocked him off balance and we staggered back against the fence next to the shop. I forced my knees to straighten and for a few seconds, as the tram clanked away towards the traffic lights, I thought that the moment of weakness was over. I would be all right.

I opened my mouth to tell him this, but the months of fear and tension and unhappiness exploded out of me in huge, juddering sobs.

'Come on, come on,' he said, patting my back. 'Let's go home.'

Half supported by him, I staggered home, weeping uncontrollably. As we went through the front door and I saw my mother's terrified face, I collapsed in the hallway, all strength gone.

'I'm sorry. I'm sorry,' I sobbed as my father carried me up the stairs.

During the night I was dimly aware that I was groaning and that my body ached and I was terribly, terribly hot. I wrestled with my bedclothes, trying to push them off, but someone covered me again and stroked my forehead. I heard voices, but when I tried to open my eyes, the light stabbed painfully.

For over four days I had a dangerously high fever. The doctor came and was unable to diagnose the cause of the fever. Meningitis and infantile paralysis were mentioned, then ruled out. My mother bathed my burning face and body with cool flannels and listened while I moaned and raved.

On the fifth day the fever broke. I stayed in bed for another five days and then on weak, trembling legs I made my way downstairs and lay on the sofa. My father sat with me and rubbed my feet gently as if he were trying to rub away all my hurt. From then on, my recovery was rapid and on the Friday, two weeks after the collapse, I wanted to go back to school.

'Not today, love. You can go on Monday,' my mum said. But she did allow Eddie to come in and talk to me that evening.

He filled me in on all the school news and then, having closed my bedroom door so that no one could hear, he told me that he was planning to go to the hospital the next afternoon to visit Cap.

'Will they let you in?'

'Dunno. Do you want to come?' Before I could reply, he went on with a passion that had been missing in him since the summer. 'We've got to go, Andy. It's our duty. It's something we can do.'

I had no hesitation. Yes, I wanted to go.

'What about Bob and Manny?' I asked.

'Manny can't, it's Saturday. Anyway, they won't want to. And it's not them, Andy – it's us. We're the ones he ... I mean, we were his ...'

He cast around for the right word and couldn't find it. I nodded to show that I understood.

24

My mother tried to stop me the next day when I said I was going out on my bike, but Eddie turned on his charm and convinced her that it would be good for me to get some air.

We cycled down to Blackford Hospital and asked at the desk for Stanley Evans.

'It's the side room, next to Westminster Ward. Third floor,' the receptionist said.

At the last moment my nerve started to fail, but Eddie wouldn't hear of leaving – 'We're doing something, at last.' – and we waited outside the ward until a nurse came out.

'He's in there,' she said, pointing to a closed door. 'But you can't really go in, he's ... Are you relatives?'

'Friends,' Eddie said confidently.

'Well, if you go and sit in the waiting room just up there, I'll tell his mother you're here.'

Mrs Evans was nothing like the old granny figure that I had pictured. She had dyed blonde hair, wore dark red lipstick and nail varnish, and was smartly dressed in a navy blue dress. Only the heavy black rings round her sad eyes were as I had imagined.

'You've come to see Stanley?' she said in a strong Welsh accent.

So, Welsh was Cap's real voice.

'Yes,' Eddie said, and then in his easy, good-mannered style, 'We're friends of his. This is Andrew Adamson and I'm Edward Williams.'

There was a moment's pause as she thought about this and then her face broke into a smile.

'Eddie and Andy,' she said. 'Well, I'll be blessed. Stanley told me all about you. The two orphan boys from Dr Barnardo's.'

Without missing a beat, Eddie said, 'That's right.'

'Oh, what pets to come and see him. Now, there's friendship for you. He'd be so pleased if he knew.'

'Can't you tell him?' I asked.

'Oh, you poor lamb, I can't, see. He's not ... awake. It's a coma, see. They're keeping him alive – breathing, like – in this contraption.'

'An iron lung?' I volunteered.

'No, no, it's a tent. Oxygen tent. They've done everything they can. They're marvellous here, real saints. But he won't last. I thought he would at first. But they've told me, see, right out – the top doctor told me there's no hope. His lungs have gone and goodness knows what else. But it's for the best. It would be no sort of life for him. I wouldn't wish that on him, poor mite, of course, I wouldn't. I keep telling him, 'Go on now, Stan, let go.

Don't worry about Mum. I can take care of myself. God's waiting for you.' But he keeps hanging on. They tell me he doesn't feel any pain, though, so there's a blessing.'

She gave a little sigh and seemed lost for a moment, then she rallied.

'Oh dear, you come all this way and I rabbit on at you.'

'That's all right,' Eddie said.

'Would you like to see him?'

We both hesitated now at the idea of seeing a dying man.

'Just peep in the door,' Mrs Evans said, reading our thoughts.

We followed her down the corridor and pressed against each other to peer round the door as she held it open. Cap was a still form in the bed, his head and shoulders largely hidden under a canopy of clear plastic. I could just make out a grey face on the pillow, but I would never have known it was him.

'I'll tell him you came to visit,' she said as we backed out into the corridor again and she closed the door. 'I don't know if he hears. But I keep talking to him. I'm not with him all the time now, though – well, I had to go back to work, see. But I'm here evenings. And weekends, of course.'

'Can we come again? Next week?' Eddie asked.

'Would you? Oh, I'd like that. There's nobody else, see. I tried to contact his father but no success.'

The next Saturday she was waiting for us in the corridor when we arrived. Her face lit up with a smile.

'You came! Want a look-in?'

Nothing had altered. Cap's grey face lay in the same position on the pillow. The hissing sound of the oxygen was still the same. Just before we arrived, though, Eddie had told me to look carefully at the lower half of the form in the bed. I checked and saw the shape of only one leg.

'Eddie and Andy,' Mrs Evans said, shaking her head in wonder, when we were all sitting in the waiting room. 'He always calls you "my mates, Eddie and Andy".'

She chuckled, then looked at us quizzically as if she was not sure if she should go on.

'I wasn't even certain if you were real or not,' she ventured. 'You know what a kidder, he is. Him and his stories?'

We nodded and she looked relieved that we knew.

'I used to tell him: "You and your stories, Stan, they'll get you into trouble one day." Missed his vocation, really. He should've been, ooh, I don't know . . .'

'An actor?' I suggested.

'Oh, he would have loved that. Films? Film-mad, he is. His dad always used to say, "I don't know about film-mad, just plain mad more like it." They didn't get on.'

She thought about this for a moment then she laughed.

'Or a politician. He could be that, with his gab gab gab! Has he told you about his precious Union lot? Mosley and them? Oh, I can't listen to it.'

'Does he really know Mosley, then?' I asked.

'Know him? Oh no. Seen him a couple of times at rallies and that.'

She showed us the originals of the photos that had been in the newspaper, plus a couple of others she carried in her bag. We learned that they'd lived in Aberdovey until Stanley was twelve, then they'd moved to Chester – there was a photo of him standing on a bridge over the River Dee – and then down to London when he was fifteen. His father had left them shortly after and gone back to Wales.

'Next week?' she asked timidly when we said we had to go.

'Of course,' we agreed.

When Cap's mother came out of the room to greet us on the third Saturday, she looked exhausted and old.

'He's still hanging on, hanging on, the poor lamb. The specialist says it could be weeks, months. You can't tell, see. The girls at my office say I should take a rest from coming, but I can't, can I?'

A nurse brought her a cup of tea and a couple of orange squashes for Eddie and me as we sat in the waiting room after our quick, ritual peek into Cap's room. The tea seemed to revive her and she began to ask us questions about our lives in the Dr Barnardo's home.

'Where exactly is it?'

'Oh, up near Croft Hill,' Eddie lied quickly.

'When did Cap – Stanley go in the army?' I asked, trying to divert her.

'The army? Did he tell you . . .? He is a naughty scrap. He never was in the army. Failed his medical, didn't he? Oh, he is naughty, telling fibs like that.'

She shook her head fondly at his little quirk, but then her expression grew serious.

'He never hurt you, did he? Never did anything ... wrong? Tell me the truth, now. No? Oh, that's a relief. He's such a funny chap, all the stories and that. His father said he's got a screw loose. But he always brought out the worst in Stan, that's why. He's a lovely boy really. Never a dull moment, you can be sure of that. And so quick at school – all the teachers said he picked things up just like that. Nothing missing in the brain department. But he couldn't abide exams. It was the discipline, I suppose – concentrating. He was never one for that. All airy-fairy, jumping from one thing to another.'

She stared at the threadbare carpet for a while, remembering. She absent-mindedly raised her cup and sipped some tea, then came back to us.

'Did he tell you he sees things? Spirits and things? I think he really can. He's got the gift. It runs in the family – not me, but my mother had it, and her mother as well. Stanley's always joking that he's a Welsh wizard at heart.'

I shivered, remembering his strange magical gesture and his warning: 'Anything happens to me and I'll come for you, one – by one – by one.'

We had wished him dead. And not telling him about the bomb was a Sin of Omission. If he died, wouldn't it be as bad as if we had actually killed him? Sins in thought, word and deed?

'Will I see you next week?' she asked when we got up to leave.

271

'It's Christmas Eve,' I pointed out.

'Is it? The seventeenth today, so … Yes, I suppose it is. What about the week after that? Yes? Oh, you are a pair of sweethearts! I'll look forward to that.'

We had forgotten that the Saturday we'd agreed to was 31 December, but we couldn't let her or Cap down, so, on New Year's Eve we cycled through sleet and blustery winds to Blackford Hospital.

When we got to the top of the stairs, Mrs Evans was waiting for us outside Westminster Ward. She waved and rushed towards us, smiling sweetly.

'I knew you'd come, so I had to be here to tell you. He's gone,' she said.

'Where?' I asked, thinking that they'd moved Cap to another ward.

'He just slipped away so easily, a week ago last Thursday the twenty-second,' she said lightly, almost joy-fully. She clasped her hands in front of her and wrung them as if in thanks. 'Pneumonia it was in the end. No pain, just slipped away, like a little boy going to sleep.'

Eddie and I could think of nothing to say.

'He's gone,' she repeated. 'Back into that great unknown from whence we come.'

She stared into the distance as though momentarily penetrating that great unknown. Then she looked intently at us. Our shock must have been showing.

'Oh, don't be sad, pets,' she said. 'He'll always be with us. His spirit will be right beside us through all our days, you see if it's not. I felt him, even at the funeral.

I would've asked you to come, by the way, but I didn't know how to contact you. It was a lovely ceremony.'

She walked down the stairs with us and outside to where we had left our bikes. She grasped first me, then Eddie, by our shoulders and pulled us to her.

'Thank you for being a friend to him. And for helping me. It meant everything. You're a credit to your ... a credit to Dr Barnardo's.'

We got on our bikes and she waved to us until we rounded the corner towards the High Street.

Bob's parents invited our families and some of the other neighbours to celebrate New Year's Eve at their house. By eight o'clock the Newmans' front living room and the kitchen were packed with adults drinking and talking while the younger people were upstairs, crowded into Bob's bedroom. Eddie gave us a nod and gathered me and Bob and Manny together on the stairs.

'Cap's dead,' he said in a low voice.

We'd kept Bob and Manny up to date with all the details about Cap and Mrs Evans after each of our hospital visits. They knew his death had been inevitable, but they were pale and wide-eyed at the news.

'We're going over to my place for ten minutes,' Eddie went on. 'I'll go first. Do it casual, so no one notices.'

Eddie's house was calm after the crush and hubbub of the party. I was the first to arrive and I sat on the stairs with Ed, waiting for the others. Manny was next to arrive, and couple of minutes later Bob came in.

We followed Eddie into the front room. The curtains

were drawn and just one side light was burning. He sat down, cross-legged, on the floor. I sat opposite him, Bob sat on his right and Manny sat on his left so that we formed a circle. When we had settled, Eddie took his penknife from his pocket, opened the blade and set it on the floor in front of us.

'We're going to swear an oath,' he said. 'In blood.'

I saw Manny flinch and look across at Bob.

'We're going to swear an oath, never to tell. Never to tell anything of what's happened. Do you understand?'

We nodded. There was no need to ask for clarification. He meant everything. Rix. Carver. The choir ban. The bomb. Cap. Everything.

'It's our secret, forever. In honour of the dead. And in honour of us,' Eddie said with his flair for ritual and ceremony.

He picked up the knife. I could see by the glistening marks on the blade that he had prepared it, sharpened it in readiness. He held up his left thumb and ran the knife sharply across the flesh. Dark blood welled out of the cut.

He looked at Manny, who licked his lips in fear.

'Hold out your thumb and close your eyes,' Eddie ordered, and Manny did as he was told.

Eddie drew the blade quickly across Manny's thumb. Manny winced and opened his eyes to stare at the blood running out of the cut.

I took the knife from Eddie, determined to make a good show. With barely a pause, I slashed at my thumb and brought the blood flowing from the wound.

I handed the knife to Bob. He pinched the skin of

his thumb, to deaden it, then sliced himself open. Blood gushed out and down the side of his thumb.

Eddie held up his bleeding thumb and pressed it against Manny's wound.

'I swear by our blood,' Eddie said.

He pressed his cut against mine, our blood mixing, and the pressure stinging me.

'I swear by our blood,' he said again.

He held his bloody thumb against Bob's.

'I swear by our blood,' he said for the third time.

Then it was Manny's turn to swear, pressing each of our thumbs in turn. Then my turn. And, finally, Bob's.

By the time we had finished, we were streaked with each other's blood and we went into the kitchen and ran our hands under the tap. Eddie had even prepared pieces of cotton wool and we clamped them on to our cuts to staunch the bleeding.

Half an hour after we had left, we were back amid the laughter and chatter of the party. Nobody had missed us. So nobody had the slightest idea of the solemnity of what we had just done.

Back then in 1949 most twelve-year-olds were expected to be in bed early, and our parents didn't make an exception for New Year's Eve. Bob went first, protesting at having to go at the same time as his younger brother and sister. Manny was next and Mrs Solomon left with him, saying that she always went to bed early on the Sabbath. Mr Solomon stayed. Shortly afterwards CL checked his watch and, with a jerk of his thumb, indicated to Eddie that he was to go home to bed. I saw my mother start to say something but I was ahead of her.

'Just going,' I said.

Eddie and I crossed the road together. It was cold and sleeting so we couldn't linger. He went into his garden and I went into mine. I was near my front steps when he called.

'Hey.'

He was leaning over the fence, his hand outstretched. I ran across to him.

'Happy New Year, Andy,' he said.

I grasped his hand and shook it.

'Yeah. Happy New Year, Ed.'

And After . . .

Bob, Eddie, Manny and I stayed friends. We saw each other as often as we could and we phoned or wrote when we couldn't meet.

Then, in 1966, Bob was killed when he fell in front of a tube train. He was twenty-eight. One of the witnesses said: 'He shot over the edge of the platform as if someone had pushed him. But there was no one near him.' The coroner talked of 'a freak gust of wind in the tunnel' and returned a verdict of Accidental Death.

In December 1977, two days after his fortieth birthday, Manny was blown up by a bomb in Israel. He was working there as a lawyer representing Palestinians who had had their lands confiscated. He left his office one evening and his car exploded. Nobody knew who planted the bomb. The Israelis blamed the Palestine Liberation Organization, and the PLO blamed Israelis who resented his work with the Palestinians.

Eddie and I thought about Cap's curse – 'I'll come for you, one – by one – by one.'

Eddie was my closest friend. He was a journalist on the Weald Times *and he loved his work. 'Meeting people and writing about their ordinary, everyday stories, there's nothing better,' he told me. In November 2003, just before he retired, he was driving to cover one of those everyday stories when someone threw a concrete slab from a motorway bridge. It hit Eddie's car and he was killed instantly.*

So, my three friends are gone and all by violent deaths. And now there's just me: the last. Do I believe in the curse? Not really. But I like thinking about it because it reminds me of the aliveness, the intensity, of those childhood days. We seemed closer to the mystery and magic of life back then. I think about it and I wonder if there is anything after we die. Who knows? Perhaps in this strange and amazing universe there actually is a life after death. Perhaps I shall wake from my grave and find myself with my friends again: with Manny and Bob and Eddie. In the sun. Together. Laughing and playing in the Bomb Building. It would be heaven.

An unbeatable bestseller from
Nigel Hinton, author of *Time Bomb*

Buddy

Buddy is filled with **fears** and **worries**.

Why has his mum left home?

Do the police know he's a shoplifter?

What's the mysterious 'job' his dad has found?

Perhaps there's an answer to all these questions in that
lonely boarded-up house in Croxley Street ...

puffin.co.uk

Psst!
What's happening?

sneakpreviews@puffin

For all the inside information on the hottest new books,

click on the Puffin

www.puffin.co.uk